D0707209

Seal Books by L. R. Wright

THE SUSPECT

LOVE IN THE TEMPERATE ZONE

SLEEP WHILE I SING

THE SUSPECT

L. R. WRIGHT

SEAL BOOKS
McClelland-Bantam, Inc.
Toronto

THE SUSPECT

*A Seal Book / published by arrangement with
Doubleday Canada Limited*

PRINTING HISTORY
*Doubleday edition published October 1985
Seal edition / June 1986*

Cover art by Christopher Zacharow.

ISBN 0-7704-42122-9

PRINTED IN CANADA

COVER PRINTED IN U.S.A.

U   11   10   9   8   7   6   5   4

AUTHOR'S NOTE

The author wishes to acknowledge the advice and suggestions provided by John Wright, Marti Wright, Evelyn Appleby, Dennis Stewart, Jerry Olsen and several members of the Royal Canadian Mounted Police; any inaccuracies are her own.

There is a Sunshine Coast, and its towns and villages are called by the names used in this book. But all the rest is fiction. The events and the characters are products of the author's imagination, and geographical and other liberties have been taken in the depiction of the town of Sechelt.

This book is for my brother,
Brian Appleby

CHAPTER 1

He was a very old man.

When he was struck he fell over promptly, without a sound. His chair made a sound—a twisted squeak of a noise—but it let him go, made no move that George could see to clasp its wooden arms around him, hold him close to its padded back, keep him firmly upright upon its padded seat. It just gave a small squeak as its rockers skewed frantically on the polished hardwood floor; then it righted itself, gently rocked back into serenity and was finally motionless and silent.

Everything was silent, then—silent in the silent sunshine. Yet George had an impression of uproar and consternation. There was a thundering in his eighty-year-old heart, a feebleness in his antiquated knees. His body had become a horrified, garrulous commentator on calamity.

He did a slow, backward shuffle, his eyes still fixed on the empty rocking chair, and lowered himself carefully onto the chesterfield, his right hand wrapped around a cylindrical piece of brass that had once been a shell casing.

He pushed himself back on the chesterfield and let his head rest against its flowered slipcover. Then he sat up to take a large white handkerchief from his pocket and spread it on the maple coffee table, next to a vase of peonies, robustly pink. He set the shell casing carefully on top of the white fabric square. He saw that there was blood on the sleeve of his V-necked navy cardigan.

He leaned back and closed his eyes. He was surprised that

his mind was so calm. He decided that his heart must be the font of whatever wisdom he possessed. It was still a place of bedlam, racketing in revulsion at Carlyle lying still and dead, half his face buried in the braided rug, bleeding neatly, discreetly, there instead of onto the hardwood floor.

But after a while even his heart became serene.

George realized that he was going to survive this astonishing thing.

He reached out and picked up the shell casing. It had a pattern of quarter-inch dots all over it, and up one side was embossed a voluptuous urn holding a single large flower. He couldn't identify what kind of flower it was supposed to be. It had thirteen petals—he counted them—and two large leaves protruded from its stem. He wondered if Carlyle had had this peculiar decoration imposed upon the shell casing, or if it had come like that from wherever he got it.

George studied this object, his weapon, wonderingly. It was a foot high and hollow, about seven inches in diameter at the base, tapering to a little less than five inches at the top. A kind of rim was formed at the base by an indentation etched all the way around, about an eighth of an inch from the bottom. He thought it remarkable that it wasn't even dented. Maybe skulls got frailer as bodies aged, he thought, and brought his left hand up to touch, cautiously, the top of his head. There was blood on the base, and bits of tissue or something. Maybe it was brain, thought George, detached, as he set the shell casing back on top of his handkerchief.

He didn't like feeling so emotionless. Yet it was a relief, too. Just as Carlyle's silence was a relief.

They'd probably have to lock him up immediately, thought George. He was sure there wasn't any bail for murderers. And he didn't plan to explain himself, either, which wouldn't help.

He was curious about prison. They might put him in one of those new-fashioned places, where you had a room, instead of a cell, and got to read and eat half-decent meals. He nodded to himself, thinking, becoming more and more certain that they wouldn't put a person of his advanced age into a maximum security facility. It might be quite an interesting experience, jail. No gardens there, though.

There was some blood on the front of his sweater, too, he noticed. It ought to make him feel sick, or panicky, but it didn't. He was quite tranquil.

He remembered his daughter, Carol, asking when she was very young if he had ever been in jail. He had assured her vehemently that he had not, but her question had shaken him badly. He remembered that she'd been surprised and disappointed by his reply; she'd gotten the idea from somewhere that all men went to jail now and then. George had worried about their brief conversation for a long time. He tried to imagine, now, her adult reaction to his arrest and incarceration, and flinched. He deserved it, no question about that. But he saw the irony in it, and Carol, of course, would not.

Carlyle's living room was drenched in sunshine. His body lay in it. The hardwood floor gleamed in it. There was a disquieting permanence in these moments, George thought. He was sure the sun would continue to shine steadily through the big window at precisely this angle. He was sure the earth had ceased its perambulations at last and come to rest forever at this specific point in its axis.

George continued to rest on the chesterfield, hands on his knees, and felt himself blinking stupidly at the sunshine, at the rocking chair, at the tall cabinet across the room which held a collection of china. There was no horror in the room, no disapproval. There was only the benign sunshine and the radiance of polished wood. The act of murder had apparently been swiftly absorbed, dispensed with; even George's own body had adjusted to what it had done. This didn't seem proper. Something judgmental ought to be happening. But the soporific sun shone in, illuminating Carlyle lying there dead with no more emphasis than it shed upon the rocking chair, or the brass-based lamp on the end table, or George's hands, resting on his knees.

The man was dead. There was no doubt about it. There was an incontrovertible sense of absence in his stillness.

George looked vaguely around the room and continued to sit quietly, waiting for some feeling to claim him. But nothing claimed him. Nothing choked his chest, not remorse or self-satisfaction. He was empty of all things important.

He thought back to the moments of the murder. He could remember each second clearly, but the seconds didn't accumulate neatly in his mind to form a definable experience.

He shouldn't have come here. He hadn't been in this house for months, and he certainly shouldn't have come today.

He couldn't remember what Carlyle had said to persuade him. He couldn't remember walking here. But he remembered arriving. The front door was ajar. On either side of the concrete steps, wide and shallow, was a pot of lemon-scented geranium. They were terra-cotta pots.

The door was ajar. Carlyle had a habit of doing things like that, leaving his doors and windows open for any bright-eyed burglar to get through. When he drove a car, he had never locked it and had often left his keys in the ignition. He was never robbed, and announced this often. "Never been robbed," he would say proudly. "Never. Trust people; that's my motto." His left eye would close, then. He probably thought he looked droll, winking like that, but to George he only looked like he had a left eye that wasn't reliable any more.

Never been robbed, thought George, sitting on the flowered chesterfield. And now he's been murdered.

Carlyle had droned on and on from his rocking chair, looking out the window at the sea. When George finally realized what he was leading up to he tried to stop him, he tried very hard to stop him, but Carlyle put up his hand and shook his head and went right on talking.

At some point George started to leave, but Carlyle said, "I'm talking about your sister, George. Your family." He turned around to smile at him. "Pay some respect, George. Pay some attention."

It was the smile, that mocking, knowing smile, which held George planted to the floor, his feet apart, a horrible prickling sensation moving from the middle of his back right up his spine.

Carlyle had turned back to the window and commenced again to talk. George, behind him, told him loudly to shut up, but still Carlyle went on, his voice flat and deadly. He admitted nothing, nothing, he said such awful, dreadful things, he was going on and on. . . . And then George looked wildly about him and saw the shell casings, two of them, identical, side by side on a bookcase shelf.

His body propelled him relentlessly toward them, his right hand grabbed one of them, he turned around and lurched toward Carlyle, who was still looking out the window, still talking, and then as if suddenly alerted Carlyle began to turn, his left hand grasping the wooden arm of the rocking chair. But the shell casing had already begun its descent. In the split second before George shut his eyes tight and the weapon crashed down upon Carlyle's skull he saw fear in Carlyle's eyes and knew he had seen it there before and tried to remember when, and where, and why he'd seen Carlyle terrified in the past, and it even occurred to him to ask Carlyle, but then of course it was too late.

The sound was unlike anything George had heard before. Once while he was unloading groceries from the back seat of his car a cantaloupe had hurled itself upon the concrete driveway. It was something like that.

George sighed, and rubbed his head, and wished he could weep.

He wanted to go home. He wasn't ready yet for the hustle and bustle of being arrested. He was too tired to answer people's questions, to explain to his lawyer, who had never handled anything more complicated than a will or a real estate transaction, that he now had a murderer for a client. He had to have time to rest, to prepare himself.

Gradually, as he sat thinking, it occurred to George that to give himself up was pointless. Even stupid. When they caught up with him, fine. He'd go to trial and to prison without complaining, with dignity, even, if he could manage it. But to spend any more time locked up than was absolutely necessary—it made no sense.

Besides, he thought, it had been self-defense, in a way. The man had been babbling wickedly about things he didn't understand and had no right to know, trying to hurt him with them, as though George hadn't been hurting always, throughout his adult life, since long before he met Carlyle. And George knew Carlyle had been going to confess, too, to things George had struggled for years to put from his mind.

It was lucky he'd worn his dark blue sweater, he thought, struggling up out of the soft-cushioned chesterfield. The spots and splotches on it could be anything at all.

He hobbled on prickly half-asleep legs into the kitchen, where a fish in a plastic bag lay in the sink. Even this, the sight of Carlyle's never-to-be-eaten lunch, couldn't move him. He rummaged around in drawers until he found some big paper grocery bags. Into one of them he loaded the shell casings; he wasn't sure why he took them both, but he did. He stuffed his handkerchief, marked now with Carlyle's blood, into his back pocket. Then he shuffled cautiously over to where the body lay. He didn't get too close to it, because he didn't want to look at any more of the head than he had to.

Carlyle's eyes were open. George's heart twisted in a sudden, painful spasm. For a moment he thought Carlyle was alive after all, and he felt an awesome relief. I'll leave this time, he told himself; this time I'll leave, quickly, before he can do any more talking, any more harm.

But Carlyle wasn't alive. His eyes were open, but he was dead. He seemed to be gazing across the floor at the heat register in the wall behind the chesterfield.

George went slowly down the hall, slightly stooped from the burden of the shell casings in the paper bag, lodged under one arm. He opened the front door, which he had closed when he entered the house.

Nothing had changed. The sea still slurped from behind the house, the bees still buzzed around the marguerites and marigolds filling the flower beds beneath the windows on either side of Carlyle's front door. He wondered how long he'd been in there and decided it wasn't nearly as long as it felt.

He went out onto the concrete step and turned to shut the door. As he turned, he brushed against the geranium in one of the terra-cotta pots, which released from its leaves the scent of lemon. It seemed to accompany him up the gravel path, through the laurel hedge, along the road, and into his own house, half a mile from Carlyle's.

It wasn't until he had washed off the shell casing and put it on his living room windowsill with its mate, changed his clothes, and put the kettle on for tea that he suddenly remembered Carlyle's goddamn parrot.

CHAPTER 2

Just north of Vancouver, there is a wide blue crack in the continent called Howe Sound, 10 miles wide. Across it, the province of British Columbia juts abruptly west and then extends northward for almost a thousand miles. Its intricate coastline is fissured by innumerable inlets and channels, cluttered by countless small islands, and is at first sheltered from the open Pacific by Vancouver Island, 285 miles long.

Highway 1, the Trans-Canada, comes to a halt on the shores of Howe Sound, at Horseshoe Bay. Ferries leaving from here provide the only access to the Sechelt Peninsula, otherwise known as the Sunshine Coast.

This is the southernmost forty-five miles of that long, long coastline. Along its seaside are towns and villages called Langdale, Granthams Landing, Gibsons, Roberts Creek, Wilson Creek, Selma Park, Sechelt, Halfmoon Bay, Secret Cove, Madeira Park, Garden Bay, Irvines Landing, Earls Cove.

Gibsons, at the southern end, has a population of 3,000 and was named for the first white settler there. Only about 1,000 people live in the village of Sechelt, which is a native Indian word that some people say means "a place of shelter from the sea." But Sechelt is in the middle of the Sunshine Coast and is a service center for several thousand more people who live and work nearby.

This part of British Columbia gets more hours of sunshine every year than most places in Canada—five hundred more hours, on the average, than Vancouver. Because its winters are also very mild, things grow here that will not grow anywhere else in the country—apricot and fig trees, even palm trees, it is said.

There is only one major road, a two-lane highway that follows the coastline for eighty miles and then ends.

In the summer the area is clogged with tourists, even though it is not a quickly accessible place. Getting there depends upon ferry schedules, and once you've arrived, traversing the coastline takes time because the narrow highway is winding and hilly.

The tempo of life on the Sunshine Coast is markedly slower than that of Vancouver, and its people, for the most part strung out along the shoreline, have a more direct and personal interest in the sea.

The coastal forests are tall and thick with undergrowth, but they come gently down to the water and are sometimes met there by wide, curving beaches. The land cleared for gardens is fertile, and the things growing there tempt wild creatures from the woods. In the sea there are salmon, and oysters, and clams; there are also otters, and thousands of gulls, and cormorants. There are Indian legends, and tales of smugglers, and the stories of the pioneers.

The resident police force is the Royal Canadian Mounted Police, with detachments in Gibsons and Sechelt. There are traffic accidents to deal with, and occasional vandalism, and petty theft, and some drunkenness now and then.

There is very seldom a murder.

CHAPTER 3

George waited for his tea to steep, and as he waited he struggled with an image which thrust itself at him again and again: Carlyle's corpse, rotting, little by little, while somewhere nearby a raucous green bird slowly starved to death in its cage.

It was ridiculous, he knew that. Nobody could rot, undisturbed, in his own house; not in Sechelt. People paid too much attention to one another, in Sechelt.

But what if, just this once, they didn't? He couldn't dislodge this possibility from his mind.

George contemplated his situation with profound reluctance. It was early June, and the Sunshine Coast was dry and warm. It didn't seem unreasonable to wait until the sky clouded over before going off to jail. This was probably the last dry sunny spell he'd know as a free man. He had no delusions on that score. He knew they'd catch up with him sooner or later. He had begun to hope, though, that he might first enjoy another season in his garden.

He poured his tea and lowered himself into his leather chair and addressed himself to the problem of Carlyle's pet.

He had seen very little of Carlyle in the last while and as little as possible before that. But Sechelt was a small place and he hadn't been able to avoid him entirely. Therefore he knew all about the bird. Its name was Tom, and Carlyle had doted on it. Since it had made no sound, neither word nor squawk, during George's time inside the house, its cage must have been covered; this, he had been told, was the only way to shut the bird up. And since George hadn't noticed a cloth-covered cage while he was there, Carlyle must have had the creature stashed away in another room. But the damn bird would be there somewhere, all right, and although George disliked parrots, that seemed a poor reason for letting it die for lack of food.

It wouldn't die, he told himself firmly, sipping his tea. Someone was bound to find Carlyle soon. Maybe he had an appointment with somebody that very afternoon. When he didn't show up, he'd be checked on, all right. Somebody was always checking on you, once you got into your eighties. And you often couldn't tell from their voices or their faces whether they were relieved or disappointed to find you still alive. He knew this from his visits to the old folks in the hospital.

How long could a parrot live without having its food and water replenished? he wondered. Carlyle might have filled up its dishes the minute before George arrived. Or he might not. It might be time for its next meal right now. Surely it wasn't stupid enough to remain silent through hunger and thirst, just because a cloth blocked its view of the world outside its cage.

George stared out the window toward his garden and the sea and concentrated. He'd have to go back there, unless he was willing to let the damn parrot die. He'd have to remove the cover from the cage and sneak away, hoping the bird's shrill cries would penetrate the walls of the house, and the laurel hedge, and catch the ears of the couple who lived closest to Carlyle.

Even if he added water and food to the cage himself, assuming he could find whatever it was the damned bird ate, he'd still have to rely eventually on the parrot's making its condition known to the neighbors. And if it didn't, then when the Mounties finally showed up they'd find one dead man and one dead bird.

After a while he got up and phoned Carlyle's house, hoping to find that the police were already there, but nobody answered. For a moment he almost expected Carlyle, dead, to pick up the phone, and laugh at him, or wheeze curses into his ear. The phone rang and rang and he imagined Carlyle's open eyes focusing, his battered head lifting, his limp white hands flexing, pushing his body to its knees; George could almost hear his breathing begin again, and the grunting sounds he would make as he dragged himself off the rug onto the bare wood floor and crawled toward the kitchen, heading for the telephone to complete their interrupted conversation.

He hung up abruptly. Eighteen rings, and no answer.

There was, of course, another alternative. He could go back to Carlyle's house and pretend to find the body. This would involve lying to the police, which he hadn't intended to do, but it was stupid to balk at lying when he'd just done murder. He didn't think his eventual punishment would be any more severe if he concealed as long as possible the fact that he'd committed the crime.

Finding the body seemed the most sensible way out of his dilemma.

He would have to put off his nap for an hour or so.

All for the sake of a smelly, mangy, pop-eyed parrot he was going back there.

George went into the bedroom and stuffed his blood-marked sweater and his handkerchief, which he had left lying on the floor, into a green plastic garbage bag, dumped his kitchen garbage on top of it, and closed the bag with a twist tie. He went into the bathroom to scrub his hands and comb his hair. He put on another V-necked cardigan, a gray one, and rubbed a brush over his shoes, which had gotten dusty on the walk to and from Carlyle's house. He washed out his teapot and his cup and saucer and dried them and put them away. Then he looked at his big, round gold wristwatch.

"Two o'clock," he said aloud. "I think I'll wander down to the library, maybe stop in on old Carlyle on the way." This rang false, but he persevered. He picked up two books that were lying on the footstool in the kitchen, pushed the garbage bag out onto the front porch, left the house, and locked the door behind him. He put the garbage bag out in front of his gate, ready for collection, and set off down the road, along the gravel shoulder, making an effort to lift his weary legs so as not to shuffle. The sun was warm on his sweatered back, and his hand was soon sweaty on the library books he carried. He liked the sun very much.

As he went along he kept an eye on the traffic but saw no car he recognized. There were already a lot of out-of-province license plates, tourists looking hard for God knew what.

George tried to keep his shoulders back and his knees high.

He walked into Sechelt whenever he could, a mile there and a mile back, because the exercise was good for him. He took his car only when the weather was bad. It was in the garage this week anyway, getting its clutch repaired.

He came to the laurel hedge, and then the gate, and went through and down the gravel path to Carlyle's front door. He was full of admiration for himself as he rapped on the door and stood back, attempting a wavery whistle as he waited for Carlyle. Passed up a hell of a career on the stage, I did, he thought, glancing casually through the kitchen window as if to spot Carlyle in there.

He simulated annoyance as he waited, and still nobody came to the door. He was lapsing naturally into his role as crotchety old man, a role he found came in handy, now and then.

George stopped whistling and banged again on the door, harder this time. No response. He hesitated on the broad front steps, between the geraniums. He started back up the path toward the gate in the hedge, stopped, turned around, retraced his steps, and followed the path around to the back of the house, where he peered into the small yard there, and onto the rocky beach, but saw nobody. He went back to the front steps, and knocked again, and then tried the door, which was unlocked.

"Carlyle," he called out irritably, but there was no reply, and he didn't hear anything from the parrot, either.

He went down the shadowed hall, calling, and emerged into the brilliance of the sun-flooded living room. It looks just the same, he thought, as when I was last here, and he blinked rapidly against the sunlight, and then he saw Carlyle's body sprawled on the braided rug next to the rocking chair.

George cried out and flung up his hands. The library books flew to the floor. His heart made a commotion in his chest.

He couldn't move. "Carlyle!" he said. "Carlyle, what the hell's the matter with you?" But Carlyle didn't stir.

(He told himself he was carrying this much too far. Did he think there were Mounties hidden behind the door, for Christ's sake? But he wasn't acting at all, any more.)

"Carlyle," he said again, angry. "What are you doing down there? Get up, man, for God's sake." He shuffled toward him and got close enough to see the open empty eyes and the dark red puddle on the rug in which Carlyle's head was resting. "Oh, Christ, he's dead; the man's dead, all right," said George. There was some relief in this. At least he wouldn't be called upon to try to administer first aid, about which he knew virtually nothing.

(He was appalled at himself; on whom was he practicing these inane deceptions?)

He stumbled backward into the hall, turned, and blundered toward the kitchen, his hands trying to grip the wall. He grabbed the telephone and attempted to dial, but he couldn't get his fingers to work. He put down the receiver and clung to the sink, looking out the kitchen window at the lawn that swept gently up to the laurel hedge. He took several deep breaths, then dialed again. He couldn't remember the emergency number so he dialed the operator. She didn't seem to mind and connected him quickly with the police.

"My name is George Wilcox," he said. "I live about a mile south of Sechelt. I came here to see—he's eighty-five—he's dead. On his floor, dead."

"Who's dead, Mr. Wilcox?"

"Carlyle. He lives halfway along the road between my house and the village. Burke, his name is. Was. Behind a laurel hedge." His teeth were chattering. He had to get outside and stand in the sun.

"Are you sure he's dead, Mr. Wilcox? Do you want an ambulance?"

"What? What? His head's bashed in, man, am I sure he's dead? This is no natural causes you've got here, somebody's bashed the man's head in!"

They took some information and asked him to wait there,

and he did. But he couldn't go back into the living room and sit around near the body. He went outside, but the front yard was partly in shade now and his teeth were still clattering in his mouth.

When the police arrived about ten minutes later, two of them, they found him in Carlyle's small back yard, hunched over on a bench, his hands between his knees, looking out at the sea.

"It was too cold in there," he said when he saw them.

One of them sat down next to him. "We're going to have a few questions, Mr. Wilcox," he said, quite gently. "If you don't mind."

"Don't mind at all," said George. "Not a bit."

CHAPTER 4

Karl Alberg was attacking his back yard with a pair of hedge clippers. All pretensions to cultivation, to horticulture, had been abandoned. It had come down to simple assault, of the armed variety.

He hadn't intended this. He had bought a book, just the day before, determined to do it right. He had rejected several he'd seen in the Sechelt bookstore; they had titles like *The Art of Pruning* and *Pruning for Bigger and Better Blooms*. Then, on a rack in a Gibsons grocery store, he saw exactly what he needed. It had lots of photographs and explanatory drawings, it was written in simple language, and it was bracketed by *All About Meatloaf* and *How to Knit*. Alberg took heart from this. He himself made an excellent meatloaf and had been taught how to knit when he was eight, by his taciturn grandfather, an Ontario farmer. So he bought the book, which was called *All About Pruning*. Last night he'd sat in his living room with his feet up, a glass of scotch at his elbow, and studied. He went to bed confident that by the end of the next day, which he had off this week, his yard would be tamed.

He should have known better. It was amazing how naive a forty-four-year-old man could be.

Poking among the rose canes in search of "outward-facing nodes," he managed only to get his hands and face and arms seared with scratches.

Peering into the massive hydrangea bushes looking for the

"main branches," he only succeeded in making the bees angry.

Climbing clumsily, saw in hand, up into the cherry tree was all to no avail because once in the middle of the tree he could no longer see the skyward-shooting "water sprouts" he was up there to eliminate.

He decided to hire somebody to look after the trees. But he was damned if he was going to let the rest of the yard defeat him. So from a pile of rusty tools in the unused garage at the bottom of the yard he hauled out a pair of hedge clippers, oiled them, and attempted to sharpen them, and then, weapon in hand, he charged the foliage which he was convinced endangered the structural stability of his small house.

He had begun this Tuesday in a state of calm. It was one of his good days. He knew right away that he wasn't going to spend any of it brooding over his mistakes or considering his loneliness.

Clad in cutoffs, a short-sleeved T-shirt and sneakers, he had stood before his bedroom mirror and not been displeased with what he saw. He was tall and broad enough, he decided, that the extra ten pounds didn't really show. Nor did the gray in his blond hair. He pulled in his stomach and turned sideways to the full-length mirror; not bad. He let himself sag and looked again. Not good. He tightened his muscles and pounded his diaphragm with a fist. Hard as a rock, he told himself. But there was no doubt about it, he was definitely getting thick and somewhat flabby around the waist. He would have to start working out again.

He peered critically into the mirror and ran his fingers over his just-shaven jaw. He didn't like his face much. It was too smooth, and it looked a lot younger than the rest of him. Only when he was extremely tired did it assume any character. You needed lines and hollows, he thought, for character.

He stood back and took one last look: the legs were pretty good, anyway. Then he had strolled out to work in his garden.

It was now afternoon. The first attack on the roses had hours before sent him retreating indoors to change his clothes. He was greasy with sweat, the knees of his jeans were grass-stained, and there was at least one rip in his long-sleeved shirt. He didn't remember ever seeing his ex-wife in this condition, after a day in the garden.

He stood in the middle of the back yard and looked around at the chaos he had created. The small lawn was buried under a mountain of debris. It hadn't occurred to him that when he had done his pruning, the greenery would still exist. There seemed far too much of it to get rid of in any usual way. And he hadn't even started on the front yard yet. He wondered if he could just leave the stuff there, to wither and turn brown and shrink into a more manageable heap.

"Jesus, boss," said a voice behind him.

Alberg turned to see Freddie Gainer on the walk that led from the front of the house. He looked startlingly clean.

"I've been gardening," said Alberg wearily. He wiped his forehead on his sleeve. "I am now quitting. And don't call me 'boss.'"

"You look like you've been in a war," said Gainer.

Clean, tireless, and young, thought Alberg, staring at him. Also—and this was illusory—authoritative, in his peaked hat, short blue jacket, and navy pants with the wide yellow stripe.

"What the hell do you want?" said Alberg. "I want a beer." He tossed the hedge clippers to the ground and headed for his back door.

Gainer picked them up and followed him. He put the clippers on the floor inside the door. In the kitchen, he took off his hat.

Alberg got a beer from the fridge and opened it. He leaned against the counter and took a swallow. "Ah. That feels good. A shower, and I'll be human again." He glanced at the constable, then looked at him more sharply. "What the hell have you done to your hair?" It clung to his head in tight, coppery curls.

Gainer's face reddened. "I got it permed."

"Jesus Christ," said Alberg. He wondered if there was anything in Rules and Regulations yet about permanents. He resolved not to find out. "Your damned hat's not going to stay on, with all that fluff underneath it."

"Yeah, it does," said Gainer, and showed him. "You can't even hardly notice it now, right?" He whipped off the hat. "What do you think, Staff? Women'll love it. I'm guaranteed."

"Then what do you care what I think?" said Alberg, irritated. "Did you get that done around here?" he said, as an afterthought.

"Yeah, in Sechelt. There's this girl I met, she's a hairdresser. She says they get as many guys as girls going in for this. It's supposed to last three months, she says. At least."

Alberg drank some more of his beer. His scratches stung. His head ached. He could already tell where he would be stiff and sore the next day. "You use different muscles," he said, feeling old, "attacking plants."

"Listen, Staff, the reason I'm here. We've got us a homicide, and the sarge said you'd want to handle it."

Alberg stared at him. "Why the hell didn't you use the telephone?"

"I did, but there wasn't any answer. I guess you couldn't hear it outside."

Alberg dumped the rest of his beer into the sink and went down the hall to the bathroom, stripping off his shirt. "Fill me in while I get dressed."

It would be a domestic disturbance, he thought, splashing his face with cool water. Some guy crying and hugging his wife while she bled to death from sixteen stab wounds and the knife lying right next to him, his prints all over it. He splashed more water under his arms, over his chest, across the top of his back. Or a brawl at a beer parlor down the highway, two good-time buddies slashing at one another with broken bottles, one a little faster, a little angrier, than the other. In his twenty years on the force, Alberg had worked on fewer than a dozen homicides which hadn't solved themselves at the scene or within twenty-four hours.

No suspicious deaths of any kind had occurred in Sechelt since he'd arrived, eighteen months earlier.

He was rubbing his face and arms dry when he realized what Gainer was telling him.

He caught sight of himself in the mirror over the sink. He

looked scrubbed and healthy and not at all tired, any more.

Gainer, waiting in the hall, wondered hopefully if Alberg would decide that the occasion called for the uniform. Hell, he thought, he's probably forgotten where he put it.

CHAPTER 5

When they arrived at the house there were two blue-and-white patrol cars parked on the shoulder. Theirs made three. There was also an ambulance. Two white-coated attendants waited, leaning against the hood, for instructions.

Alberg saw an elderly couple watching from the end of the driveway which led into the yard next door. Across the street, a woman looked out from a window. A small boy cycled past, slowing to get a better look at what was going on.

Alberg and Gainer went through a gate in a tall laurel hedge and down a crushed gravel path to the front of the house. A constable was stationed at the door. Sid Sokolowski was giving instructions to a dark-haired, blue-eyed corporal when he saw them approaching. "Okay, Sanducci," he said, "get at it," and the corporal went off purposefully toward the far side of the house. Alberg was convinced on little evidence that Sanducci was far more impressed with his own good looks than he ought to have been. He found the young corporal irritating.

Sergeant Sokolowski came up to him, a massive, muscular man whose notebook looked tiny clutched in his large paw. "It happened within the last few hours, Staff. The guy's name was Carlyle Burke. He was eighty-five. Guy who found him isn't a hell of a lot younger—George Wilcox. He was a friend of the victim, lives down the road a ways. Dropped in to say hello and found a corpse."

"Where's Wilcox now?"

"Around back. Redding's with him."

"Okay. Go on."

"The victim was struck on the head. No sign of a struggle, no sign of a break-in or a weapon. This Wilcox called in at two thirty-seven. Sanducci and Gainer got here in eight minutes. It's Sanducci's Italian blood. He oughta be a race-car driver." The sergeant was fond of categorizing people by blood. Mediterranean types were notoriously fast-moving and quick-tempered; Englishmen were cold and logical; the French couldn't tell the truth to save their lives; and then, of course, there was the lusty Slav. . . .

"What else?" said Alberg.

Sokolowski checked his notebook. "I've sent Sanducci out to start looking for the weapon. Called the detachment, got more guys coming to help him and talk to the neighbors. Next I was figuring to get on the blower to Vancouver."

It was a small but rambling house, comfortably sprawled upon a large lot. The laurel which hedged the property on three sides was eight feet tall and about six feet thick. The yard and the house were sleek, well maintained.

"Yeah," said Alberg. "Get on to Vancouver. But all we want is an ident man. If he moves his tail, he can make the four thirty ferry. Anything else?"

"The old fellow who found the body says the victim had a habit of leaving his doors open." Sokolowski was sweating in the afternoon sun. "We oughta get him to take a look around, see if anything's missing. Doesn't look like it to me, but you never know."

They heard a car pull up with a squeal of brakes. It's going to look like the detachment parking lot out there, thought Alberg.

"Okay," he said. "Sounds good. Get the reinforcements to work fast. We want the weapon, and we want something from the neighbors—an individual, a vehicle, sounds from the victim's house—whatever we can get."

Three constables and a corporal arrived through the gate in the hedge and stood nearby, waiting to be dispatched.

"I'll talk to Wilcox," Alberg went on. "Get Redding to call the district coroner's office. Gainer, go tell those ambulance guys not to hold their breath out there. Get the place roped off and sealed," he said to the sergeant. "And Sid, when the guys check the neighborhood, don't let them forget the beach. Anybody wandering around out there, any boats close to shore."

Sokolowski nodded. "There's one thing," he said. "A salmon in the kitchen sink. In a plastic bag. Looks like he bought it today, or somebody gave it to him, and he never got around to putting it in the fridge."

"Did Wilcox bring it?"

"He says no."

"Okay. Good." Alberg grinned. "So we've got something specific to ask the civilians: Any salmon peddlers around today?"

Gainer returned from talking to the ambulance attendants. "They say they'd just as soon hang around," he said. "The hospital can get them on the radio, if they need them."

Alberg sighed. "Better get the ropes up fast, Sid. This place is going to be the A Number One attraction around here. Come on, Freddie. Let's take a look inside."

The flower beds in front of the windows were undisturbed. The concrete steps were unmarked. The constable standing by the half-open door stood stiffly aside as Alberg approached. He looked a bit pale.

"This your first homicide, Constable?" Ken Coomer had joined the detachment in January, after a two-year posting in Prince Albert, Saskatchewan.

"It's the first one I've actually been involved in, Staff. That is—I mean, the first one I've been on the scene of." He looked to be about sixteen, which of course was impossible. "I've seen road-accident stuff that's a lot worse than this. It's just that— it's deliberate, you know what I mean, Staff?" His forehead crinkled as he tried to explain. "I mean, it's just a lot different, that's all, when it's deliberate."

Alberg nodded and went past him, into the hall, followed by Gainer.

The house smelled of flowers. That was the first thing he noticed.

At the end of the hall he stood looking at the body, which

lay directly ahead, on a rug in front of a large window. Then he gazed around the room. It was remarkably serene. The sweet scent of blossoms was stronger; apparently it came from a vase of large pink flowers, lush and frilled, that stood on a coffee table in front of a chesterfield. Alberg could see nothing in the room that hinted of violence or even dissonance; nothing but the body. And two books on the floor nearby, one of them splayed open, face down.

Gainer was breathing heavily at his shoulder. Alberg, hands in his pockets, walked closer to what had been Carlyle Burke. He lay on his right side, almost graceful, a tall man, thin, legs arranged with peculiar elegance on the polished hardwood floor, head and upper torso resting on a brightly colored, home-made-looking rug. Very near him was a rocking chair, half on and half off the rug, one of its motionless rockers poised above his left hip.

"It's neat, for a homicide," said Gainer behind him. Alberg glanced over his shoulder at the constable. "Tidy, I mean," said Gainer, almost cheerfully.

There were no rings on the dead man's fingers. Carlyle Burke had been wearing a pair of white trousers and a pale blue shirt when someone shattered his skull. There wasn't much blood on his clothes, but his head, which was almost bald, lay in a pool of it. Sokolowski was right; he hadn't been dead for very long. His left eye looked hopelessly out across the floor. Alberg reached down, gently, and brushed the lid closed.

Nothing appeared out of order in the rest of the house. In the bedroom, a single bed, a straight-backed chair, a small dresser with a mirror. On the dresser sat a large rectangular lump, covered with a red-and-white checked cloth. Alberg lifted a corner of the cloth. Beneath it was a cage containing a large green bird with a hooked beak. It let out a shriek. "Jesus," said Gainer, whirling from the closet, which was full of clothes hanging from rods and stacked in drawers. Alberg dropped the cloth, and the bird was silent. In another room they found a great many bookshelves and a large ivory piano.

In the bathroom, clean towels. In the kitchen, the salmon in the sink.

"Okay, Freddie," said Alberg. "Let's go see this Wilcox."

"What's your rank?" said George Wilcox. He was sitting on a bench in the middle of a small lawn behind the house.

Alberg noticed more flower beds, and a tall pine tree close to the beach, and under it, set upon wooden blocks, an overturned aluminum rowboat. He heard the sea washing upon the sand.

"I'm a staff sergeant," he said. "The fellow with the curls here is a constable."

The old man was probably in his late seventies, not very tall, maybe five feet seven or eight, 160 pounds or so, with longish white hair that curled out from the sides of his head in waves. He had bright brown eyes and looked strong and fit, despite his age. He was slightly pale but composed. He watched Constable Redding disappear around the front of the house. "Where's he going?"

"The sergeant's going to put him to work."

"Going to be a hell of a hullabaloo around here, once people find out what's going on," said George Wilcox. "They must know something's up already. Those fellows, they came up here with their lights flashing and all that, did they?"

"Probably," said Alberg, thinking of Sanducci. The old man seemed relaxed as he sat there, hands on his knees, peering up at them. He was enjoying the fact that he'd sent for them, and they had come.

"And now you two. You're the boss, right? That why you aren't wearing a uniform?"

"Yeah," said Alberg. "I'm the boss." He pushed his hands into his pockets and continued to study George Wilcox, content to let him chatter on. The man wasn't disheveled. His gray sweater, white shirt, and gray trousers bore no stains, his face and hands were unmarked.

"They said you'd want to ask me some questions," the old man said.

Alberg nodded. "First I'd like you to show me how you happened to find him. Can you do that?"

"Of course I can do it." George pushed himself up from the bench. They walked around to the front of the house, single file, Gainer leading the way, George in the middle.

On the steps, Constable Coomer stepped back to let them through.

George Wilcox leaned shakily against the doorjamb. "Give me a minute," he said.

Alberg stood waiting, polite and watchful; he was suddenly aware of his own excitement, which was almost predatory.

George straightened, tried to smooth his white hair. "Okay. Let's go in."

"Just a minute," said Alberg. "Was the door open like this when you got here?"

"No. Closed. I banged on it, no answer, started back up the path. Then I decided I'd better check up on him. He's eighty-five, you know. Was."

"Was he in ill health?" said Gainer. Alberg's quizzical glance seemed to confuse him.

George Wilcox stared up at the constable. "Ill health? How the hell should I know? I just told you, the man was eighty-five." He jabbed a finger against Gainer's blue-jacketed chest. "The fact of the matter is, sonny, at eighty-five the whole shitteree is fast wearing out. Any minute, something essential could go on you." Again he tried to tame his hair, but the waves sprang back, undeterred. "How do we go about this, then?"

"You started back up the path," said Alberg. "And then you decided you'd better check on him."

"Yes," said George Wilcox, nodding. "I came back to the door and banged on it harder, and hollered, but nothing happened. So I tried the door, and it opened. He never locked his doors."

"Okay," said Alberg. "When you went outside, after you called us, did you close the door behind you?"

The old man shook his head. "Didn't think about closing it. Must have left it open."

"Now," said Alberg. He motioned inside. "Go ahead. Show us."

George Wilcox stepped across the threshold into the hall. "I came in here," he said, and immediately lowered his voice. "I came in here, and I called out to him. No answer. So I walked down the hall." He stopped and said over his shoulder, "I knew he wasn't in the kitchen. I'd looked in the kitchen window, waiting on the step." He began walking again. "So I came down the hall. 'Where are you, Carlyle?' I said, or something like that, and I got to the living room." He emerged into the sunshine and stopped. "Had to blink my eyes a few times. The sun made me blurry for a minute. And I looked around, and I saw him lying there."

He started to point; then his hand began to shake. "His eyes were open," he said in a whisper, "I know they were." He turned to Alberg. "You'd better check," he said urgently. "Maybe he isn't dead after all. His eyes were open, I know they were."

"We checked," said Alberg gently. "He's dead. I closed his eyes."

George Wilcox shut his own eyes for a moment. When they fluttered open, Alberg said, "He was a friend of yours, right?"

"I knew him," said George.

"Do you know the house well? Did you come here often?"

"Sometimes. I used to come here sometimes. Not very often."

"Okay. Look around. Take your time. Tell me if you see anything unusual, anything that's out of place, or anything that seems to be missing."

"That," said George, pointing at the body. "That's unusual."

"Right," said Alberg, soberly. "Anything else?"

With an effort, George Wilcox looked away from the body. For a few seconds he seemed to have difficulty actually seeing anything. His eyes skittered over chesterfield, china cabinet, flowers in the vase, bookshelves, without focusing. Then they concentrated on the rocking chair.

"That," he said finally. "It's supposed to be facing the window more. He sat in it, watched the boats go by or some damn thing, I don't know."

He could have been sitting in the chair when he was struck, thought Alberg; or maybe he fell against it.

"Anything else?" he said.

The old man studied the room. He had regained most of his self-control. "Those books on the floor, there. Those are mine. Library books. I dropped them, when I—when I saw him lying there." He shivered. "Bloody cold in here, don't you think?"

"Just a few more minutes, Mr. Wilcox. Look carefully. Do you see anything else?"

"It all looks just like it ought to," said George. "No, wait. He got himself a parrot lately. I don't see the parrot."

Gainer cleared his throat. "It's in the bedroom."

George looked at him sharply. "Is it dead, too?"

Gainer was nonplussed. "No, sir," he said. "It's fine, I think."

"What are you going to do with it?" George demanded. Alberg watched him, curious.

Gainer glanced at the staff sergeant. "Call the S.P.C.A., I guess. Unless he—Mr. Burke—maybe he's got a friend, or a relative—"

"We'll take care of it," said Alberg.

George turned away from them. "That's it," he said. "Can't tell you anything else."

"Okay, then, Mr. Wilcox. We can get out of here now."

"Fingerprints," said George, on the front steps. "You'll want my fingerprints, I guess. For comparison."

Alberg led him up the path toward the hedge and stopped halfway to the gate. He could see the police investigation ribbon strung across it. "First of all, Mr. Wilcox," he said, "why did you happen to call on Mr. Burke today? You say you don't come here often. Why today?"

George Wilcox shrugged. "Spur of the moment. It was one of those spur-of-the-moment things."

"Did you bring him a salmon? On the spur of the moment?"

George looked astonished. "What would I be doing with a salmon?"

"Maybe you caught it. Do you fish, Mr. Wilcox?"

"I'm a gardener, Staff Sergeant, not a fisherman. I'm not fond of fish, myself."

"Okay," said Alberg equably. "Now, would you tell us, please, where you were today, and what you were doing, before you came here to see Mr. Burke."

Gainer pulled a notebook from his jacket and clicked open his ballpoint pen. George, hearing this, shot him an irritated glance.

"It would be a great help," said Alberg smoothly. "Start from when you got up and just go through your day for us."

George shoved his hands in his pockets and looked down at the gravel path. "I got up early. Around seven. Went out to turn the sprinkler on in my garden." He looked up. "Best time of the day to water, early morning. You wait until the sun's hot, the plants get burned."

Alberg stored this information away. It might be useful, in the unlikely event that he should ever find it necessary to water his jungle.

"Let's see." George Wilcox looked up at the sky. "Then I had breakfast. A bun and some coffee and I think an orange. By this time the paper had come, so I had some more coffee and read it." He looked at Alberg. "You really want to hear all this?"

Alberg smiled. "Please."

"He's not writing much of it down." He glared at Freddie Gainer.

"I use a kind of shorthand," said Gainer apologetically.

"What time was it when you finished your second cup of coffee?" said Alberg.

George thought about this. "Must have been about nine o'clock. Then I turned on the radio. I don't want to hear anybody talking to me until I've had two cups of coffee and read the paper. Then, it's okay, it's company. So I turned on the radio. And then what did I do." He considered. He turned quickly to Alberg. "I forgot to tell you. When I went out to get the paper, I turned off the sprinkler. That would be about eight o'clock. An hour's plenty of watering." He looked relaxed, almost mischievous, and Alberg felt a spurt of annoyance.

"Very good, Mr. Wilcox," he said calmly. "And how did you spend the rest of your morning?"

George turned away restlessly, as though suddenly tired of the game. "I worked out in my garden, that's what I did. I weeded and dead-headed, planted some more annuals. Used to grow my own annuals, when I had a greenhouse. Anyway, I planted some, mostly in the back, and—oh, I sprayed, too. Got some aphids on the goddamn roses, and the broccoli. Came inside at noontime, washed up, changed my clothes, got me some lunch—you want to know what I ate?" he said, aggressively.

Alberg, who didn't, said that he did.

"Vegetable soup, four soda crackers, three pieces of cheese, and a glass of milk," said George Wilcox, angry. "And I took my vitamins then, too, in case you're interested. Did my dishes. It'd be about one o'clock now, I guess. Then I lay down for an hour. I usually lie down for an hour, most afternoons." He looked at Freddie Gainer. "It'll happen to you too, one day, sonny. Then I got up," he said to Alberg, "and decided to go to the library. Thought to myself that I'd stop in on old Carlyle, seeing it's on the way. There," he said defiantly. "You got it. An ordinary day in the ordinary life of an ordinary old person. Until I banged on his front door." He rubbed at his face. "Should have minded my own business. Should have kept right on going. Shouldn't ever have gone in there, not ever."

Alberg nodded, sympathetically. "You live alone, do you, Mr. Wilcox?"

"I do."

"Did you notice anyone passing by while you were out in your garden or having your lunch? Somebody selling fish, for instance?"

George looked at him with interest. "That salmon in the sink. The one you thought I brought. Good lord, you've got yourselves a suspect already, and old Carlyle's not even stone cold yet." He grinned and shook his head. "Nobody came by trying to sell me fish. I was in the back, mostly. The kitchen's in the back, too. Didn't see anybody. Nobody came banging on my door, peddling fish."

"Did anyone at all visit you during the day? Or phone? Did you see anyone, any of your neighbors maybe, while you were working in your garden?"

George looked at him, then at Gainer, then back at Alberg.

"It's just routine, Mr. Wilcox," said Alberg. "We'll be asking everyone who knew him. You just happen to be first, because you found him."

George was expressionless. "Nobody visited me, and nobody phoned. I don't remember seeing anybody while I was in my garden. My fences are high. What about my library books?"

"I'm afraid they'll have to stay where they are for now," said Alberg. "We'll make sure you get them back as soon as possible. One more question, if you don't mind. Do you know anyone who might have wanted Mr. Burke dead?"

George shifted his weight heavily from one foot to the other, and Alberg saw how weary he was. "I didn't know him all that well."

The staff sergeant considered him for a moment. "But what you knew, you didn't like much, did you?" George looked up, and Alberg gave him his sweetest, most compassionate smile.

"No," said George Wilcox quietly. "I didn't." He looked extremely worn. "But us old-timers, you know how it is. We usually don't like to see each other get bashed on the head."

"And that's another thing that bothers me," said Alberg.

"It bothers me too," said George, wiping at his forehead.

"Why were you so sure he'd been bashed on the head?"

George looked at him. "Well, he sure as hell didn't have a heart attack."

"It could have been an accident, though, couldn't it?" Alberg was watching George curiously. "He could have stumbled, fallen, hit his head. Homicide," he said gently, "isn't usually the first thing that comes to mind, when someone's found dead."

George shook his head stubbornly. "There wasn't anything

near enough for him to have landed on. There wasn't anything knocked over, as though he'd fallen on it. And there wasn't any blood, anywhere, except on him, and that rug." He was pale and agitated.

"You're very observant, Mr. Wilcox," said Alberg.

"A thing like that, finding a thing like that . . . it gets burned into your brain," said George to the gravel on the path. "I'd like to go home now."

"Sure," said Alberg. "Thanks for your cooperation. Constable Gainer will give you a lift. We'll want to talk to you again, though."

George squinted up at him. "I don't know any more than I already told you."

"We'll be asking you about Mr. Burke. Who his other friends were—things like that."

George looked at him for a moment, then turned without a word and plodded up the path.

Gainer followed him, shoving his notebook and pen back in his pocket, freeing his hands so he could move the ribbon from across the gate and let the old man out.

CHAPTER 6

The following day, Cassandra Mitchell sat in her car outside the Pacific Press building in Vancouver. There was a bundle of letters in her lap. She dug her sunglasses out of her purse and put them on; then she picked up the topmost envelope. BOX 294, THE VANCOUVER SUN, it said, in block letters written with a blue ballpoint pen. She couldn't tell much from that.

She ripped it open and pulled out a small folded piece of notepaper, and as she did so, something else fell out of the envelope. She picked it up and saw that it was a photograph. She stared at it. It was a waist-up picture of a hairy, muscly man in his early thirties, apparently wearing nothing but his self-satisfied grin. Cassandra felt herself flush. She put down the photograph with care on the seat next to her, wondering if she really wanted to read the accompanying message. "Be brave," she mumbled to herself.

Dear Box 294. I have never answered an add in the paper before, but I knew as soon as I read yours that your the one for me. I'm younger than you said but not much and believe me it wont matter. Let me know your number and I'll phone you so we can meet and get together and get to know each other. You wont regret it and I know I wont either. Love, Brett.

"'Love, Brett,'" said Cassandra. She scrunched up the letter, tossed the rest of the pile on top of the photograph, and started up the car with a roar.

The Hornet churned across the Granville Street bridge, and the breeze from the open window blew Cassandra's dark hair around her head. A total of fifteen letters she'd had, counting today's four, from two advertisements. It had cost her a packet and she hadn't even wanted to meet most of the men who had written to her.

She inched her way through the rush-hour traffic wondering why on earth she had done such a thing: advertised in the paper, for God's sake, for a man.

Yet she had. She had delivered the advertisement to the newspaper in person, as was required. She had slunk in and out of the building, hidden behind her sunglasses and a guilty slouch. In due course she returned, to pick up the replies. While waiting for her turn at the counter she watched a man walk away with a pile of letters almost high enough to make him stagger. Eagerly she gave her box number to the woman behind the counter, who disappeared briefly and returned with six envelopes. Cassandra looked at them incredulously, then at the middle-aged woman with ferociously yellow hair who had given them to her. "I know, dearie," the woman had said, "it's the men get all the answers." The next time, there were only five letters; and this time, four.

Phyllis Dempter, small, blond, and restless, married to a preoccupied Gibsons dentist, had encouraged her in this madness. In fact, Cassandra reminded herself, amid bumper-to-bumper traffic on the Lions Gate bridge, the whole thing had been her friend's idea.

"You're giving up too soon," Phyllis had said calmly when Cassandra flapped before her eyes the dispiriting replies to the first ad. "These things take time. You've got to go through a lot of chaff before you get to the wheat."

"Chaff," muttered Cassandra, turning off the bridge onto Marine Drive, the road still bottlenecked. "Wheat."

She had made several self-conscious forays into Vancouver for encounters set up in awkward telephone conversations during which she strained (with notable lack of success) to put appropriate faces to unfamiliar male voices. So far she had met and conversed reasonably politely with a chartered accountant who had never been out of British Columbia, a fact he stated with bewildering pride; a sixty-five-year-old businessman who had felt it fitting not to have previously revealed the disparity in their ages because he was "young at heart"; and a teacher who told her immediately that he was married but enjoyed a "nonthreatening" relationship with his wife.

None of them had stirred her blood.

She had seen none of them twice.

She was on the Upper Levels highway now, heading through much lighter traffic for Horseshoe Bay and the ferry that would take her across the sound. Far below to her left lay the blue-silver sea.

Her ad had made it clear that she lived, inconveniently, on the Sunshine Coast. Three of her replies had been from men who also lived there, which for some reason she hadn't expected. Cassandra had responded to only one of these, a man whose letter had piqued her curiosity because it revealed nothing about him but his first name. *I enjoyed your ad and would like to meet you,* he had written, and he'd put his telephone number below his signature. She had eventually called him and they arranged to meet in Sechelt for lunch, but he had canceled their appointment twice, and if he didn't show up the next time, on Friday, she was going to tell him to forget it. It was probably a lousy idea anyway, she thought. Too close to home. Every time a male person of the right age came into the library she blanched a little, wondering if he was the one and hoping he was not.

She remembered the three unopened letters on the seat beside her and permitted herself a small surge of hope.

She waited patiently in line for the ferry and, when she had driven aboard, sat in the car until everybody else had scurried off to find the cafeteria or the sun deck, and then she opened the rest of the letters.

There was one from an X-ray technician who enjoyed walking in the woods and listening to hard rock; one from an insurance salesman who liked women and cats but expressed disapproval, entirely unsolicited, of children and dogs; and one from a tuna fisherman whose wife had left him and who was too shy to try to find a prostitute. Cassandra, disheartened, tore them up, decided not to show Phyllis the picture of the naked hairy man after all, and tore that up too.

She passed up the cafeteria and stood out on the sun deck, wrapped in a sweater against the wind, during the half-hour trip to Langdale. She watched a tugboat hauling an enormous log boom, and sailboats dipping in the wind, and the mountainous coastline pressing at the sea.

It would soon be nine years since she'd moved to Sechelt. Although she enjoyed the village, she didn't want to spend the rest of her life there. This had proved enormously complicating to her sex life. Nine years ago she was thirty-two and considered still of marriageable age by the few men there over thirty and unattached. They were surprised—even shocked—to discover that she had no interest in marrying one of them and settling down for good in a small town on the Sunshine Coast. It was impossible to explain why. "I'm just waiting for my mother to die," she could have said, cheerfully, "and then I'll be off." Impossible. Eventually all the men had drifted away and gotten married to women younger and less disconcerting than she.

Cassandra turned her back on the water and stretched her arms along the railing of the sun deck, surveying the other people there, checking them out from behind her sunglasses. A few she recognized: an elderly couple who lived in the same senior citizens' complex as her mother; a lanky, black-haired woman who lived alone above the Sechelt hardware store and whose balcony was crammed with potted flowers from March until November; the cheerful, overweight, perpetually perspiring man who operated the service station across from the hospital. There were some children running up and down the deck, too—it was a wonder dozens of them didn't catapult themselves overboard every year, especially in the tourist season.

Cassandra sighed and faced the sea again, letting the wind whip her hair back, instead of forward around her face. She began to think about the men she had loved, even merely enjoyed the company of, during the course of her life; but soon gave this up, because she believed in looking firmly ahead, preferably with an optimistic heart.

They were passing Keats Island, now. Only a few more minutes.

Traveling down the three escalators that led to the car deck, Cassandra decided that it might be worth one more try. She would get Phyllis to help her rewrite the ad. Maybe she had made too modest a self-presentation. God knew, she didn't mind admitting it, she would dearly love to meet an agreeable male person. It had been far, far too long.

At seven that evening she was in the library, and at seven thirty George Wilcox came in, a bunch of irises in his hand.

"Cassandra," he said, presenting her with the flowers. "I like saying your name. Never known another girl with that name."

"I'm not fond of it, actually," she said, smiling at him. "I'd have preferred being called something more ordinary."

"It's got a nice lilt to it," said George, "you've got to admit that. How would you like to have a name like mine, now? George. In your case it would be Georgina, or Georgette, or some damn thing. It sounds like your mouth's full of porridge, George does."

"But it's what it means that's important," said Cassandra. "Not what it sounds like." She put down the irises and whisked a dictionary out from under the counter. "Mine means the unheeded bearer of bad tidings, that's what it comes down to. But yours—" She looked it up. "Earthworker," she announced, triumphantly.

"Farmer," said George.

"Or gardener," said Cassandra. She closed the dictionary with a snap and stuffed it back under the counter. "It suits you."

"Maybe," said George, grudgingly, and he wandered off among the books.

When the library had moved two years ago from its old, cramped, musty quarters in the basement of a church to the new building, Cassandra, eyeing the six wide floor-to-ceiling windows, had gone off immediately to buy several large plants. Included in the order were three *Ficus benjamina*, five or six feet tall, shivery and graceful. Two days after they were set in place, they let loose a shower of leaves. George Wilcox was waiting at the front door when she arrived to open the library that day and was witness to her dismay.

"They don't like being moved, that's all," he told her. "Just leave them alone. Mist them a lot—squirt them with water. They'll be all right."

And they were. Cassandra took to consulting him whenever she had worries about the plants, which she considered a far weightier responsibility than the books, since she knew nothing about them.

George Wilcox was one of her more regular customers. His preference among books was biographies, while hers was novels. Eventually, casual conversation as he checked out his books led to her reading some that he recommended and to his trying an occasional work of fiction.

He had started bringing her things a year ago: flowers from his garden, interesting shells from his beach, sometimes small potted plants which he told her sternly were for her house, not the library. When his wife became ill in November, Cassandra helped him choose books for her. And when she died, in March, Cassandra appeared at his door with a chicken casserole, feeling stupid and helpless, and in his kitchen she wept with him, and he patted her shoulder and made her coffee.

She wondered now, putting the irises in water, what he would think if he knew about her ad in the paper. They had had few personal conversations—although he had once told her, uneasy but determined to speak his mind, that he was sure her mother would survive quite happily in Sechelt without her. Cassandra, shocked to find he had read her situation so accurately, didn't reply, and he hadn't mentioned it since.

She put the vase of flowers on the counter and went to hunt up three romance novels for Mrs. Wainwright, whose husband would stop by later to pick them up for her. Mrs. Wainwright, a bustling, large-boned woman of fifty, was a practical nurse whose hours seldom allowed her to visit the library in person.

Cassandra found George Wilcox scanning the shelves of mysteries and was surprised.

"It's that business with Carlyle," he said, by way of explanation. "It's turned my mind to crime." He jabbed his finger toward the shelves. "Who's good, here?"

She picked out a book by Julian Symons and another by Ruth Rendell and handed them to him.

"They're both English," he said, studying the jackets. "Doesn't surprise me. All those bizarre murders they get over there. Ever noticed that? You see a headline in the paper— 'Eviscerated corpse found in bog,' say—and you know right away they're talking about England."

She walked with him back to the checkout counter. "I heard about Mr. Burke. It's terrible. So much more awful than if he'd died of an illness."

"Quicker, though," said George, getting his library card from his wallet. "He probably never knew what hit him."

"Do the police know yet?" said Cassandra. "What hit him, I mean?"

"Who knows? It only happened yesterday. And they're going to be vague about it, even if they do know something. A secretive bunch, those Mounties."

She pushed the books across the counter to him. "He must have surprised a robber, or something."

He loaded the books, the two mysteries and a biography of Mozart, into a crumpled plastic grocery bag which he'd pulled from his pocket. "He wasn't robbed. That's what they say." He shrugged. "Somebody must have had it in for the old bugger. That's all I can figure." He grinned at Cassandra. "You didn't notice. I haven't brought my last ones back."

"That's all right. You've only had them for a couple of days."

He leaned over the counter. "The police have them now. They're scene-of-the-crime evidence, your books."

"Good heavens," said Cassandra, mildly.

"I dropped them." He pointed to the floor. "Right next to the body, I was."

"Good heavens," said Cassandra, weakly.

"Not to worry," said George. "They flang themselves in the other direction."

Cassandra saw that there was sweat on his forehead. She thought his eyes looked feverish. Only his white hair, sweeping in flamboyant waves out from the sides of his head, appeared unaffected by his experience. His neck suddenly looked too thin and scrawny to hold his large, well-shaped head erect. He had to look up at her; Cassandra wondered if, in the physical prime of his life, he had been taller. "It must have been dreadful for you," she said softly, "finding him like that."

He looked out the window. "It wasn't so bad. No more than I deserve." He turned back to her. "And don't waste your sympathy on him, either. He was one first-class Grade A son-of-a-bitch, was Carlyle. He got exactly what was coming to him." He started for the door, his back straight, his legs in baggy trousers slightly bowed.

Cassandra was astounded. "You don't mean that," she said. "You can't mean that."

He turned back, hesitated, seemed about to go on, but when he spoke he said only, "It's time you had another look at my garden. The roses are grand this year, just grand. Stop by. I'll give you some lemonade." He waved at her and was gone.

CHAPTER 7

If he had been the first of the men she'd met through her ad he would have been a disappointment. But her standards had plummeted, or at least her expectations had.

She was relieved that he was neither too young nor too old, and not ugly, either. He wasn't what she would call extremely attractive, but at least he was tall enough, and big, though not overweight.

His taste in clothes wasn't anything to lift the spirits. He wore a suit, which in Sechelt was unusual to the point of being extraordinary—a dark gray one, with a plain white shirt and a maroon tie that was much too wide.

Cassandra approached him, walking briskly, holding out her hand and grinning at him. He seemed astonished, possibly by the wideness of her smile, but rallied enough to smile back as he rose from the table to greet her.

"The more nervous I am," she said to him, "the bigger I grin."

"You must be Cassandra." He shook her hand, then pulled out a chair for her. "I'm Karl."

"With a K," said Cassandra, sitting down.

"With a K," he agreed.

He had white-gold hair, not a sign of a wave in it, and pale blue eyes, and his face was a collection of planes. She wondered if she would feel any physical attraction for him, by the time lunch was over.

"You do have an Aryan look about you," she said.

They were almost alone in the restaurant, which was a place with overgrown ferns hanging from the ceiling and a view over the water.

The waitress approached, a petite, curvaceous young woman with a tumble of wavy auburn hair. "Hi, Cassandra," she said with a grin. "How's your life?" Her eyes skittered to Alberg.

"Just fine, thank you, Rosie," said Cassandra briskly.

"You two gonna have a drink? Maybe a bottle of wine?"

"I was thinking more of coffee," said Cassandra. "And then maybe some food."

"Oh. Right. I'll go get a couple of menus, then."

"Librarians," muttered Cassandra as Rosie turned away, "can't slink among the stacks smelling of gin."

Alberg was observing with interest Rosie's undulating progress across the room.

"She's studying psychology," said Cassandra.

Alberg looked at her. "I beg your pardon?"

"Rosie. She's a psychology major. At U.B.C. Her parents own this place. She works here in the summers."

"Ah."

Rosie returned with menus. "The clam chowder's good today. So I'm told."

"I'll have it," said Cassandra promptly. "And coffee."

"Me too," said Alberg. He smiled at the waitress as he handed back the unopened menus, but at least this time he didn't goggle at her as she walked away.

"I hate this," said Cassandra with passion.

Alberg leaned forward politely. "What do you hate? Having lunch? Restaurants with ferns? Or meeting strangers?"

"Meeting strangers." She took a drink of iced water, wishing it were wine.

"I liked your ad," he said after a while.

"Why? What made you like it?"

"It had a nice, sunny sound to it."

Rosie returned with two bowls of clam chowder and a basket of rolls and butter. "Have a nice lunch, you two," she said sentimentally.

Cassandra stared indignantly at her back.

Alberg laughed. "Hey, look," he said. "Relax. Enjoy yourself. You never have to see me again, if you don't want to. Meanwhile"—he waved his spoon at her—"she's right, it's good clam chowder. You can tell by the smell." He closed his eyes and leaned over the soup and sniffed, blissfully.

"I'm sorry," said Cassandra, smiling. "You're right." She began to eat.

"Tell me about yourself," he said.

"I'm a librarian. Here in Sechelt. That's what I meant in the ad, when I said—"

"'Books are my work, my comfort, and my joy.'"

She looked at him curiously. "What did you think of that?"

"I thought you were probably a librarian." He took a spoonful of soup.

Cassandra laughed. "I could have been a writer. Or a bookbinder."

"You could have been. But it seemed unlikely. What else?"

"What else? Well, let me see." She broke open a roll and buttered half of it. Then she put the roll back on her plate and her hands in her lap and spoke rapidly. "I'm forty-one years old, financially secure though not much more than that, never been married, came here from Vancouver almost nine years ago—God, I can't believe that—I've got a mother who lives in Golden Arms and a brother who lives in Edmonton, I go back to Vancouver once a week if I can to remind me that these villages up and down the coast are not all there is." She picked up her soupspoon and the buttered roll.

"Golden Arms? Oh, that senior citizens' place."

"Yes, that's right. They live there on their own, but somebody's there to sort of watch over them. Now you. Tell me about you."

"I'm a police officer."

She looked at him blankly. "A police officer. A cop. Are you a Mountie? Up here, you must be a Mountie."

"R.C.M. Police. Yeah. I hate 'cop.'"

"A policeman. R.C.M.P." She chewed her roll thoughtfully. "I use marijuana sometimes. Nothing else, though, not for a long time. I've had a few speeding tickets, too."

"This is obviously not going to work out." She looked up to see him smiling; she hadn't heard a smile in his voice. The smile altered her entire impression of him. There might be some exuberance in there, after all.

"What else?" she said. "I mean, there's got to be more to you than being a policeman."

"Not much."

"Well, what do you like to do," said Cassandra patiently, "when you're not on duty?"

"I think I like having lunch with librarians," he said. "Or dinner." It was the first thing he'd said that sounded awkward. He pushed away his bowl. "Do you mind if I smoke?" She shook her head, and he lit a cigarette. "I don't read much. I like to go to the movies, sometimes. I like to travel. I like to sail."

"Are you separated, or divorced, or something?"

"Divorced."

She felt considerable relief. "Why are you divorced?"

"We get moved around a lot. My wife finally got tired of it. I don't blame her. We were in Kamloops before I came here. We'd been there five years, and she'd started a little business, a boutique. She didn't want to give it up."

Cassandra waited, but he didn't go on. "Do you have any kids?"

"Two. They're in university now. In Calgary. That's where their grandparents live. My ex-wife's parents."

Cassandra looked out over the water. She wondered why his children hadn't wanted to go to university in Vancouver, where they could be near their father. "Where did you learn to sail?" she said.

"On Lake Ontario. That's where I grew up. Toronto."

"What kind of a policeman are you? You don't give out traffic tickets and things like that, do you?"

"No." He smiled again. "This is my detachment. Sechelt. I do whatever comes along."

"If this is your detachment," she said hesitatingly, "then you must be involved in that awful thing, that poor old Mr. Burke."

"Yeah."

"The man who found the body—he's a friend of mine."

"George Wilcox?"

"He comes into the library a lot. We've become friends." She felt an uneasy sense of caution. "He was quite upset, I think."

"I'm sure he was."

She finished her lunch in silence. He doesn't talk about his work, she thought. She wondered if this was because she was a stranger to him, or if he hadn't even talked about it with his wife. She'd read somewhere that a lot of cops—police officers, she corrected herself—were like that.

Over coffee they discussed the Sunshine Coast, and Vancouver, and sailing. Cassandra kept trying to imagine him brandishing a revolver and shouting, "Stop in the name of the law!" He looked a bit old to be doing that sort of thing, actually. Maybe he just did administrative work and delegated all the other stuff.

"How many ads have you answered?" she asked him.

"Oh, two or three. Maybe four."

She wanted to ask how successful these other meetings had been. "Have you put in an ad of your own?" she said instead.

"No."

"Are you going to?"

"I don't think so."

"You'd get more replies than I have," said Cassandra glumly. "There are hordes of women out there, just hordes of them."

"Yeah," said Alberg, "but they all want to get married."

Cassandra looked at him with interest. "Oh, do they?" she said casually. She glanced at her watch. "My God, I've got to get back to work."

"Me too," said Alberg. He put his cigarettes and lighter in his pocket and laid money on top of the bill. He got up and pulled back Cassandra's chair for her.

Outside the restaurant he walked her to her car. "How long have you had this thing?" he said, looking critically at the Hornet.

"All its life. Nine years." She put an affectionate hand on its hood.

"I'd like to see you again," he said. "But I won't call you if you've already made up your mind that you don't want to see me."

Cassandra lowered her head to fish her sunglasses from her purse. "Go ahead and call," she said carelessly.

He opened the door for her. "You ought to lock it, you know."

"I ought to exercise, too, and eat more salads." She climbed in and slammed the door.

"Thank you," said Alberg through the window. "I enjoyed myself."

"Are you off duty?" said Cassandra. "Is that why you're wearing that suit? If you don't mind my asking."

"I don't mind your asking. I'm going to a funeral." He smiled. "I'll call you."

She watched him drive away. She didn't know yet whether she liked him or not. She certainly didn't *dis*like him.

She started the car. It wouldn't hurt to see him again, she thought, driving back to the library. Even though she'd never been all that fond of blonds. And she'd certainly never imagined herself dating a cop. A police officer.

CHAPTER 8

"Helen Morris, please."

"This is she."

"Mrs. Morris, I'm Staff Sergeant Alberg of the R.C.M. Police in Sechelt."

"Oh, yes, Mr. Alberg." Her voice was thin, gray. "I think I remember you. Tall and fair-haired."

"Right."

"You paid your respects, as I recall. When I was there to—make the arrangements."

"You didn't stay for the funeral," said Alberg.

"No." There was a pause. "It was today, wasn't it."

"I kind of expected to see you there. I've got a few questions—I'd hoped you'd be able to help us out a little more."

"I don't see how I could," she said. "As I told your sergeant on Wednesday, I hadn't seen my brother in more than twenty years. I haven't the faintest idea what he's been doing, who his friends were."

"Not even Christmas cards?"

She didn't reply.

"You didn't even exchange Christmas cards?"

"No, Mr. Alberg. We didn't."

"Were you surprised to hear that he'd died?" Alberg leaned back in his chair and put his feet on the desk. He shifted the phone to his other ear.

"Not particularly. He was eighty-five, after all."

"How old are you, Mrs. Morris?"

"I'm seventy-six. But healthy."

"Were you surprised by the will?"

She laughed. "As you've just discovered, he never even sent me a Christmas card. Why should I be surprised that I don't figure in his will? I wouldn't have taken anything from him, anyway."

"Were you surprised to hear how he'd died?" Alberg squinted his eyes almost closed, as though by diminishing his vision he could make his hearing more acute.

He heard her sigh. "Of course I was surprised," she said irritably. "I'm not accustomed to having acquaintances who get themselves murdered."

"Acquaintances?" Alberg let his voice fill with amazement.

Another silence. "He wasn't much more than that, Mr. Alberg. I regret having to say so, but it's true."

"Do you have any other brothers? Any sisters?"

"No. There were just the two of us."

"So he was your only living relative."

"In the sense you mean it, yes. I have three children. My husband died several years ago. Forgive me, but I really don't see the point of your questions."

"I was just thinking that it must be very sad to have been estranged for so long from your only brother. It must have been a great sadness in your life, and in his." He winced, telling himself not to overdo it.

"Estrangement, Mr. Alberg, implies a previous affection. There was never any affection between Carlyle and me. Therefore we were never estranged, and the situation was never a sad one."

Alberg removed his feet from his desk and sat up. "What *was* the situation between you, Mrs. Morris?" He went on quickly, before she could tell him it was none of his business. "You see, so far we don't have any suspects in your brother's homicide. In order to try to find out who did this to him, it's necessary to know something about him. What kind of man was he? Did he, for example, make friends easily?"

He waited, and the long-distance seconds ticked by, but she didn't reply.

"He lived here for five years, Mrs. Morris," he said. "Played the piano at the old folks' dances, sang in the men's choir down at the Old Age Pensioners' hall, played bingo nearly every week, even went on a couple of bus tours to Reno." He paused; no response. "Quite a sociable fellow, your brother." He picked up a pen and began doodling on a routine letter from division headquarters. "Yet you know, the funny thing is, he doesn't seem to have had any particular friends. He only did things in groups. Does that sound like your brother to you?"

"I keep telling you," she said sharply, "that I hadn't seen him in twenty years. You could tell me anything at all—I'd have to believe it. The man was a stranger to me."

He liked the sound of her voice, as he had liked the brief glimpse of her which she had permitted the village during her quick trip to arrange for her brother's burial. She was tall and straight and thin, well dressed, with coiffured white hair and a lift to her chin. She had been brisk and businesslike, in Sechelt.

"It wasn't that people didn't like him, exactly," said Alberg thoughtfully. "Most people described him as the life of the party, that sort of thing." He tossed the pen aside and leaned back. "But there were a couple of people who told us they felt kind of uncomfortable with him. And this interests me, as you might imagine."

"Really," said Carlyle Burke's sister, politely.

"Yeah. That's all we've got. Some people felt uncomfortable with him. They said things like..."—he shoved the defaced letter aside and ruffled through the file on his desk—"I'm quoting, now. 'He made me nervous with all his boisterousness.' And, 'It was like he was always acting a part, and you'd wish and wish he'd give it a rest now and then but he never did.' And, 'I don't like to speak ill of the dead, but whenever he asked me to dance I'd try to find an excuse; the way he liked to fling people around when he was dancing—well, it was too much for me, I'm seventy-eight years old.'" Alberg rubbed his forehead and closed his eyes and waited. "Nothing serious there," he said absentmindedly. "It just got me thinking, that's all."

"No," said Mrs. Morris. "No, it doesn't sound particularly serious."

Alberg sat up. "In the twenty years since you saw him," he said amicably, "who did you talk to about him, and what did you tell them?"

"What makes you think I *ever* talked about him? To anyone?"

"I don't know. But I'm sure you did."

He imagined her sitting at a small desk under a window. There would be white curtains at the window, the kind that hung straight to the floor. Maybe the desk had pigeonholes. It was probably made of dark wood, and it probably shone in the light from the window, or the lamp that would be standing next to it. He saw her fidgeting with the telephone cord, wrapping it around her fingers, unwrapping it, wrapping it again around her fingers, marking them.

"I can fly out to Winnipeg to see you," he said softly, "if that would be easier for you. Maybe talk to your children, too, while I'm there."

"There's no need for that," she said coldly. "They never met him. They never laid eyes on him. I made sure of that."

He waited again, and when she finally began to speak her voice was toneless. She spoke quickly, and Alberg gave an inaudible sigh of relief.

"He was nine years older than I. He taunted me when I was a child, baited me when I was an adolescent. My parents punished him, but it didn't do any good. He didn't like me, that's all. Maybe if I had been born when he was younger, or older. . . . I'm trying to be charitable. Really, I don't believe it would have made the slightest difference. He just didn't like me, that's all. So of course eventually—it didn't take long— I didn't like him, either. It's as simple as that."

"Was he physically cruel to you?"

"Oh, not really. It was nothing like that," she said quickly.

"Did he get into trouble at school, for the same kinds of things?"

"I don't know. I don't remember. I was nine years younger than he; that's a big difference, when you're children."

"Was he ever married?"

Another pause. "Good heavens, Mr. Alberg. He was married to George Wilcox's sister. I'm astonished that you didn't know."

Alberg stared blankly at the photograph of his daughters that hung next to his desk. "Jesus. So am I."

"But perhaps it isn't so surprising after all," she said, almost comfortingly. "It was a long time ago—thirty years ago. And the marriage only lasted two years. Audrey was killed in a car accident."

"Thirty years ago. You mean he was fifty-five before he got married?"

"Yes."

"Why did he wait so long?"

"I really haven't the faintest idea." She sounded cool, now.

"Did you go to his wedding?"

"I hadn't any choice. My mother was still alive—it would have upset her if I'd stayed away."

"You met his wife, then, and her brother?"

"I met Audrey. I don't remember meeting George. I remember that she spoke of him with great affection, and that he gave her away, but I don't remember him."

"Did you see him this week, while you were in Sechelt?"

"No."

Alberg frowned, irritated. All this was very interesting, but what the hell did it mean, if anything?

"Tell me about Audrey," he said.

"I only saw her a few times, over a period of a couple of days. She was lovely." Alberg could hear her smile. "Absolutely a lovely person. Not so much in the way she looked, although she was very pretty. It was more—oh, a kind of singing in her, if you know what I mean." Alberg wished he could see her face. "I was amazed that she was going to marry Carlyle—she was twenty years younger—and that she behaved so fondly toward him, and seemed so happy." She gave a bitter laugh. "But nothing lasts, does it, Mr. Alberg? Two years later, she was dead."

"Some things last, Mrs. Morris," said Alberg gently. "You hated him, and that sure lasted, didn't it?"

She sighed. "I can't help you," she said wearily. "I have no idea who could have killed him. You'll probably find it was one of those senseless acts of—of random violence. There's a lot of that, these days, isn't there?"

When he'd hung up the phone, he sat back with his feet up on the desk and his hands behind his head.

His office was small, containing in addition to his desk and swivel chair a filing cabinet, a large bulletin board, some bookshelves, a deep black leather chair with an aluminum frame, and next to it a small, scarred coffee table.

Maybe he'd try to get back out to Toronto later in the summer, to see his parents, he thought. Maybe he could pry his daughters loose from Calgary and take them with him.

He swung around in his chair to look at the photograph. He found himself studying it intently.

They were young women in their late teens, standing in front of a tall, smooth-trunked tree. Unsmiling, grave, they seemed to bend slightly toward each other, like dancers. The girl with shorter hair and larger eyes was deeply tanned; she stood behind her younger sister, her right shoulder pressing lightly against Diana's left. Diana, hair long and sleek, the color of taffy, faced the camera almost straight on. Her head and neck and shoulders were aware of her sister; she had an air of guarded protectiveness. They were bare-armed, wearing dresses, and Janey's tan was very dark against Diana's ivory skin. They looked straight out from the photograph, straight into his eyes, and they weren't smiling. He had taken the picture the summer before he left Kamloops. Had they broken into laughter when the picture-taking was over? He couldn't remember. Or had they turned their backs on him and walked away down a tree-arched road into their own futures, abandoning him as he was about to abandon them? . . .

He became aware of an unfamiliar scent and sniffed suspiciously, his eyes darting around the office. In the middle of his small coffee table stood a pot of white flowers. He got up quickly, picked up the flowers, and strode out into the reception area, where he set the pot down hard in the middle of Isabella's desk. She looked up at him, annoyed. From the cage on the card table next to her desk, Carlyle Burke's parrot shrieked at him.

"You startled him," said Isabella disapprovingly.

"Keep your damn plants out of my office," said Alberg. "And keep that damn bird quiet." He turned to leave and then came back. "What are they, anyway?"

"Stock," said Isabella. "Nice smell, eh?"

Alberg put his hands flat on her desk and gazed into her eyes. "Every week, Isabella, you clean my venetian blinds with vinegar," he said. "Nobody asked you to do that. It's not part of your job to do that. And I appreciate it. It's very nice to have clean venetian blinds. Only, Isabella, my office smells like a pickle jar. And when you add the smell from these flowers—they combine in the air, and the result is nauseating." He removed his hands from her desk and stood up.

"I never thought of that," said Isabella. "The question is, do you want clean blinds or nice fragrant flowers that bring a whiff of summer into this joint?" She frowned, pondering.

Isabella Harbud was a tall, lumpy woman married to a chiropractor. She had long thick hair, once brown, now becoming unapologetically gray, and she wore it down, which Alberg thought inappropriate in a woman of late middle age. Her front teeth protruded, and she didn't care much about the way she dressed. She was usually cold, even in summer, and had a selection of thick sweaters which she grabbed from her closet without any apparent consideration as to what she planned to wear underneath. Today the sweater was turquoise, and partly obscured a red and black striped dress. She had the most beautiful eyes Alberg had ever seen: gold, flecked with brown; they were what he imagined a tiger's eyes must look like.

"You want clean blinds," said Isabella, decisively.

"Right," said Alberg, with gratitude.

"I'll bring you in one that doesn't have a smell."

"I don't have any room in my office for any plant. No room."

"Sure you do," said Isabella comfortingly, going back to her typing.

"When you go home," Alberg yelled as he went down the

hall, "make sure you cover up that damn cage."

Sokolowski appeared from somewhere and followed him into his office. Alberg swung his feet back up onto the desk and linked his hands behind his head. "What've we got, Sergeant? Fill me in. Bring me up to date." He tossed him the file. "Let's go over the whole damn thing, one more time."

Sokolowski settled himself in the black chair and opened the file. His big thighs strained the fabric of his dark blue uniform trousers, his legs were stolidly apart, feet planted heavy on the floor. "Victim died between eleven A.M. and two P.M. on Tuesday, June fifth, from a blow to the head. Death was probably instantaneous. The coroner says the weapon was a metal object, rounded, with some kind of rim. Very little spattering. Probably some blood got on the perpetrator's clothes, but not much. No forced entry into the house." He droned on, shifting his feet a little. "Nothing missing as far as anybody can tell."

"I know all this," said Alberg, staring at the ceiling.

"Several neighbors saw the fish guy's truck, four of them saw the fish guy." Sokolowski looked up. "You want their names and addresses?" Alberg shook his head, slowly. "Vehicle described as an old VW van, couldn't pinpoint the year, just old, painted silver, paint flaking off, orange paint underneath, they think, but they aren't sure; van's got a big rainbow painted on each side and some birds; rainbow's all colors, birds are blue. No sign of the vehicle yet. I got on to the mainland, just in case it got by the ferry types, which wouldn't be hard in my experience."

"Sid, Sid," Alberg chided, still staring at the ceiling.

"The fish seller," the sergeant went on, "he's a guy about thirty-eight, forty, got a beard, wore a pair of jeans and a light shirt and smelled like fish, which isn't surprising. Soft-spoken kind of guy, say the citizens. One of them bought a salmon from him, why not." Sokolowski shrugged. "He's not a licensed peddler, so what else is new." He looked up at Alberg, exasperated. "The woods are full of them. Guys selling salmon, crab, oysters, fruits, vegetables, you name it, not a license between them."

"I know all this too," said Alberg. He sighed and sat up. "Go on, Sid."

"The fish seller's our best lead. We're combing the bush for him. Checked the town first, got on to Gibsons, but he's probably camped up on Crown land someplace; we'll find him when one of the lumber companies moves in someplace new with chain saws."

Sid Sokolowski was a few years older than Alberg, a ponderous, suspicious man, but thoughtful. He was comfortable only with other police officers and with his family, which was large. He and his wife had five children, all girls. The gender of his progeny was a source of hurt and bewilderment to Sokolowski, who understood perfectly well that it was his sperm or chromosomes or something which were responsible for his situation. It gave him, he thought, something in common with Alberg. He and his wife had decided not to have any more children, but Sokolowski waffled about this confidentially to Alberg every now and then, saying he'd like to try once more. Surely the odds would be much more in his favor, he argued. But Alberg on these occasions would reply that they had been more in his favor the last time, too, and even the time before that. "You were a man meant to have daughters, Sid," he would tell him. "Stop trying to argue with fate."

Alberg had a great fondness for the sergeant, but he wasn't someone Alberg could confide in about personal things. Not that he'd ever done much confiding anyway, he thought now, looking at Sid bent over the Burke file; not even with his wife. And maybe that was a more serious problem than he'd realized. He had wanted to have things all figured out before talking about them with Maura. As a result, he was always presenting her with faits accomplis. He had thought he was saving her worry. But maybe he'd been wrong.

"Did the neighbors see anybody on the road that day," he asked the sergeant, "besides the fish guy and George Wilcox?"

Sokolowski shook his head. "Nobody we haven't accounted for. The fish seller we haven't found yet—he was there at just about the right time, between eleven thirty and twelve thirty.

And Wilcox...well, actually we've got some disagreement there."

"What kind of disagreement?"

"Two witnesses, including the woman who lives across the street from the victim, say they saw Wilcox go through the hedge into Burke's front yard at about two fifteen, two thirty, somewhere in there. And this checks with his call to us at two thirty-seven. But one old fellow—Frank Erlandson, his name is—he says he saw the same thing, only two hours earlier, at about twelve thirty." He shrugged. "He seemed kind of confused. He's probably just misremembering." He tossed the file folder onto Alberg's desk.

"What about the seaward side of things?"

"Nothing. Nobody seen prowling the beaches, nobody out on the water at the right time except for a couple of kids nine and ten in a dinghy, and a guy fishing from a rowboat. We checked them out."

"The old fellow who says he saw Wilcox at twelve thirty," said Alberg. "Let's talk to him again. Try to get that straightened out."

The sergeant was nodding. "Yeah, I think so too. Problem is he's been in the hospital since Wednesday afternoon for some kind of tests. He's supposed to be home Saturday. Tomorrow."

"Okay. I'll do it myself, since I'll be seeing Wilcox later on today." He got up and stretched. "Sid. I just talked to Burke's sister, Mrs. Morris. She tells me Burke was once married to George Wilcox's sister. She's dead now. Do you find that interesting?"

"Kind of a remote connection, Staff," said Sokolowski reluctantly. "Can't see anything in it, myself. Despite the will." He retrieved the file. "I looked into him," he said, shuffling through the pages in the folder. "Here he is. Wilcox. Not rich, but he's got money in the bank. House paid for. And he gets a pretty good pension. Well spoken of by neighbors and friends. According to them, he wasn't a special friend of the victim." He closed the file. "It's a toughie. My money's on the salmon seller." He looked up at Alberg. "Christ, it's been three days. It's gotta be the salmon seller."

"Yeah, Sid, but why? He didn't take anything from the house. What was the motive?"

"He went berserk," said Sokolowski promptly. He spread his hands. "It happens, Karl. You know it happens."

"Okay, but if he went berserk it must have been as soon as he walked in the door," said Alberg dryly. "He'd been to—what?—three houses before Burke's. And he wasn't berserk then. He wasn't armed, either. What did he hit him with?"

"Maybe he found something in the house," said Sokolowski, after a moment's thought. "And then took it away with him. And Karl, it's kind of peculiar, isn't it, that he didn't stop at anybody's place after Burke's? People up the road saw his van drive by, but he didn't stop."

"Maybe he ran out of fish." Alberg sighed. "Yeah, okay, I agree, he's our best bet. For the moment." He got his suit jacket from the rack in the corner.

"Who'd you have lunch with?" said the sergeant, grinning.

Alberg looked at him coldly.

"It's a small town," said Sokolowski. "So who was it?"

"A librarian," said Alberg, with dignity. He threw his jacket over his shoulder. From the reception area, the parrot squawked. "Jesus," said the staff sergeant.

CHAPTER 9

"Is it always this busy in here?" There was nobody in the library except Cassandra, and now him.

She turned quickly from the cart filled with books ready for reshelving. "Oh, heavens, yes. We're a regular beehive of activity." She smiled, automatically. He wasn't at all sure she was glad to see him.

"It's a very nice library," said Alberg.

"I get the feeling you haven't been in many."

"Of course I have," he said, irritated. "It's not where I spend most of my time, maybe, but I use the library, just like anybody else." He wondered why he hadn't thought to go there for a book about pruning.

She went back to putting books away. "This is the slowest part of the day. The old people come in the morning, usually. The kids come in after school. And working people come in the evenings, or on Saturdays. I'm surprised to see you again so soon. I thought you had a funeral to go to."

He watched her shelve a biography of Churchill. "I did. I went. It's over. Doesn't anybody else work here?"

"I've got a couple of volunteers. That's all. But from two until four every day, I'm usually on my own. Whose funeral was it?"

"Carlyle Burke's. Did he come here in the mornings?"

She looked puzzled.

"You said the old people usually come to the library in the mornings." He took from the shelf a book entitled *The Life of*

Catherine the Great and hefted it in his hand as if trying to determine its weight.

"Oh. Yes." She reached down to get two more books from the cart. "But not him. I don't remember ever seeing him in here."

"You didn't know him, then." He noticed that as she shelved the books she pulled some slightly farther out and pushed some farther in, to even them out, and then, unthinking, ran her fingers along the spines as if playing a harp.

"No, I never met him," said Cassandra. "I think my mother knew him, though. She knows everybody."

"How about George Wilcox? Does he come in the mornings?"

She pushed the cart across an open space furnished with easy chairs and low tables to a row marked SOCIOLOGY. "Mostly in the mornings," she said, "but evenings, too, and sometimes afternoons. It depends on the weather. He spends a lot of time in his garden."

Alberg walked aimlessly to the window. A tall plant stood there, in a big white pot. Its huge wide leaves looked glossy, almost wet; he touched one of them curiously.

"I can't imagine," said Cassandra, "finding a body. Well, I *can* imagine it. . . ."

He rejoined her just as she was ready to move the cart again. He got out of the way and followed her to the fiction section.

"I can't understand why anybody would kill an old man," said Cassandra, looking up at him from her crouched position on the floor by a lower shelf. "What reason could anybody possibly have for doing a thing like that?"

"Same reasons people have for killing anyone."

"It wasn't robbery, was it," she said, and added quickly, "that's what I heard, anyway." She was standing, shelving books rapidly, confidently. The cart was almost emptied.

"Might have been attempted robbery," said Alberg. "All we know is nothing seems to be missing."

"That means somebody might have gone to his house *meaning* to do it, doesn't it?"

"Could be. Right now," said Alberg grimly, "anything's possible."

She reached for the last two books on the cart and put them away. Then she pushed the empty cart back to the front desk. Again Alberg followed, feeling inexplicably exasperated.

"He used to be a teacher," said Cassandra, lifting the hinged section in the U-shaped counter and pushing the cart through. "So did George Wilcox. He's the one who told me. They'd known each other for years. Since long before they came here. But I assume you know all that."

"No," said Alberg. "I didn't know they'd known each other for years. Not until today."

She adjusted some tall purple flowers that stood in a vase on the counter. "They taught in the same school in Vancouver for a while. A long time ago. That's how they met. Then they must have lost touch, because I don't think they'd seen each other for years when Mr. Burke came here to live."

"Did they become friends again, then?" Alberg wondered if she knew they had been brothers-in-law. If so, she wasn't telling him. He found this mildly depressing, even though he hadn't convinced himself yet that the old relationship between the two men had anything to do with Burke's death.

Cassandra looked at the irises. Some of them were beginning to wilt. She heard it again: *He got exactly what was coming to him.* She had never before heard George Wilcox say anything so unfeeling. It must have been the shock, she thought. The poor man, he was probably still in shock.

"Well?" said Alberg. "Were they friends, here in Sechelt?"

She smiled at him. "Are you poking around for information? Is this an interrogation?" She clasped her hands on the countertop and put an eager look on her face. "Anything I can do, Officer, to assist you in your inquiries—anything at all."

Alberg was slightly flustered. "I'm just curious, that's all. And I'm trying to find out who's committed a homicide around here. Yeah, I'm poking around for information, of course I am. That's not why I came in here, but—" He shrugged.

"To answer your question," said Cassandra carefully, "no, I don't think they became friends again. George didn't mention Mr. Burke often. At least, not to me."

She touched an iris, and the light stroke of her finger against the petal of the flower suggested to Alberg his own gesture to brush closed Carlyle Burke's eyelid; there was great gentleness in it.

"He brought me these flowers," said Cassandra. "George Wilcox did." She turned to Alberg. "He's a very interesting man. He taught history. He's still curious and impatient. Until his wife died a couple of months ago, they traveled a lot." She smiled suddenly. "Only in winter, though. He doesn't like to be away from his garden." She looked at Alberg curiously. "If you didn't come here to ask me questions, why did you come?" Safe behind the counter, she seemed amused.

He had passed the library on his way to Wilcox's house. He was driving slowly, not wanting to arrive early, and when he saw the empty parking spaces, he drove in. He sat there for a few minutes admiring the building. It had lots of windows, and greenery, and he could see the low shelves filled with books, and this pleased him. He didn't go to church, either, he told himself, but he liked the fact that there were a few of them around.

"I came for a library card," he told her. He watched her push her dark hair away from her neck. It curled a little, where it sprang away from her face. He noticed several gray hairs. The skin next to her eyes was crinkled, and there were two horizontal lines in her forehead. Character, he thought, with satisfaction. Her eyes were wide and hazel. Her mouth was wide, too, but her nose was small. He saw her face become pink and realized that he'd been staring at her. He looked away, up at the clock on the wall. "I've just got time, before I get back to work."

She got a blank card from a desk drawer and sat down at a manual typewriter. "Full name, please," she said briskly.

"Alberg, Martin Karl." He rested his elbows on the counter and leaned over to watch her type. She was wearing a blue and white pinstriped dress. There was a gold chain around her neck and gold watch on her wrist; gifts, he wondered? No rings, and her nails were short; she used colorless polish on them. She was tall, about five feet nine, and weighed about 140 pounds.

He didn't know why he said it. He didn't often act on his more mischievous impulses. "Are you looking for a husband?" He watched her face, knowing that his own was smooth, expressionless.

She looked up at him quickly, and although her face burned with embarrassment she didn't look away. Her hands were poised over the typewriter keys. "Are you looking for another wife?"

He shook his head.

"Then you have come," she said coldly, "to precisely the right place." She turned back to the card in the typewriter. "Address, please."

"The directors' house, Gibsons."

"And is this the book you wish to take out?" She pointed to *The Life of Catherine the Great*, which lay on the counter between them.

He looked at it in astonishment, unable to remember how it had gotten there. "Yes," he said humbly. "I'll start with this one. Has it got anything about pruning in it, do you know?"

She gave him not the glimmer of a smile.

CHAPTER 10

He went from the library to George Wilcox's house and parked his car on the verge of the road twenty feet from the gate leading to the old man's front yard. It was his own car, a 1979 four-door Oldsmobile, nothing splashy, nothing special, except for the police radio.

Alberg crunched along the gravel shoulder toward the gate. The fence was sturdy, but in need of painting. There was a well-trimmed evergreen hedge behind it, and between the hedge and the front of the house was five feet of neatly clipped lawn. The house itself was short and squat, with small windows and a small square porch; it, too, could have used a few coats of paint. And who am I, thought Alberg gloomily, to talk about decrepit-looking houses. At least this one had a neat border of flowers in front of it, instead of a tropical thicket.

He turned into the yard, closing the gate behind him, and went up a cracked concrete walk to the porch. The door was opened before he could knock. George Wilcox peered up at him. He didn't say anything.

"Hi," said Alberg, finally.

"Why don't you ever wear a uniform?"

"It's distracting."

"No uniform, no police car. How am I supposed to take you seriously?"

Alberg thought about it. "I've got my badge," he said, and showed it to him. "Does that help?"

"What about a gun? You got a gun?"

"Not with me. Why, do you think I'll need one?"

"No need for sarcasm, sonny. The badge will do." He stepped back and opened the door wide.

Alberg squeezed through the tiny hall and into a narrow living room. The high small windows admitted very little light. An oatmeal-colored sofa and a matching armchair, and two occasional chairs upholstered in red wool, sat on the dark brown wall-to-wall carpeting. The windowsills were cluttered with objects: two fat-cheeked Toby mugs; a brass candle snuffer and two brass candlesticks, empty; what appeared to be a wooden salt shaker and pepper mill; a pair of shell casings— standard mementos of the Second World War, except for some unusual decorative work; a pipe holder containing no pipes; two china figurines, possibly Hummel; three china roses in a marble base. There was a television set in one corner, and a collapsed card table leaned against a wall. Everything seemed very dusty.

"Don't use this room much," said George Wilcox. "Come on into the kitchen." He waved Alberg on toward the back of the house.

The kitchen was a bright, sunny square, painted yellow. A worn leather chair sat at an angle to the large window, which looked out upon a small garden and the sea. Next to the chair stood an old-fashioned tobacco cabinet. There was a footstool in front of the chair, piled with magazines and a section of newspaper folded to the crossword puzzle. A TV tray stood nearby. There was no table in the kitchen. The yellow walls were grimy with accumulated dust and splotched with grease near the four-burner electric stove.

"You might as well see the rest of the place, now you're here," said George. He opened a door and Alberg followed him into a small beige-carpeted room. Two walls were lined with bookcases, a desk and chair sat by the window, several comfortable chairs were scattered around, and there was a fireplace.

"This is where you live," said Alberg.

"Here and in the kitchen." George went through a doorway

in the corner of the room, into a short hall. "Here's the bath-room," he said, waving to the right, "and straight on here is the bedroom."

Alberg stood in the doorway and looked around. Small win-dows again, almost as though the room were in a basement. A large four-poster bed, two dressers, a half-open closet door. On one of the dressers was a framed photograph of a woman. It was angled slightly away from him, and Alberg couldn't see it clearly.

"That's it," said George, reaching in front of Alberg to close the door. "The grand tour." He went back down the hall and through another doorway which led into the living room, then turned left back into the kitchen. "Fellow who built this place," he said, "was awfully fond of doors. I took some of them down, you probably noticed. Doorways is one thing, doors is another. Take up too much room. Sit down there, by the window. I'll make some coffee. Eight of them, there were, when we bought this place. Not counting the outside ones, or closets. Eight doors, in a house this size."

He filled a percolator with water, poured coffee into the basket, and set the pot on the stove. Then he went into the study and hauled out the desk chair. Alberg, standing by the window, made a move to help. "Sit down, sit down," said George Wilcox. "No, not here—in the leather chair, there. Sit."

Alberg sat. George took the straight-backed chair.

"Now," said George. "What questions?"

He was alert and unruffled. Alberg glanced wistfully at his thick white hair. He himself was sure to be bald, eventually. All the men in his family had gone bald. He checked once or twice a week, and his hairline had already begun to recede. It had started about twenty years ago.

"What do you know about Carlyle Burke?" he said.

George Wilcox sighed. "What's this in aid of, anyway? I can't figure it."

"When you're trying to find out who killed somebody, you've got to poke around in his life a bit."

"Is that so?" said George. "Is that the way it's done, then."
He rubbed one scuffed slipper against the linoleum. "Got any
suspects?"

Alberg hesitated. "Not really. Not yet."

"You're pretty damn calm about it," said George. "If I were
a cop, and I had me a murdered body and no suspects, I don't
think I'd be so damn calm about it."

"I'm not calm," said Alberg. "I just look calm. Actually I'm
irritated. And extremely curious."

"Curious." George chortled. "I'm curious, too." He leaned
forward. "I supposed you've looked at the obvious. You know,
milkman, postman, paperboy—that kind of thing. And of
course the most obvious thing of all, your basic hoodlum,
possibly drug-crazed." He sat back, complacent.

"Yes, Mr. Wilcox," said Alberg. "We've looked at the
obvious."

"How?" said George. The water in the coffeepot began to
burp. He got up and turned down the burner.

He had wide, strong shoulders, Alberg noticed. Probably
all that gardening. His own shoulders were still stiff and sore,
from Tuesday's efforts.

"What have you done, exactly?" said George, sitting down
again. "Besides take the fingerprints of innocent bystanders,
I mean. Did you photograph the corpse? Query people up and
down the street?"

Alberg nodded. He told himself that he had lots of time.

"You found that fish seller yet?"

Alberg shook his head.

"Probably in Vancouver by now," said George. "Or on his
way to Calgary or someplace. What else? What do you know?
The autopsy, for instance. There must have been an autopsy.
What did that tell you?"

"He was struck on the head. It killed him."

George looked at him for a long moment, then sat back and
folded his arms. "I always said you were a secretive bunch,
you Mounties. In *or* out of uniform."

Alberg couldn't help but grin. "There's not much to tell
you. Really. Okay. There are a few things." He counted them

off on his fingers. "One, the perpetrator didn't force his way in. Two, the victim was struck from behind, while sitting down. Three, no damage was done—"

"Except to Carlyle," said George.

"—to the house. Four, nothing was stolen, that we know of. Of course the forensic guys found some fingerprints. The victim's, a cleaning woman's, yours."

The coffee was bubbling now, its fragrance drifting through the kitchen. George got up and took two mugs and a sugar bowl from the cupboard and a small container of milk from the fridge. He smelled this cautiously before putting it on the counter.

"What do you figure from all that?" he said, taking the pot off the burner and placing it in the middle of the stove.

"An unknown person went to Mr. Burke's house, armed with a blunt instrument. Mr. Burke let him in. He sat in his rocking chair looking out over the water. The unknown person struck him, from behind. He died almost instantly."

George poured the coffee and put the mugs down on the crossword puzzle on the footstool. He went back for the milk and sugar and two spoons. "Help yourself," he said, and shoveled sugar into his mug, and stirred it vigorously. "Why the hell would Carlyle let the fellow in," he said, "if he was carrying a blunt instrument?"

"That's an interesting question," said Alberg, reaching for his coffee. "Maybe he didn't recognize the object as a weapon," he said, looking at George. "Or maybe the killer used something he found in the house."

George sipped at his coffee, staring at the floor. "Have you found it?" he said finally. "The object? The weapon?"

"No."

George looked up. "It's probably out in the middle of the ocean by now," he said comfortably.

Alberg observed him grimly. "You can be a very irritating man, Mr. Wilcox. Did anybody ever tell you that? I bet they did."

George grinned. He drank some more coffee, added a small amount of milk, and stirred it again. He put the spoon down on the newspaper. "Okay. So you want to know about Carlyle."

"Right."

"You been down to the Old Age Pensioners' hall? He was in a choir there. Played bingo or checkers or something, too, I think."

"Yeah, we've done all that. Didn't help us much."

George looked at him shrewdly over the top of his mug. "How come I rate the big cheese, by the way?"

"You found the body."

"That was just my bad luck," said George. "I told you, I didn't know him all that well. How well do we ever know anybody, when it comes right down to it?"

Alberg put his coffee down on the TV tray. He took from an inside pocket an envelope on which he had scribbled a list.

"We went through the house pretty thoroughly, of course," he said, and looked up to see George Wilcox watching him warily. "He had a lot of stuff, did Mr. Burke. A stereo, very good speakers."

"Huh," said George, contemptuously.

"A twenty-six-inch remote control color television set. An aluminum rowboat. An upright grand piano, white."

George grunted.

"A whole lot of silverware: flatware, a tea set, trays and things. A bunch of china—that might be valuable too."

"Is that what you've got written on that envelope?" said George irritably. "You got a list of his assets there, or what?"

"And then of course there's the house," said Alberg. "It's mortgage free. All paid for."

"Huh," said George. "So's mine."

"He didn't leave much actual cash," said Alberg regretfully. "But there are some Canada Savings Bonds, a few stocks—about twenty-five thousand dollars' worth, all told."

"Christ," said George. "Spare me."

Alberg put the envelope back in his pocket. "He left it all to you," he said.

For a second George's expression didn't change. Then the sneer slipped away, and his mouth fell slightly open. He leaned forward and cocked his head, looking intently at the tobacco stand next to the chair in which Alberg was sitting, as though it were that which had spoken. "What?" he said, staring at the tobacco stand.

"You get it all, George," said Alberg. "The whole shebang."

And he watched, bemused, as George collapsed in a fit of laughter which Alberg briefly thought might choke him.

"You all right now, George?" he asked softly, when the old man's wheezing had subsided. "Because we've got a lot to talk about, you and I. And there are a couple of things we should get straight, before we go on.

"First of all," he said, leaning forward, "I don't want to waste any more of my time with this cantankerous-old-man act you have so much fun with. And second of all, I know Carlyle Burke was your brother-in-law."

He sat back. "So let's get on with it, shall we, George? Tell me why you didn't get along so well with old Carlyle. And tell me what your fingerprints were doing not just on the phone but all over the damn kitchen. And then tell me why he left everything he owned to you, this fellow you didn't care for. Okay, George? Start talking."

CHAPTER 11

Alberg, sitting in the worn leather chair, fingered the stuffing which oozed from a crack in the seam of the right arm and kept his eyes on George Wilcox.

After a minute, George settled back and folded his arms. "My fingerprints are all over his kitchen because, I don't mind saying it, I was—I was somewhat discombobulated," he said, "seeing him lying there. I grabbed at things to hold me up, on the way to the phone. I grabbed at the wall, I grabbed at the sink...." He lifted his shoulders, let them drop.

The late-afternoon sun struck into the room at a steep angle; the windows were marked by the rains of spring and probably winter, as well. Tumbleweeds of dust lay in the corners of the floor.

George sighed. "I met Carlyle a few years after the war," he said. "Must have been '48, '49. Myra and I wandered out here from the prairies. Saskatoon." His folded hands rested comfortably in his lap. "I was born out here. Went to Saskatchewan about 1930. A bad time to head out there, as it happened, but we survived. I even went to school, eventually, got to be a teacher. Met Myra, got married, et cetera, et cetera." He shrugged. "Anyway, we got tired of the cold, that's what it was. Myra's people had retired out here. I didn't have any family left by then, except my sister, Audrey. She lived with us." He shifted a little in his chair. His feet were flat on the floor, toes pointed outward, heels about eight inches apart.

"Myra's people lived in the Fraser Valley," he went on. "She wanted me to get a job out there. But I considered myself a city person. There were lots of jobs, back then. I could take my pick, pretty well. I picked Vancouver." He tipped his head at Alberg. "Are you a city man, Staff Sergeant?" He leaned toward him. "Is that what I call you? Staff Sergeant?"

Alberg nodded.

George sat back, slowly. "You don't want my life history. I got a job in a high school, teaching history. Carlyle was on the staff. That's how I met him." He turned his head to look out the window. "He taught music."

"And?" said Alberg, after a couple of minutes.

"And what?"

"Come on, George."

"You're calling me George now? Have *you* got a first name? What is this 'George' all of a sudden, anyway?"

"Sorry. You've got more to tell me. Go on."

"Go on, go on," said George. "As though all I've got to do is push a button somewhere and out it comes." His face was flushed. He leaned forward, his elbows on his knees, and studied the floor. "After a while Carlyle met Audrey, God knows how, I can't remember how. And it ended up they got married." He glanced at Alberg, outraged. "I was suddenly his brother-in-law, for Christ's sake. Couldn't believe it."

"Right from the start, then, you didn't like him," said Alberg.

George sat up straight and looked out the window again, concentrating. Several moments went by. Alberg waited.

"He played the piano," said George, finally. "He could play anything. Sometimes he'd go to the music room. . . . I'd be going down the hall, wide and empty, the kids gone for the day, the floor all scuffed; I'd hear him playing. It came soaring out from behind the door and filled every nook and cranny in the school. That's what it felt like. Mozart. Or Chopin. Or Beethoven. As long as I couldn't *see* him playing, it was like some angel had sneaked in to try out the piano." He sat quietly for a moment. Then, "Ah," he said, and pushed himself up. He picked up his coffee mug and went over to the kitchen counter. "It was the man's one redeeming characteristic," he said. "Didn't seem right, that he could play like that. But he could."

"What was it that you didn't like about him?" said Alberg.

"Didn't trust him," said George promptly. "Never trusted him. He came over all friendly to me the first day I got there. I took one look and said to myself, 'I don't trust that man.'"

He went back to his chair and lowered himself into it. "When he married my sister I had to overlook all that. Never got to know him well; closely, I mean. Never wanted to. I had a big resistance to Carlyle, all the time I knew him." Quite suddenly, he looked exhausted.

"How long was he married to your sister?"

"Two years."

"What happened?"

"She died. In a car crash." He rubbed his face, pale and strained. "We were out of the country when it happened, Myra and I and our daughter, Carol. I was teaching in Germany." He straightened and rubbed the small of his back with both hands. "That's what it must have been, you see. He never got married again, didn't have any family except that sister in Winnipeg and they couldn't stand each other. He must have figured I was the closest thing to kin he had." His voice shook a little. "The crazy old bastard."

Alberg felt depression nudging him, gentle little pushes that made him feel slightly sick. He struggled against it, looking around the room for something to hook on to. "This place could use a good cleaning," he said disapprovingly.

George looked at him, startled, and grinned. "Myra was quite a one for the cleaning. I've barely touched the place since she took ill, last November thirteenth " He glanced around the kitchen. "You're right, though."

They sat quietly, and Alberg became aware of the sound of the sea's incessant surging against George's beach, and the occasional cry of a gull. He saw that the waters were calm; there was a tremble upon them, that was all. George's garden, between his house and the beach, was an orderly riot, not a weed in sight, just lush growth and colors that were almost audible. He saw this through the streaked window of George's kitchen, and had an urge to go out there and see it all clearly, watch the leaves breathe and smell the roses.

"When did your wife die?" he asked.

"On the twentieth of March, this year," said George.

"Do you still miss her?"

George looked at him with distaste and didn't reply.

Alberg didn't know where to go from here. He felt almost stupefied, sitting in George's kitchen, nestled into the worn leather chair, and thought if he stayed there much longer his eyelids would grow heavy and his head would drop back.

"So you met a man you disliked on sight," he said, trying to organize his thoughts. He ought to get up, thank George Wilcox for his time, and leave, that's what he ought to do. But he felt the interview had been sloppy. Maybe there wasn't anything more to be learned here, but he was uncertain about exactly what he *had* learned. He wrenched his mind into action. "You instinctively distrusted him," he said doggedly. "But you taught at the same school. I presume you were polite, never let him know how you felt. Is that right?"

"Oh I think he must have known how I felt, all right," said George. "He kept asking me out for a drink, and I'd hardly ever go, and sometimes he'd call me at home and invite Myra and me to dinner, and I don't think we ever went." He looked at Alberg, not seeing him, remembering something. "That's how he met Audrey," he said dully. "How could I forget that? Every year we had a staff party, on the last day of school before Christmas. We always invited him because we always invited everybody, but usually he couldn't come, because he went away for Christmas and had to catch a train or a plane for somewhere. But one year he didn't go away, so he came to our party. And Audrey was there, of course. That's how he met her. In my house. Christ."

"When you did have a drink with him," said Alberg, "what did you talk about?"

"Women. He liked to talk about women. They liked him, women did. He was a good-looking man," he said grudgingly, "and he played the piano, I told you that. Talked a lot, made jokes, flattered, smiled. I didn't trust him."

"Did you tell your sister that you didn't trust him?"

"What the hell do you think?" said George, agitated. He got up and rubbed his sweatered arm vigorously back and forth across the window, smearing the dust and accumulated grime which until then had been almost invisible, obscured by the dried streaks made by the rain on the outside of the glass. "Of course I told her. But she was a grown woman. She was thirty-five years old, for Christ's sake. I told her she was making a terrible mistake; the man was twenty years older than she was, into the bargain. And she just laughed and sparkled, all excited she was." He slumped back on the chair. "Myra gave me a talking to. She liked him," he said, glaring at Alberg. "She actually *liked* him, Myra did."

"Were they happy? Carlyle and your sister?"

"Almost as soon as they got married, we left. Didn't plan it that way. Got the job in Germany—I'd been trying for it for a couple of years. A few months before we were supposed to come home, she was killed. . . .

"I'll tell you, Staff Sergeant, I'm feeling kind of pooped. Could you come back some other time?" He looked small and fragile, slumped in the straight-backed chair, and his face was gray in the sunlight.

"Just a couple more questions. Did you ever talk to anybody else who felt the same way about him that you did?"

George appeared to give this serious consideration. "Women liked him. I told you that." He thought some more. "Except for his sister."

"What about the other men on the staff? How did they feel about him?"

"I don't know," said George wearily. "I don't remember. It was a long time ago. I don't want to talk about him any more."

"When you got back from Germany," said Alberg, ignoring his exhaustion, "did you return to the same school?"

George slowly shook his head. "We went to California for a year. Then I got a job in a school in a different part of Vancouver."

"Did you do that deliberately? To avoid teaching on the same staff as Carlyle?"

"I didn't ever want to lay eyes on the man again. And I didn't, not until 1979. Myra and I had been here in Sechelt ten years by then. One day I'm walking along the road heading for town and who comes popping out of those laurel bushes down the way but Carlyle." He shook his head disbelievingly. "He retired to Arizona or someplace, then suddenly got homesick, came back to B.C. and bought himself that house not half a mile from mine. I scooted straight home to tell Myra." He looked up at Alberg and grinned, wryly. "She didn't mind. Only I minded."

"It must have been hard to avoid him, here in Sechelt."

"Damn near impossible," George agreed. "Everywhere we went, there he was, playing some piano, cracking his awful jokes." He shivered. "I made the best of it," he said grimly.

"Had he changed much?"

"Hard to say. I told you, I never knew him well to begin with. No better than I had to." George got up, restless, and threw open the door to the back yard. The sound of the waves on the beach was immediately louder. The fragrance of the garden wafted into the kitchen.

"You tell me you never trusted him," said Alberg, exasperated, "and at the same time you tell me you never got to know him. Then maybe you were all wrong about him."

George nodded. "That could be," he said seriously. "That could well be."

Alberg got up. There was a tingling in his thighs; he felt like he'd been sitting for hours. He towered over George. The kitchen ceiling seemed to lower itself as he stood.

He clomped through the house, following George, feeling enormous and clumsy. At the door he stopped and looked slowly around the living room. "What are you going to do with all your loot?" he said.

George looked at him with disgust. "Loot," he muttered. "Loot. What the hell would I do with a white piano?"

"There's the house," said Alberg. "And some money, too."

George flushed. "I don't want it, policeman. I'll sell it all and give the money away, or something. Maybe I'll give the house to his sister. He sure as hell wouldn't like that much."

In his car Alberg opened the window wide and sat for a while without turning on the motor.

He'd been wasting his time, he thought. He ought to be out on the back roads himself, bumping into cool clearings circled by towering fir, and cedar, and spruce, looking for a decrepit old van with bluebirds and rainbows painted on its sides, looking for a middle-aged, quiet-spoken seller of fish whose fingerprints would match those on a plastic bag in Carlyle Burke's kitchen sink.

But he had delegated that responsibility and kept Wilcox as his own, and he had to finish up with George before he pointed himself in another direction.

He started his car, threw it into gear, and pulled off the shoulder of the road onto the pavement. He saw George motionless on his porch, watching him pass. Neither of them waved.

CHAPTER 12

On Saturday morning when George awakened, he thought at first that the hot dry spell had ended and the clouds had come, and then he realized that he'd closed his bedroom curtains. He didn't usually do that on clear nights. He liked to see the starlight and the moonlight, if there was any, before he went to sleep.

He got slowly, stiffly, out of bed. It took a while to get the circulation going—a little longer every day, he thought. He reached up to pull back the curtains and there was the morning sun, and another clear sky above the top of his neighbor's house. He would put on his bathrobe and stand outside for a few minutes, letting the sun oil his hinges. He shuffled back to the bed and picked up his robe, sprawled at the bottom, and noticed that he had hardly disturbed the covers in the night.

And then he remembered.

He sat heavily on the bed and looked at the worn carpet, and at his splayed and lumpy feet with their thick horny nails. He thought for a while it was a dream he was trying to get out of. But he got to his feet and forced himself into the living room and there he saw them, on the windowsill: Carlyle's shell casings.

It was as though he'd slept, dreamed, these past four days—Carlyle, and the funeral, and the interrogations of that smooth-faced, unyielding, disconcerting staff sergeant.

He blamed the sleeping pill, one of four left over from a prescription forced upon him at the time of Myra's death.

George leaned heavily against the doorjamb, staring at the shell casings, and wondered how he'd gotten through these days. And whatever had possessed him to put the shell casings on his windowsill, like an obscene trophy?

He pushed himself back into the bedroom and got dressed. His fingers were numb as he worked buttons into buttonholes and pulled up the zipper in his pants and thrust his feet into socks and slippers; he didn't want to fumble helplessly with the laces in his shoes.

He went straight outside to his garden and sat in his canvas chair.

It would be nice to have a greenhouse again, he thought, but there was no room for one, not even a small one. Maybe he should sell this house and get another one, smaller inside but with a bigger yard, away from the sea. His proximity to the sea limited what he could grow in his garden. And it was almost blinding sometimes, the sunlight on blue rippled water. He would miss the sounds the ocean made, though, and the smell of it, and the things it left on his beach: nice pieces of wood and interesting shells.

A four-foot-high stone wall protected his garden from the strong breezes that sometimes blew in from the water. George got up to inspect the things that grew behind the wall.

The peas were five feet tall and covered with swelling pods, their stalks twining around thick white cord strung tepee fashion from the top of a long pole. The beans were up high, too, and his single zucchini was thriving. His vegetable garden was much smaller than last year's. There was no point in growing a lot of stuff he'd never eat. And it was hard to give vegetables away. Almost everyone had a garden. He could keep up with the zucchini, though; he'd eat it every day and be sorry when it was gone. He liked peas, too. The beans he grew only because they had been Myra's favorite.

He looked out to sea, bewildered. He seemed to recall having talked to that Mountie about his garden. He seemed to recall telling him he had broccoli in his garden. He was astounded at himself; he hated broccoli. Why on earth had he told such a stupid lie?

George brushed his hand over his thick white hair and realized that he hadn't even combed it, yet, or brushed his teeth, either, or even gone to the bathroom, though his bladder had been full from the minute he'd awakened. He went slowly into the house to take care of these things.

Later, he sat in his leather chair sipping coffee and trying to get his mind working right. It's that damn pill, he thought; it's made me logy.

He had to get rid of the shell casings. They were shriveling up the whole house, sitting there. Which one of them had he hit Carlyle with? he wondered. He tried to remember bringing them home and putting them up there but he couldn't quite do it, couldn't quite remember. He *knew* he'd done it; put them in a paper bag he'd found in Carlyle's kitchen and lugged them home and set them up on the windowsill. He could *see* himself doing it. But he couldn't remember what it had felt like, or what he had thought while he did it.

He drank his coffee and tried to take stock. He had struck Carlyle on the head, and Carlyle had died. Then Carlyle was buried. Then the policeman came and told him that Carlyle had left him all his belongings—and some money too, he thought, but he wasn't sure.

George felt cold sweat under his arms. He must have been in shock. Doing a thing like that—it would be enough to put anybody in a state of shock. But for *four days?*

What he ought to do was get up right now and find the telephone and call that Mountie and confess to his crime. That was the right and proper thing to do.

He looked out the window and blinked at the sunlight and didn't move. How would he explain keeping his mouth shut for four whole days? The man's going to think I'm a nutter, he thought. But that wasn't what bothered him, not really, not if he was going to be absolutely honest with himself. What bothered him was the humiliation he would feel, capitulating to a remorse which he still didn't fully accept, four days after the fact.

He tried to work out what he'd say. "I'm your man, Staff Sergeant. Can't stand the guilt any longer " Lord, there was no dignity in that. If he'd confessed promptly, as soon as he'd done the deed, that would have been different; that would have been all right.

The point is, though, he told himself, you killed somebody, and you can't remain unpunished.

He sat very still, thinking about it. It was perfectly true. But it wasn't all there was to say about the situation. It wasn't as though he was a danger to anybody, sitting here free. He probably wouldn't live long enough to get to trial anyway, the way they dragged those things out.

Yet he knew he was rationalizing. The plain truth was that he didn't want to make a public spectacle of himself, and he didn't want to go to jail. They'd catch him eventually; that pale-haired Mountie would catch him for sure, somehow. There was no need to force upon himself today something that was going to happen anyway, in the impartial fullness of time.

And he knew already that he didn't need the R.C.M.P., or the Canadian justice system, to ensure his punishment.

George put down his coffee mug and rubbed his head. His arm felt heavy as iron.

He deeply regretted having committed murder. He didn't believe in it, and he never would have believed himself capable of it. But it didn't surprise him that Carlyle had been murdered. Carlyle had deserved it. He straightened a little in his chair and looked calmly out through the window at his garden. It was true. Carlyle had deserved it.

He got up, and went back outside, and looked this time at the flowers that grew in the bed against his house. He'd put out his bedding plants more than three months ago, as if sub-consciously predicting the unusual warmth and dryness of the spring. He had accepted the weather with pleasure and equa-nimity. Perhaps it was his last summer; perhaps it was nature's final gift to him. Except that he didn't deserve any gifts from nature. Not now.

It occurred to him, however, as he bent over his marigolds, that a vengeful God might well give him a present for getting rid of Carlyle.

George had to brace himself against the side of the house

for a minute, to catch his breath and let some dizziness pass. And he closed his eyes, then, and thought of Audrey. A great surge of relief swept through him that he could still remember her, holding an armful of deep purple lilacs and laughing her pleasure. She had been the real gardener in the family. It was only after her death that he took it up, grimly at first, in deliberate homage and apology to her, then gradually finding in it his own personal joy.

He remembered toiling in the vegetable garden in California, after she died. He had dug up far too much of the lawn. It was a gigantic garden. And of course he'd had no idea how quickly things grew down there. Myra would come out to him, bringing him iced tea or lemonade, never scolding him although she worried. She would wipe his dripping forehead with a cloth carried from the kitchen and put her arm around his shoulders and kiss him.

He shivered, leaning against his house, as the sea breeze stroked the side of his face, and he thought how lucky he had been to have had Audrey in his life, and then Myra, who had never resented his devotion to his sister, even though he knew she had never quite understood it.

George opened his eyes and shoved himself away from the house. Marigolds smoldered at his feet, and sweet peas draped themselves along his fence, and the rosebushes along the fence on the other side of the yard were laden with blooms.

The only blight upon his entire life had been Carlyle. It may have been a desperate, bloody, brutal, and uncivilized thing to do, but at least he'd done something, finally, about Carlyle.

He decided he would row out into the bay and dump the shell casings overboard. He would have to use Carlyle's boat, since he had none of his own and didn't want to call attention to himself by renting one; it was only fitting, he thought, that Carlyle's boat, now his, should be the one he used.

But he couldn't do it during the day, and he knew he wouldn't have the strength to do it that night, and the next night was Sunday, which although he was not religious was still not appropriate. He would do it on Monday.

Yet he couldn't stand the thought of those shell casings sitting in his house one more second. He might be unrepentent about his act, but he wasn't proud of it, and he didn't want to be reminded of it every time he went through his own living room.

He went inside to fetch them. He would bury them in his garden until Monday night. It wouldn't hurt the zucchini to be uprooted for a while. Not if he made sure to water it as soon as he planted it again.

But when he got into his kitchen, his life in its entirety was waiting for him, and it toppled upon him—he put up his hands to ward it off, and stumbled to his leather chair to hide and huddle there, but it swept implacably upon him, his entire life. It was a lie, of course, that Carlyle was the only blight upon it; a lie that Carlyle was his only guilt. With his face in his hands he sat, rocking himself back and forth under the pain that stretched back over so many years. All his attempts to make things right had failed; worse, they had brought death, and more death, and finally this death, Carlyle's, and all that was left for him now was his own.

George sat for a long time. When he finally lifted his head, his face was dry again.

Had he misjudged his duty, throughout his life? Or had he simply been unequal to it?

It was midafternoon when he finally dragged himself from his chair and went to get the shell casings.

CHAPTER 13

"We should question the bird," said Freddie Gainer that same morning as he peered into the cage. "Parrots talk. Could be he saw something."

"Good idea," said Sokolowski. "Go ahead, Freddie. You want to take him into an interview room, or what?"

"He didn't see anything," said Isabella, over the clackety-clack of her typewriter. She worked Saturday mornings and took Wednesday afternoons off. She said it suited her. She took karate lessons in Gibsons on Wednesday afternoons.

"How do you know?" said Freddie.

"He'd be upset. Disturbed. Something. He's a feeling creature."

The parrot sat silently on his perch. Alberg was over at the duty corporal's counter, getting the name and address of the man who'd said he'd seen George Wilcox enter Burke's front yard at twelve thirty. He glanced at the bird uneasily. He didn't like the way it cocked its head at him, staring at him through eyes like tiny black marbles.

"Does it ever say anything interesting?" said Gainer.

"I think it's very interesting that he says anything at all," said Isabella. She whipped a sheet of paper from her machine and inserted a clean one. "But I admit, his vocabulary is limited."

The parrot gave a sudden squawk. It was a loud, shrill sound.

"There," said Isabella proudly.

"There what?" said Sokolowski. "What did it say?"

"He said 'Tom.' I think that must be his name."

"Sid," said Alberg. "If you can drag yourself away from that damn bird for a minute...." He went down the hall to his office.

The parrot was Isabella's latest self-assumed responsibility. When Gainer had delivered it to the detachment office Tuesday afternoon, Isabella had snatched the cage from his hand and plunked it on her desk. She then picked up her purse and hurried off to the pet supply store, where she had a conference with the owner and purchased from him sufficient quantities of food and vitamin supplements to last several weeks.

Next, in Alberg's absence, she whisked away his coffee table and spread upon it a white cloth she had picked up from her house. She put the table next to her desk, and the cage on the white cloth.

Alberg retrieved his coffee table that evening, leaving the cage on the floor. The parrot shrieked when he did this, even though the cage was covered.

Sometime Wednesday morning he ventured out into Isabella's domain and saw that the cage was now sitting upon Sokolowki's table. The sergeant kept his table against the wall next to his desk in the main office, behind the counter, and used it as a place to drop things he'd finished with but didn't want to put away yet. It took him several hours to realize that the table was missing, and he was piling things up on the floor.

"Shit!" Alberg heard him cry. "Where's my table?"

On Thursday he and Alberg found themselves going shopping for a card table for the parrot. "Why the hell are we doing this, Karl?" Sokolowski complained as they drove. "What's that parrot doing here anyway? Why don't we just turn it over to the S.P.C.A.?"

But they couldn't do that. The parrot was part of Carlyle Burke's legacy to George Wilcox, and Wilcox refused to decide what he wanted done with it, except that he didn't want it in his house and he didn't want it given to the S.P.C.A., in case they took it into their heads after a while to have it put away.

Now Sokolowski followed Alberg into his office, which seemed to shrink as he came in, and sat down in the black chair. It was getting hot in there, too. The sun shone in through the window from late morning until midafternoon, which was nice most of the time but not in the heat of summer, and the heat of summer had begun early this year. Alberg's shirt was sticking to his back, and the waistline of his pants dug into him uncomfortably. He thought with dismay that he must have put on yet more weight.

He peered out through the slats of the venetian blind. A couple of squad cars sat in the parking lot, glinting in the sun. Alberg's Oldsmobile was out there, too, along with Isabella's well-used Mercury—doesn't she ever wash that damn thing? he thought irritably. The road led off through scattered groups of houses and stands of fir and fields cleared for strawberries or orchards or kitchen gardens, then down the hill into the village and straight to the sea.

"No word yet on the fishmonger, I suppose," said Alberg moodily, trying to spot the roof of the library.

"You'll be the first to hear, Staff," said the sergeant.

Alberg fiddled with the cord on the blind, lessening the glare. Then he turned from the window. "I've got another thing or two I want you to look after."

"Yeah? What?"

"First, check old Carlyle out on the computer."

"For what?"

"I'm just curious, that's all," said Alberg. "Why doesn't anybody seem to have liked him much, why didn't he get married until he was fifty-five, why did he never get married again—that sort of thing. You probably won't find anything. But have a look, would you?"

"What, you think he was a fag?" said Sokolowski, showing more interest.

"I don't know. I'm looking for anything, anything at all."

"Those fags carry grudges, all right. Like I told you, I worked in Vancouver for a while, before I joined the force. In the West End"—he shuddered, fastidiously—"they're worse than married people, those fags. The way they bash each other around, cut each other up." He sounded massively disapproving.

"His wife's name was Audrey," said Alberg. "Burke, née, of course, Wilcox. She died in a vehicle accident, this was about twenty-five years ago. See if you can find out what the circumstances were."

"Twenty-five years ago? Come on, Staff."

"Give it a try, Sid, okay? It happened in or around Vancouver. The records will be around somewhere."

Sokolowski was nodding thoughtfully. "I like the fag angle." He stood up to leave. "Tell you one thing. If it wasn't a fag thing, and it wasn't the fish seller, it must have been a crazy or a shitrat or two."

"It wasn't messy enough for crazies or shitrats, Sid."

"There wasn't any profit in it—except for Wilcox and the will, and you said that surprised the hell out of him—so it wasn't a criminal, either."

"Let's find the fish man," said Alberg, "and go from there." He got up, straightened his tie, and put on a light jacket. "Meanwhile, I'm off to talk to—" He consulted a small notebook. "To Mr. Frank Erlandson. Gotta tie up all the loose ends, Sid. I'd sure hate to trip on a loose end."

Frank Erlandson sat on his porch on a cushioned wicker chair. He was a tall man with long limbs, a slight potbelly, and an open, freckled face. When he occasionally uncrossed his legs and recrossed them, or lifted a hand to stroke his nonexistent hair, he moved slowly and cautiously; Alberg thought he might be anticipating pain. He looked older than George Wilcox and was certainly not as strong.

His widowed sister, Molly Newell, lived with him in a house across the street and two doors up from Carlyle Burke's. She was knitting as they talked, her hands moving the needles slowly and awkwardly; the knuckles of her fingers were swollen. But she was younger and more robust than her brother.

She had served them iced tea and brought one of the dining room chairs onto the porch for Alberg before settling into a wicker chair of her own. They had discussed the weather, and Alberg had inquired politely about the state of Mr. Erlandson's health, which was apparently not good.

"If you could just go through it for me once more, Mr. Erlandson," Alberg said now, taking his notebook from his jacket pocket.

"As I told one of your men on Wednesday morning," said Erlandson, "I'd hardly be likely to mistake either the date or the time, given the circumstances." He pointed to the laurel hedge across the road. "I saw George come walking along there, from the direction of his own place, and I saw him go through the gate into Carlyle's front yard, and it was just a few minutes after twelve thirty P.M."

"I'm going to be patient, here, Frank," said Molly Newell to her brother, "but I'm bound to tell you, Sergeant, that we disagree on this matter, Frank and I."

"Yes, I understand that," said Alberg. "I wonder, though, if I could hear Mr. Erlandson's account first, and then yours. People often see the same things and yet make different observations. It's very common," he told her reassuringly.

She looked at him for a moment through gold-rimmed bifocals. Her long gray hair was done up in a neat bun at the back of her head. Her blue eyes were brilliant against her tan; she was not smiling, and he could see delicate white lines in the wrinkles around her eyes.

"I'm perfectly aware of that, Sergeant," she said. "However, that's not the kind of thing I have in mind. Not at all." She lifted a hand from her knitting—Alberg thought it was a square meant for an afghan—and waved it at her brother. "Go on, Frank."

Erlandson reached for a glass of iced tea sitting on a wicker table, took a slow sip, and carefully replaced the glass. "As you suggested, Mr. Alberg, I'm going to retrace my day for you; last Tuesday, that is, the fifth day of June." He dabbed at his lips with a tissue from the pocket of a light sweater he wore over a white shirt.

"It's my usual habit to have lunch with Molly, here, at noon precisely. We have lunch at the kitchen table and we listen to the twelve o'clock news. This has become routine. Immediately after lunch, which lasts about half an hour, it is my custom to go out into the back garden while Molly does up the dishes. I walk around making mental notes of the things that need to be done out there; this usually takes me about twenty minutes, or perhaps half an hour, if I should happen to sit down in one of the patio chairs for a few minutes."

Alberg nodded soberly. He was fervently grateful for the large cedar tree that stood in Erlandson's front yard, spreading shade over the end of the porch where the three of them sat.

Mrs. Newell dropped the completed square into a basket at her feet which contained several similar squares, some brown and some rust-colored, and began casting on stitches for another one. Alberg thought of his grandfather, who had provided his entire family with afghans, over the years.

"Now on this particular day," said Erlandson, "my normal routine was shot to ribbons." He spread his hands on the broad arms of the chair and recrossed his legs, slowly. "Usually, after my walk around the garden, I go indoors and rest for an hour or so, and when the hottest part of the afternoon has passed I go back outside to do some chores. But on this particular day—" He looked coolly at his sister. "And I remember it quite, quite well," he said. She ignored him, bent over her knitting. "On Tuesday I had my usual one fifteen P.M. doctor's appointment, and"—he looked unhappily at Alberg—"I knew what he was going to say. He was going to tell me I had to go into the hospital for tests. So I found it quite impossible to follow my regular routine. Right after lunch I came out onto the porch and sat here, just thinking. A few minutes—no more—after I sat down, I saw George coming up the road, heading in my direction." He nodded to himself. "I like George. He's a bit gruff, but I like him. I know he goes to the hospital regularly, once a week, to read to some of the patients, visit them, that sort of thing."

Molly Newell interrupted to agree with him. "He's a good man, George. Ever since his Myra died—no, before that," she said to Alberg. "Ever since she got sick in the first place, he's been spending time at the hospital. Go on, Frank. Get on with it."

"As I said, I saw George coming up the road. I assumed he was walking into the village, and I decided to hail him as he passed me." He rested his head against the wide, curving back of his chair. "I think I wanted some reassurance. I think I wanted him to tell me the hospital wouldn't be so bad after all." He lifted his head and focused again on Alberg. "But I didn't get a chance to call out to him. He went through the gate in Carlyle's hedge."

"How long did you sit out here, Mr. Erlandson?"

"Not long. Maybe fifteen minutes or so. Then Molly came out and told me I'd better get ready for my doctor's appointment."

"So you didn't see George come back out through the gate?"

"No."

"Did he often visit Mr. Burke, do you know?"

"He and Myra used to drop by sometimes, I think, before she took ill. But I haven't noticed him going there since. He comes here, to us, every now and then."

"Not often, though," said Mrs. Newell, her hands motionless in her lap. "He keeps to himself, now that Myra's gone. Except for visiting the hospital, once a week like clockwork, I'm told." She shook her head and resumed her knitting. "It's a sad thing. All he lives for now is his garden, it seems to me."

"True," said Erlandson sorrowfully.

The ice in his tea had melted, but Alberg drank it anyway. "Now, Mrs. Newell," he said, "in what way does your memory of that day differ from your brother's?"

"He's got the time wrong," she said immediately. She dropped her knitting into the basket and pushed her glasses farther up on her nose. "His doctor's appointment on Tuesday was at three thirty, not one fifteen. He's been going every week, recently, and usually it's at one fifteen, but this week it was three thirty." She turned to her brother and spoke gently. "That's what's gotten you confused, Frank, as I keep telling you. They changed your time this week, that's all."

"So, you mean..." said Alberg.

"I mean that, yes, he was sitting out on the porch on Tuesday, and, yes, he probably saw George go through the hedge, but he's got his times mixed up. After lunch on Tuesday he went out into the back garden as usual, and then he lay down for a while as usual, and then he got up, at about two fifteen, and I reminded him about the doctor's appointment at three thirty, and *then* he came out here onto the porch." She reached over to pat Erlandson's hand. "It was the *next* day, Frank, *Wednesday*, that you were sitting out here early, right after lunch, thinking about your tests. The day the policeman came to talk to us in the morning. And then at four o'clock I drove you to the hospital. Don't you remember?"

Alberg noticed that his heart hadn't sunk. Did that mean he'd stopped thinking seriously of George Wilcox as a suspect? Or maybe he didn't want the old man to have done it....

Erlandson wore an expression of great stubbornness. "Then I must have come out here twice on Tuesday," he said crossly. "It was right after lunch when I saw him. How would you know, anyway? You have a rest after lunch too, same as I do."

Mrs. Newell sighed and glanced apologetically at Alberg.

"What does George say about all this?" said Erlandson, irritably. It didn't seem to have occurred to him that, if accepted as truth, his account of things might get his friend in trouble.

"Mr. Wilcox says he found the body," said Molly Newell quietly. "At about two thirty." She turned to Alberg. "Isn't that right, Sergeant?"

Alberg agreed.

For the first time, Erlandson seemed bewildered.

"What was he wearing when you saw him, Mr. Erlandson?"

He concentrated. "Gray pants and a sweater. Dark. I don't remember exactly what color, but dark."

"What kind of 'dark?'" said Alberg. "Dark red? Dark green? Dark brown?"

Erlandson was shaking his head. "No, no, no. Dark blue, I think. I'm not sure."

"Could it have been gray?"

He thought about it. "Maybe. If it was a very dark gray. But I think more likely blue."

Alberg put away his notebook and stood up. "Thank you both very much indeed," he said.

"What do you think of cremation?" said Erlandson suddenly, looking up at him.

"Frank, really, for goodness' sake," said Molly Newell in horror.

Alberg stuck his hands in his pockets and watched a loud-mouthed bluejay chase a sparrow away from a birdfeeder that hung from the corner of the porch roof. "I think it's fine," he said, "for dead people."

Their laughter followed him to his car.

He found Cassandra next to one of the potted plants. Her nose and forehead glistened, and the hair around her face was damp and more curly than usual.

"You're going to roast yourself," he said.

She turned, a cloth in her hand, and he was happy when she smiled at him. She wiped the back of her hand across her forehead.

"What are you doing, anyway?" said Alberg.

She gestured to a pail of water on the floor. "I'm sponging their leaves."

"Do you have to do it when the sun's pouring right through the windows at you?"

"I have to do it while there's somebody else here to take care of the customers," she said. He'd noticed when he came in that a teenage girl was busy behind the counter, checking books in and out. There were a dozen or so people in the library. This gave Alberg an illogical pleasure.

"Can you have dinner today?" he said. "Or tomorrow?"

"Good heavens. Wasn't it just yesterday that we had lunch?" He ignored this, waiting. "Not today," she said. "Tomorrow I spend the afternoon with my mother. I have dinner there, too. Every Sunday."

His disappointment was intense. He hadn't thought beyond tomorrow. What was she doing tonight, to make her unavailable? He didn't know what to say next.

She hesitated, the cloth in her hand. There was a trickle of sweat on her left temple. He reached over and flicked it away.

"God, I must look a mess," said Cassandra cheerfully. "I'll tell you what. How about you pick me up at Golden Arms—say, about six thirty—and we'll go for a walk on the beach."

"Okay," said Alberg, slightly cheered. "Golden Arms. Christ."

"How's the—uh, the investigation going?" she asked, as she walked with him to the door.

"Which one?" said Alberg. "The log thefts? The vandalism? The stolen four-by-four? The tourist yacht that got crunched by a fishing boat?"

"Actually," said Cassandra, "I was thinking of the murder. Remember the murder? Or have you handed that over to someone else?"

He stopped and leaned against the end of one of the shelves in the BIOGRAPHIES section. "Your friend George is Carlyle Burke's heir," he said. "That's the news from that particular investigation."

She was astonished, of course, but he was surprised to see that she was also uneasy. She stared at him for several seconds.

"Does that make him a suspect?" she said finally.

Alberg pretended to think this over. "Not really," he said. He moved out of the way of a young man in jeans and a David Bowie T-shirt. "It seemed to come as a big shock to him, as a matter of fact."

Cassandra pushed her hair away from her face and then realized she'd done this with the cloth she had been using on the plants. She stared at it uncomprehendingly. Alberg began to laugh. She looked at him, blank-faced, and seemed to become agitated.

He put his hand on her bare arm. "What is it? Is something wrong?"

Cassandra tried to laugh. "No, nothing. It's just the heat." She gently dislodged his hand. "I'll see you tomorrow."

He watched her go through the hinged section in the counter, speak to the volunteer, and disappear into an office behind the shelves of reserved books.

"Okay," he said finally, out loud. He looked around him. "Okay," he said again, and wandered out of the library into the heat of the late afternoon, and decided he might as well go home.

CHAPTER 14

Alberg lived in Gibsons, at the southern end of the Sunshine Coast, about fourteen miles down the narrow winding highway from Sechelt. He preferred to have a little distance between himself and the detachment office.

His house was known as the directors' house because for several years it had been rented by the C.B.C., for use by television directors in town briefly to shoot episodes in a series called *The Beachcombers*.

The place had about it an air of preoccupation, of distraction. Alberg had marveled when he moved in at the things abandoned there by harassed people to whom the house had been mere shelter, less than a hotel. They had spent very little time there, and yet some had managed to leave things behind.

There was a single serving size box of Rice Krispies in the kitchen cupboard, open but empty, the knocked-over box surrounded by mouse turds. On the floor of the bedroom closet in furry gray globs of dust, Alberg found a gold Cross ballpoint pen. Under the bed huddled a threadbare pair of white jockey shorts. In the bathroom medicine chest sat a lonely, sticky bottle of cough medicine and a half-used roll of antacid tablets. On the small table next to the lumpy bed someone had left a paperback copy of *Worlds in Collision*.

Alberg had been in a hurry to move in and told the owner not to bother having the place cleaned, he would see to it himself. It took him several evenings but he was glad, later, that he hadn't hired someone else to do the job.

He found nothing in the house that would identify its former occupants as practitioners of the art of television, yet the things he found caused him to create people in his mind as he swept and polished. There wasn't enough evidence for legitimate deduction, so he just made them up, and he became fond of these people, so that in the end he didn't throw away anything but the cereal box. He put the cough medicine and the antacid tablets and the jockey shorts and the Cross ballpoint pen and *Worlds in Collision* into a small cardboard box, which he then kept on the shelf in his bedroom closet.

It comforted him to keep nearby these reminders of some of the other temporary occupants of the house. It was almost as though he expected one winter evening to hear a knock at the door and, when he opened it, holding an open book in one hand (he would have been sitting in front of the fire, reading, for once), there would stand one of the directors, who would apologize for intruding and begin a stammering inquiry about an object he had only recently discovered was missing. (It would be the pen, probably; hardly the jockey shorts.) Alberg would invite him in, return the object to his delighted visitor, and they would sit together in front of the fire and have a drink and talk about television until the director had to leave to catch the last ferry back to the mainland.

But nobody at all knocked on his door, that first winter. It had been a very lonely time. Work had kept him busy during the days, but the evenings were bad.

It seemed to rain incessantly. Sometimes there were winter storms, and that was all right, a fire in the fireplace and candles to eat by and the excitement of wondering whether the huge Douglas fir across the road was tall enough to crash into his house, if uprooted by the raging winds. But mostly it just rained, straight down, no breeze to angle it, bathing his house and trickling down his windowpanes and pattering on the foliage with a sound like eternal grieving, and it was this, the rain, with which he struggled as he wrote upbeat affectionate letters to his daughters and occasional notes to his wife which he hoped were graceful as well as businesslike. He would look up from the paper, after signing his name to these missives, and there was always a moment of shock as he looked blankly around him, and this was followed by a jolt of pain so severe that the first few times he had seriously considered seeing a doctor.

One day in February he had noticed on his way out to his car an unfamiliar fragrance in the air. He looked carefully about him but couldn't see anything unusual except a few small green shoots. Their presence in the earth of his front yard surprised him until he realized that the Sunshine Coast had had only a few nights of frost, and that was back in December.

On a Saturday in early April he glanced from his kitchen window and found that growing things had thrust themselves high enough to almost block his windows.

That was the start of his battle with the greenery which last year had threatened to swallow up his house. He was determined it wasn't going to happen again.

The house was on the side of a hill that reared up out of Gibsons. It looked down upon a disorganized tumble of small houses, and below them the town's main street, and beyond that the government wharf and a wood-piling breakwater that protected several finger floats. The back yard wasn't large, and most of it was lawn. A lopsided wooden fence surrounding the yard supported the climbing roses, which, when untended, went mad. Until Alberg's attack with the hedge clippers on Tuesday, some of the canes had stretched twelve feet into the air, clawing wildly at nothing when the breezes blew in from the ocean.

He pulled up late this Saturday afternoon in front of the house, which faced Schoolhouse Road sidelong, thrusting a suspicious shoulder at the traffic. A fence in dilapidation similar to that in the back yard offered yet another line of defense, and hydrangea bushes grew in glorious disarray along the fence and across the front of the house, encroaching upon the somewhat rickety front porch.

It was a small house, but he liked it. He was now even thinking about buying it. He toyed with the idea each time he thought of requesting a permanent posting to Sechelt, which had first occurred to him about a month ago.

There was a sun porch at the back, on the southwest side, and through its wide windows he got his best view of the town, the wharf, and across Shoal Channel to Keats Island. He had noticed during his preliminary inspection of the house that there was a hole in one wall of the sun porch, where it met the floor. He also noticed a large battered cardboard carton in which lay some rags, and a scratched blue bowl next to it.

The first evening after he moved in he was standing in the sun porch looking down at the town and at the black sea, on which floated the running lights of a few invisible boats, and listening to the rain, when he heard a scrabbling sound. He got a flashlight and found in the box of rags a thin gray cat who remained for a moment pinioned by the beam of light and then leaped from the box and disappeared through the hole in the wall. Before he went to bed that night he filled the blue bowl with milk. In the morning the box was still empty, but so was the bowl.

The cat hung around for a few days, then disappeared. Alberg left the box of rags, and filled the blue bowl with fresh milk each night, but months passed and he didn't see the animal again. Finally he repaired the hole in the wall.

But late in the summer the cat returned. He heard meowing, and scratching, and went outside to see her (if it was, in fact, a she) trying to claw her way into the sun porch where the hole had been. He left the screen door propped open, put out some milk, and went to bed.

This continued until fall, when once more the cat vanished. Alberg thought she must have discovered in her feline wisdom a way to escape the wet British Columbia coast winters for a dryer, warmer place. So far she hadn't come back again, but he left the box and the rags out there, just in case, and had begun in April to call her softly before he went to bed.

Now in the kitchen he boiled water for instant coffee and looked in the fridge for a while, but he didn't see anything that interested him. He shouldn't eat anything anyway, he thought; not with an expanding waistline.

He took his mug of coffee into the living room and settled down at the heavy round dining room table he'd put at one end of the room. He brought with him his notebook and a pen, intending to make notes about the Burke homicide.

He had lived through that first awful winter with a minimum of furniture, only what the house itself provided. But when spring came and the sun emerged he began buying things. At first he felt uncomfortable, going shopping alone, with only himself to please. But eventually he began taking pleasure in surrounding himself with things that satisfied his own tastes. These tastes sometimes astonished him, as if they were new ones, as perhaps they were.

Restless, the page in his notebook still blank, he moved to a wingback chair near the window and put his feet up on a hassock.

It would be extremely convenient, he thought, if a satisfactory relationship should develop between him and Cassandra. He'd started answering ads only a couple of months ago. When he first arrived in Sechelt he was too busy with his job and too unhappy and bewildered in his personal life to seek female companionship. He wasn't sure he remembered how to do that, anyway. Eventually he began spending an occasional weekend in Vancouver, frequenting the singles bars. He felt excessively middle-aged in those places. He ignored this for a while, because he did manage to meet women there, all right. But it soon became depressing. The sexual experiences were more reassuring than anything else, and while he had badly needed that reassurance, he also needed somebody female to talk to and laugh with. He probably shouldn't have given up on those bars so soon. He thought it must have been the music in those places that finally sent him fleeing.

So next he tried answering ads. He met a lot of the same kind of person he'd met in the bars—bright, well-dressed, much too young—and he also met a great many women whose ages and personalities suited him better but whose loneliness had made them desperate. Their desperation caused him great discomfort, knowing how close he was to desperation himself, and he saw few of them more than once.

All he wanted was friendship and sex combined in women

who were content in their singleness. He hadn't expected this to be so difficult to find.

He couldn't figure what the hell it was that kept an attractive, intelligent woman like Cassandra Mitchell buried alive on the Sunshine Coast. Still, he told himself, she must have her reasons. Just as he had his.

He hoped her friend George was no longer even a remote contender as Sechelt's felon of the year.

But he made a note—finally—in his book. He'd have to check out that business of the color of Wilcox's sweater. He was pretty sure Frank Erlandson had gotten his times mixed up, all right. Yet if he and his sister both took naps after lunch, it was just possible that he'd sat out on his porch twice that day and had seen George the first time.

But that didn't make sense, Alberg thought impatiently, closing the notebook. If Wilcox had killed the old man, why the hell would he come trotting down the road two hours later to find the body?

Alberg stood up and stared out through the window. It's got to be the fishmonger, he thought. And we'll find him. It's only a matter of time.

He noticed the sunlight slanting into his front yard, shining almost amber upon his hydrangeas. He felt a sudden inexplicable exhilaration. The flowers were larger than they had been four days earlier, and beginning to show their blueness. He was very happy that he hadn't gotten around to chopping them down.

CHAPTER 15

The weather was holding. Sunday was again hot and dry, with not even a sea breeze to temper it. Nothing but total immersion in the cool waters of the Pacific Ocean, thought Alberg, baking in his back yard, could bring his body temperature down. Yet he wasn't complaining. This kind of heat was unusual in Sechelt at any time of year, rare indeed in June, and unusual weather heightened his awareness of things and increased his interest in them.

Besides, the waitress at the diner where he'd had a late breakfast had told him it wouldn't last.

"Watch the sunset," she'd said, lifting his coffee cup to wipe up the liquid she'd sloshed into the saucer. "It'll be clear as a bell, not a cloud in sight. But it'll be the last one like that for a while." She tossed the cloth into the sink behind her, put her hands on her wide hips, and inspected the street outside the window; Alberg could almost see the heat shimmering there. "Tomorrow'll start out just like today, get even hotter, probably, but by evening the clouds'll start coming and you'll see, we'll have rain by Tuesday."

"And how long will the rain last?" said Alberg.

She calculated, her hennaed finger waves shining in the sun. "A week," she said firmly. "Maybe longer."

He ate a sandwich and drank a can of beer for dinner and tried calling the cat again. He had a tin of tuna for her if she showed up. But there was still no sign of her.

He dressed carefully before going to meet Cassandra in tan

chinos and a green shirt and, because they were going to walk on the beach, sneakers. He looked at himself, dissatisfied. Finally he rolled the sleeves of his shirt up to just below his elbows and undid the first two buttons, revealing some of the blond hair on his chest. He combed his hair, wishing it were thicker, and checked under the clump that fell over his forehead, but decided, probing cautiously, that it hadn't receded any more under there since the last time he'd looked. He studied himself somberly in the mirror for another minute, thinking about Freddie Gainer's hair, which certainly looked a lot thicker since he'd had that damn permanent.

Alberg was suddenly embarrassed by his absorption in his physical self. He actually glanced around him, as if someone might be watching and finding great amusement in his performance. Then he shook his head to unsmooth his hair, did up the second button on his shirt, and left the house.

Golden Arms was a place created by one of the local service clubs for elderly people still self-sufficient but aware that they were losing the confidence necessary to live alone. It was a single-story complex, U-shaped, with a large lawn in the middle. The units at the end had small patios with sliding doors and were occupied by couples.

Alberg hadn't given much thought—until he found himself walking down one side of the U, looking at the numbers on the doors—to the intimacy his picking up Cassandra there might imply. He felt there were people peeking at him from behind their curtains, up and down the rows on either side of the large lawn, and called himself paranoid.

When he had found the right door, and knocked, and been admitted by Cassandra, he completely filled the dining area of Mrs. Mitchell's kitchen. She was sitting in a chair by the window in the living room, to his right, fanning herself with a magazine.

"I won't get up," she said. "If I did, one of us would have to move outside." She was a small, rotund woman with gray hair cut like Prince Valiant's. She wore glasses and smiled at him with an air of cool speculation that made him uneasy.

Cassandra introduced them, leaned down to kiss her mother's cheek, and reached around Alberg for a straw handbag sitting on the kitchen table. She seemed anxious to leave.

In the car, he made a polite remark about her mother.

"She prefers my brother," said Cassandra. "But he's in Edmonton, so she has to make do with me."

This would have been a provocative and interesting remark, coming from a stranger. From a potential lover, it was disquieting. He made no response, and she said nothing more.

They drove to Davis Bay, where the main highway dipped close to the sea. Alberg parked the car, and they crunched down the gravel to the beach. They walked out to the end of a long wharf, passing amateur fishermen and kids in bathing suits who were running up and down and yelling, causing the wooden flooring to spring beneath their feet.

"Up that way," said Cassandra, pointing northwest, "is Selma Park. It's in the next bay. There's a stone breakwater there. Have you seen it?"

Alberg nodded.

"There was a luxury yacht named the *Selma*," she said, leaning on the wharf's railing. "In the 1880s. It cruised the Mediterranean, sometimes with Edward the Seventh and Lillie Langtry aboard." She grinned at Alberg. "Must have been fun, huh?" She turned back to the sea. "Anyway, the *Selma* went around the Horn to British Columbia eventually, I can't remember why, and ended up plying the run between Vancouver and Powell River. The land near the breakwater was bought by the shipping line. They used it as a picnic ground for the steamship passengers."

"It's very handy," said Karl, "knowing a librarian."

"Actually it was George Wilcox who told me all that."

They began walking back down the wharf toward the beach. But he stopped halfway and turned around to look out at the ocean, and almost due west, a clump of rocks protruding from the sea.

"That's Trail Islands," said Cassandra at his elbow. "In the winter you can hardly see the rocks. They're covered with sea lions."

He smiled, remembering his first sight of it.

The water was stitched with silent sails. He could hear the raucous murmur of powerboats. He looked far off across the water and saw on the horizon the mountainous outline of Vancouver Island, hazy in the distance.

They left the wharf and wandered north along the beach, which became sandier as they walked closer to the water. The evening was very warm; sunlight flashed from the sea, and when Karl half turned his back on it, he saw that there was a golden glow over everything.

They were walking close together, but not touching. The air was so filled with other scents—salt and seaweed and the pine trees they were slowly approaching—that he couldn't tell whether she wore any perfume. He felt mildly helpless, a tourist. But he thought he probably didn't look much different from anybody else on the beach. Except that he wasn't wearing shorts. He hadn't been able to imagine wearing shorts while meeting somebody's mother.

Suddenly Cassandra began to run. He watched in exasperation as she pelted up the beach, her straw bag bouncing on its long braided straps, her skirts flying out every which way. If she thinks I'm going to chase her, he thought in disgust—she was a grown woman, for Christ's sake. He glanced around in embarrassment, but nobody seemed to be paying any attention. A group of small tanned children ran in and out of the water, screaming. Some adults sat on towels on a big log, eating hot dogs. And still Cassandra ran, growing smaller as she increased the distance between them.

Finally she whirled around and bent to put her hands on her knees, catching her breath, he figured. She stood up and waved him energetically forward. He couldn't see her face clearly, but he thought she was smiling. He began a slow, sedate jog, holding onto his dignity and his disapproval. She waved again, impatient. He jogged a little faster. The soles of his sneakers grabbed confidently at the gravel and tossed it behind him. He felt himself start to grin, and he ran faster. Cassandra urged him on with shouts and gestures. Soon he was flying up the beach. She grew larger and larger; he could hear her laughter clearly. When he reached her he threw his arms around her, panting, and her hands grabbed instinctively at his now sweaty back.

"Jesus," he gasped, "I'm out of shape." He was leaning on her; she pushed him away gently, smiling at him. His heart was thumping quickly and he felt triumphant.

"George Wilcox lives up there a way," said Cassandra, pointing beyond the end of the beach. "I'd like to stop in to see him. He's got a lovely garden. Are you game?"

Where the curve of the beach ended there were trees and houses that backed onto the sea.

"Isn't it all private property, past here?" said Alberg.

She laughed. "Yes, but I don't think anybody's going to mind. Come on."

They clambered along a much rockier, narrow beach that led behind lawns and gardens, some well cared for, some not. The sun was lower now, getting ready to drop behind Vancouver Island. Alberg wished devoutly, as he stumbled over the rocks, that they were back in his car, heading for his house, or hers.

"How much farther?" he called out, as they rounded a slight curve and came within the gaze of a middle-aged couple sitting in lawn chairs.

"Not far," shouted Cassandra, who was some distance ahead of him, and she waved at the couple, who waved back, mildly surprised.

"Here we are," she said a few minutes later. Karl caught up to her and stopped, panting and grateful. He took a few seconds to recover his wind and then looked curiously at George Wilcox's house, set back about a hundred feet from the water's edge.

A lawn sloped gently up to a garden buffered from sea winds by a low stone fence built across half the width of the property; some tall plants rose above the fence, swaying idly. Flowers grew against the house, and there were more next to the fences that separated George's house from those of his neighbors. There was a small toolshed at the end of the lawn, to Alberg's left. On the grass to the right, near the back door, sat a some-what threadbare canvas chair and a small table. The large window which Alberg knew was in the kitchen, and the smaller one next to it, in the den, were veneered with gold from the slow-sinking sun.

Cassandra was advancing across the lawn toward the door. Alberg followed, ill at ease. She banged on the door.

George Wilcox opened it and looked at her in amazement.

"I hope you don't mind," said Cassandra. "We've come to see your roses."

George's gaze shifted to Alberg. "The Mountie," he said. "You've brought the damn Mountie."

"I'm not on duty, Mr. Wilcox," said Alberg, furious now with Cassandra and with himself.

"Well, I can see that, can't I," said George, eyeing the two of them.

"He's actually a very nice man," said Cassandra.

"That may be," said George, holding on to the door.

"We were walking on the beach," said Cassandra. "At Davis Bay."

George looked at Alberg. "*You* want to see my roses? I find that hard to believe."

"Well, I'll tell you, Mr. Wilcox," said Alberg. He had thought of his hydrangeas and felt suddenly like a normal person. "Cassandra says you're a gardener. I need all the help I can get."

"What do you mean, help?" said George suspiciously.

"I'm living in a house in Gibsons with all sorts of things growing in the yard, and I don't even know what most of them are, let alone what to do about them."

"What house in Gibsons?"

"The one they call the directors' house."

George snorted. "That place has been going to rack and ruin for years, ever since the C.B.C. got its hands on it."

"Well, I've got it now. I'm only renting it, so far. But it's still my responsibility. And I'm not really up to it."

George Wilcox joined them on the grass, leaving the door

open behind him. He was wearing his gray sweater. It was dark enough, Alberg supposed, halfheartedly, to be taken from a distance as blue.

"You've got some dandy hydrangeas there," said George, "if I remember the place rightly." He shuffled over to the corner of his house, next to the neighbor's fence. "These are hydrangeas," he said, pointing to an enormous group of shrubs about four feet tall. He reached into the middle of a bush and stroked a faintly blue blossom much larger than any on Alberg's plants. "In a couple of weeks these will be so big," he said, indicating with his hands a six-inch circle. "Blue, then purple-ish. Last the whole summer. You got these in your yard?"

Alberg nodded. "They're growing along my front fence. I think they're going to bring it down."

"Damn things'll grow into trees if you let them," George agreed. "Cut them back. Be brutal. But don't do it now. Do it in the fall, when they've finished flowering." He moved on. "Now these, these are roses. Climbers. They grow up along the fence, you see that? You've got to tie them, though."

"I've got some of those, too," said Alberg. "I cut them back last week. Flowers and all, I'm afraid. They were about twelve feet high."

"Climbers are a bit tricky," said George, inspecting the leaves. "See this?" Alberg leaned closer. "Aphids." He wiped them off with a gnarled thumb, stooped to wipe his thumb on the grass. "Climbers are tricky. Some of them like to be pruned and some don't. If yours grow back and bloom again this summer, then they're the kind that like to be pruned. If they just show you a lot of leaves, then you did the wrong thing. You did it at the wrong time, anyway, that's for sure. It's too late in the year. You can't go hacking things down when the flowering season's under way. It's not natural."

"I'll remember that," said Alberg.

"Instead of pruning them, you could have bent them down and tied them to the top of your fence." He had begun walking across the grass toward the stone fence; he stopped and threw

Alberg a curious glance. "You ought to get some books out of the library," he said.

"I just got my card the other day," said Alberg.

The sun was low and saffron in the cloudless sky. The sea had darkened almost to violet, and the air was golden. It was as though the scene had been lit for a photograph, Alberg thought, looking at the bent old man leaning over his vegetables and Cassandra leaning next to him, holding back her chestnut hair. They were absorbed in the plants which grew in the shade of the low stone wall. Yes, thought Alberg, the scene looks lit, for a family photograph or a sentimental movie; there was an artful glow about it. The lawn beneath his feet was soft, springy, fragrant.

"I've got a couple more chairs around somewhere," said George. "Probably in the toolshed. Why don't you dig them out?" he said to Alberg. "I'll go get us some lemonade."

The toolshed was small and weatherbeaten, standing on the lawn between the stone wall and the beach, under a wind-twisted arbutus tree. Inside, gardening supplies were arranged on shelves, gardening tools hung from large nails, a ladder leaned against the wall. There were also a small push lawn-mower, a wheelbarrow, a large half-empty bag of lime, another of fertilizer, and a lot of odds and ends. Pushed into a dusty corner, Alberg found three canvas chairs like the one outside. He set up two of them in a semicircle with George's, out on the grass, and placed the small table handy to them all.

Cassandra had gone indoors to help George. Karl stood on the lawn looking at the garden. He wondered how difficult it was to keep flowers blooming serenely against the side of the house; he liked their vivid colors. Behind him the sea washed upon the beach with a rhythmic, whooshing sound.

George came out bearing, incongruously, an elegant crystal pitcher. Cassandra brought three ordinary glasses on a tray. George poured, a bit unsteadily, holding each glass over the grass so the spillage wouldn't get on the tabletop. He was careful to pour the same amount of lemonade into each glass. He put the pitcher down carefully and sat, gripping the wooden arms of the canvas chair, and then rested his hands on his thighs.

He had told Cassandra in the kitchen that the crystal pitcher was forty-five years old, a wedding gift. She thought he looked weary and more stooped than usual, and wondered how long his strength could endure in the face of his loneliness. She wanted to touch his hand as it lay upon his thigh, but she didn't.

"My mother grew a lot of geraniums," said George. "And sunflowers, and hollyhocks. She probably grew more than that, but that's all I can remember."

They listened to the sea and welcomed the cooling brought by evening.

"Was your father a gardener too?" said Alberg, stretching out his long legs, crossing his sneakered feet at the ankles.

George looked at him for a moment. Alberg couldn't read his expression. Then he looked away, and for a while there was silence, and then George began to speak. He looked at the grass as he talked, or at the white-cord tepee upon which the peas were climbing, and sometimes he shaded his eyes with a hand and looked out at the sun, still glinting from behind the hazy mountains on the horizon.

"There's a lot of peace to be found in gardening. I didn't discover that myself for years and years; just watched other people do it and wondered why they bothered. But I found out there's a lot of peace in it. That might be something you'd appreciate, Mr. Alberg."

Karl looked over at him thoughtfully.

"When you plant a seed," said George, "it almost always comes up, and turns into a plant, and gives you flowers or something to eat. When you accidentally put a bulb in upside down—a daffodil or a tulip, for instance—it comes up anyway, most times, making a half-circle under the earth, heading for the sun it can't see.

"Gardens are magical places. Marigolds all orange and gold bring exuberance and joy into your patch of earth, but if you plant them in with the vegetables, they also keep away the carrot rust fly. Picking peas, eating them straight from the pods—nothing in the world tastes as good."

There was very little expression in his voice. Cassandra felt that he was speaking by rote and yet had an urgent need to say these things. She glanced at Alberg, who was looking out to sea, his feet outstretched, hands linked behind his head.

"You've got roses in your garden, Mr. Alberg," said George. "Look closely at them, sometimes. Touch the softness of them, and smell the perfume, and see the shades of color—you won't find that particular kind of beauty in anything but roses.

"Sometimes you get infestations of things; you're in for a real battle, then. You can buy chemical sprays that choke your throat when you use them. Don't use them, if you don't have to. Wash the aphids away with soap and water."

Cassandra, watching him intently, saw that he never looked directly at either of them. His white hair gleamed in the dying sunlight; she saw only his profile as he looked away from them, out toward his garden or the ocean.

"As you said, Mr. Alberg, you've got a responsibility for the plot of ground you occupy. You share it with lots of other living things. Your responsibility is to keep a balance out there, like nature does.

"Maintenance, that's the thing to remember. Ten, fifteen minutes a day, that's all it takes, once things are under control. More in the planting season, of course. And you've also got the spring and fall cleanups to do." His voice fell away for a moment; they waited, wondering if he was finished.

"I like that part of it, though," said George, heavily. "I like digging in compost, raking up the leaves, ferreting out the stones. Because it's part of the tending of the earth."

There were bees in his garden and birds in his arbutus tree. For a few minutes, when he stopped speaking, Alberg heard them clearly, above the swishing cadence of the sea.

"It's hard to tell if your interest is genuine," said George, and now he was looking straight at Alberg. "It's hard to tell if you're the kind of man likely to become a gardener."

Karl cleared his throat and nodded.

George blinked out at the sea, and at the sun, which had almost disappeared. "It's going to be another hot one, tomorrow."

Alberg put two of the canvas chairs back in the toolshed and closed the door firmly. It had no lock. He joined Cassandra and George in the kitchen, where George was carefully rinsing out the pitcher and Cassandra was putting the clean glasses away.

"What did you think of that lemonade, eh?" said George.

It was delicious, they told him.

"Came out of a can. Frozen stuff. You add three cans of water and mix it up."

He walked them through the house to the front door; it was getting too dark, he said, to stumble along the beach over all those rocks. They paused before they left to thank him and say goodbye.

Alberg turned to follow Cassandra out the door, then turned back. He looked around the living room, puzzled.

"What's the matter?" said George.

"You've changed something."

George followed his glance. "Nope," he said.

"There's something different," Alberg insisted.

"Nope," said George.

Still Alberg hesitated, looking around the room.

"You're imagining things," said George quietly. "I ought to know. I'm the one who lives here."

Alberg turned back to him. He grasped George's hand; it was gnarled and knotty, but his grip was firm and strong.

"Your garden's very beautiful," said Alberg. "It seems to give you a lot of happiness."

"It used to," said George hoarsely, and pulled his hand free.

Alberg thought of his ex-wife, no longer his but at least alive. He thought of his daughters, no longer near but still his. He thought of the years he had to live before he would reach George Wilcox's age.

"Where's your daughter?" he said. "Carol; is that her name?"

"She's in Vancouver. Lives near Stanley Park."

"Do you see her often?"

"Sometimes. She lives in an apartment. I'm not fond of apartments." He was clutching his hands tightly in front of him. They seemed to be trembling.

Again Alberg hesitated. He wanted to say something comforting, but this wouldn't have been appropriate. It was an impulse with no genuine substance; he had known the old man for too short a time, under circumstances which had not been friendly, and suddenly realized now that he knew him not at all.

Finally he just thanked him for the lemonade and left, hurrying along the walk to catch up with Cassandra, who waited for him on the shoulder of the road.

CHAPTER 16

Alberg was feeling pretty good when he went to work the next day. He'd been hungry when they left George's house, so they went to a restaurant near Davis Bay. He had a meal and Cassandra had oysters on the half shell and they shared a bottle of wine and talked and found things to laugh about. By the time he took her home he knew he wanted to go to bed with her, but she didn't want to do any more than kiss him, sitting in the car. Her face was hot next to his, and he felt her tremble (although this morning he hadn't been totally certain about that). He was disappointed that she hadn't let it go any further, but it was going to happen eventually, he was convinced of it, and he had decided to try to be patient.

He liked her. That was the most important thing.

It was another bright, cloudless day and he was filled with optimism.

When he came into the office the parrot was shrieking and squawking.

"I don't know what to do about him," said Isabella, worried. "He isn't happy, poor thing."

Alberg got down on his haunches next to the cage. "Come on, bird," he said, "what the hell's the matter with you?" He spoke soothingly and stretched out his finger, thinking to stroke its feathers, show it some kindness.

The parrot lunged forward, snapped up a morsel of his flesh, and hopped back onto its perch, letting out a piercing scream.

Alberg in his astonishment sat down hard upon the floor, clutching his injured hand.

Isabella quickly threw the red-and-white checked cloth over the cage, and the bird's shrieks subsided to an ominous chatter. She whipped from her desk drawer a first-aid kit and knelt beside Alberg.

"My, my, my, broke the skin and everything," she said, dabbing iodine upon the wound, which was in the fleshy part of his hand. "Ignored the finger and went straight for the meaty stuff." She slathered on another layer of iodine.

"Jesus," said Alberg, breathless, "haven't you ever heard of Mercurochrome?"

"We'd better call a vet," said Isabella. "See if you can get rabies from a parrot." Deftly she unwrapped a Band-Aid and smoothed it over his hand.

"Rabies," said Alberg, faintly.

Sid Sokolowski came through the door, ushering before him an elderly woman who, when she saw Alberg and Isabella upon the floor, shrank back against the sergeant and then attempted quickly to turn around. Sokolowski grabbed her by the shoulders, gently, and propelled her inside, but he was looking disapprovingly at Alberg, who scrambled clumsily to his feet.

"Thank you, Isabella, that's fine. I appreciate it."

Isabella gathered up her supplies, packed them back into the first-aid box, and replaced it in her desk drawer. Alberg had disappeared down the hall.

"That's his bird under there, isn't it?" said the elderly woman. "A thoroughly unpleasant beast, that. He likes a bit of cheese now and then. It seems to calm him."

"Would you have a seat for a minute, Mrs. Harris?" said Sokolowski. He pointed to a long wooden bench under the window. It was padded with green cushions. At either end was an ashtray on a stand. "I'll be back in a minute."

He went to Alberg's office door. "What the hell was all that about, you and Isabella rolling around on the floor?"

"It's that goddamn bird," said Alberg, red-faced. "This is no place for a goddamn parrot. Force it on Wilcox. Give it to a zoo. Turn it loose. I don't care what you do with it, but do something. Get rid of it."

"Bit you, did it?"

"Yeah, it bit me. Get rid of it."

"What did you do, stick your finger in its cage? Okay," he said hastily. "Okay. Listen." He came into the office and sat down. "That woman out there; she was Burke's cleaning lady."

"Make her take the parrot."

"She gave the place a going-over once a week, on Wednesdays. Come last Wednesday, the guy's dead. When I interviewed her she said she couldn't believe it, such a fine man and all that, it must have been robbery.

"She called me up the next day to say it all again. I told her according to the victim's lawyer nothing's missing, and she said how could we be so sure, she knew the house and its contents better than anybody's lawyer, there were a lot of valuable things around the place. I said they're apparently all still there. Anyway, the long and the short of it—"

"The short of it, please."

"—is that I took her over there this morning. She kept calling, you know? Kept bugging me. So I drove her over there to take a look around." He hesitated. "She says she reads a lot of crime books."

Alberg groaned.

"I figured what she really wanted was to have a gander at the scene of the crime, get a glimpse of the blood on the rug, that sort of thing. Something to tell her cronies about. Still, I said to myself, you never know."

"I don't want civilians at a crime scene," said Alberg furiously. "What is this, a circus? Jesus Christ, Sergeant."

"Would I bring her here if it wasn't important?" said Sokolowski, calmly. "We just got back from the house. I want you to hear what she's got to say."

"Jesus Christ." Alberg sighed. "All right, bring her in."

He waited without moving, trying not to think, trying to concentrate on the pain in his hand; but it was almost gone. It would be too much to hope for, he thought, that she could have seen anything significant. . . .

"I thought I might be of some help," said Mrs. Harris. She was about sixty-five, not much more than five feet tall, with curly gray hair. She wore glasses with extremely large, round lenses. The frames were studded with rhinestones. "He didn't have many visitors," she said, "as far as I could tell. I told your man that last week. Poor Mr. Burke, such an awful way to die. It isn't natural, Inspector," she said, rather dramatically. "It just isn't natural. That's what bothers me."

"Staff Sergeant, actually, Mrs. Harris," said Alberg.

She scrutinized him disapprovingly and glanced around his small office. Clearly, she would like to have asked to see his superior.

"He's the boss here, like I told you, Mrs. Harris," said Sokolowski. "Go on. Tell him about when you went into the house. Sit down, why don't you?"

She sat in the black chair. She was wearing brown shoes with laces, and brown polyester slacks, and a brightly embroidered white short-sleeved sweater. "This gentleman accompanied me," she said, indicating Sokolowski, "and a good thing, too. I'm not one of nervous spirit. But a man met death in there, death by misadventure. There's no way you could have persuaded me to enter that house alone, even though the sun was shining and it looked as peaceful as ever."

She took a deep breath. "The parrot was gone. I noticed that. But then this gentleman informed me he'd been taken off to police headquarters." She settled herself more comfortably in the chair, adjusting her large handbag in her lap.

"Was anything missing, Mrs. Harris?" said Alberg.

"At first everything looked exactly the same, except for the rug." She shuddered.

"I walked through the whole house," she said, "concentrating, concentrating. Before I went into a room I'd stop outside the door and squeeze my eyes shut and picture it in my mind, all the furniture and the doodads and the drapes and what-have-you, then I'd march in there and have a look round and it all looked just the same as always."

Alberg glanced at Sokolowski, who was standing next to Mrs. Harris, impassive.

"Finally," said Mrs. Harris, "I went back into the living room. Where the rug is. I just ignored it this time. Got firm with myself. Steeled myself, you might say. I shut my eyes and thought hard and opened them again—and there it was. An empty space where there didn't used to be one. It isn't important, though, I suppose. It wasn't anything valuable."

"Tell me about the empty space," said Alberg, studying his hands clasped on his desk.

"There used to be two things there, exactly the same. Souvenirs, he said they were, from the war. He must have meant World War Two. He couldn't have been in World War One. Well, I guess—he was eighty-five, born in 1899—I guess he could have got in on the last days of World War One. I would have thought he'd be too old for World War Two, starting as it did in 1939 and going on to 1945. That makes him forty when it started and forty-six when it ended. I would have thought that was too old. But anyway, they were souvenirs of the war, that's what he said."

"What were they?" said Alberg.

"I don't have any idea."

"What did they look like?" said Alberg, patiently.

"Oh, about this tall," she said, measuring the air with her hands. "They stood about so tall, a foot, maybe. Not too heavy, I remember. I had to lift them up to dust under them. They were hollow."

"How big across, would you say?" said Alberg.

She measured again. "About like that. Maybe—what, three inches? About like that."

"Would you recognize them if you saw them again?"

"Oh, yes, certainly," she said. "They had a peculiar design on them: a big flower, something like that. Ugly things they were, that's my opinion. It's funny they're gone, isn't it?" She leaned forward. "Could they be valuable, do you think?"

"I doubt it, Mrs. Harris," said Alberg. "They sound like shell casings. They were a dime a dozen around here, after the war. Lots of people have them."

"I've got a couple," said Sokolowski. "My father got them. Had them made into bookends."

Mrs. Harris sat back, disappointed. "Oh. Still, it's odd they're gone, isn't it?"

"Maybe he got rid of them himself," said Sokolowski. "Just got sick of looking at them and pitched them out."

"Oh," said Mrs. Harris. "Well. Anyway, that's all that's missing, as far as I can tell, and who could tell better. And I went through that house so concentrated I was shaking when I came out."

Sokolowski saw her out and came back to Alberg's office.

"I think there's some Greek blood in her someplace," he said. He sat down. "So what did I tell you. He used something he found in the house, right?"

"Yeah," said Alberg. "It looks like it."

"He bashes him, then takes the weapon away with him."

"And its mate, too," said Alberg. After a minute he said, "How are we doing on that guy?"

"We've found lots of people up and down the coast know him by sight, or his truck. People tell us he lives in the bush, all right—he's an old hippie, they think. Name of Derek something. You know these people, Karl. They hop from one thing to another. They're always selling something, everything from handmade pots to Okanagan apples to honey to fish. And they don't work according to any schedule. Just whenever they've got something to peddle. But we'll get him. No word from the mainland, so he's got to be around here somewhere."

Isabella appeared in the doorway. "Have you called the vet?"

Alberg rubbed the Band-Aid on his right hand. "No, I have not called the vet. I am not going to call the vet."

"I'll call him," said Isabella, and retreated.

"Jesus," said Alberg. "I'm going out for lunch."

He drove down the hill into the village, his arm out the open window, preoccupied. He was trying to imagine Carlyle Burke sitting in his rocking chair, looking out at the sea, while somebody sneaked up behind him to bonk him on the head with one of his own shell casings.

He tried to imagine the conversation that might have preceded the attack.

He tried to imagine the attacker, to put a face on him, to find his shape, his substance, and the nature of his fury.

CHAPTER 17

George Wilcox sat outside in his canvas chair until it got dark.

He sat quietly, with his hands in his lap, and watched the sun lower itself behind Vancouver Island. The sun was much larger than the inch-high mountains on the horizon. For a while it appeared that it was going to sit all night on the ground behind them, letting most of itself continue to light up the sky. But then it began to settle lower, and lower, and finally it was gone. George looked straight above him and saw faint stars.

He continued to sit, wrapped in his gray cardigan, watching the western sky fade. The bees had gone back to their hives for the night and most of the birds, too, were still. Lights went on in the houses next to George's. Quite early they went out, in the house of one of his neighbors, but continued to burn in the other house. George began to feel cool and went inside to put on his pea jacket; he was already wearing his gardening shoes, which had thick rubber soles and were old and comfortable.

Finally his other neighbors put their lights out, too.

He hadn't gone to the hospital today, he realized. It was the first Monday in six months that he hadn't gone to the hospital.

George got up from the canvas chair and went to his toolshed for a spade and two burlap bags. He spread one of them on the lawn next to his vegetable garden, carefully dug up the zucchini and moved it with its root ball of heavy moist earth onto the burlap. He dug deeper and unearthed the shell casings. He shook dirt from them and wiped more away with his hands. He wrapped them in the second burlap bag, making sure there was burlap between them so they wouldn't clank around. Next he scooped some earth into the hole in his garden, and carefully replanted the zucchini, brushing dirt from its leaves as he did so. The light from his kitchen window shone upon him as he worked. He shook the dirt from the first burlap bag into the garden, then put the burlap-wrapped shell casings inside it and pulled taut the strings. He went inside and filled a watering can and watered the zucchini. Then he washed his hands and turned off the kitchen light and went back outside, closed the door, and locked it.

George put his keys in his pocket, picked up the burlap bag, and adjusted it over his right shoulder. He walked down the lawn to the beach and turned toward Carlyle's house.

The moon was full, and it caused the rocks on the beach to cast large shadows, which George sometimes mistook for more rocks. He went slowly, frequently stopping to shift the bag to his other shoulder. He didn't bother to look up at the houses he passed, in some of which lights still burned. If somebody opened a door and called out to him, "Hey, who are you? What are you doing out there?" he wouldn't stop but he'd say loudly, "It's George Wilcox, and I'm going to throw Carlyle Burke's shell casings into the drink." He didn't care. Christ. He just couldn't have them contaminating his garden. Enough was enough.

Alberg was in his living room. He had called the cat, and gotten no response, but had automatically put fresh milk in its bowl anyway. Now, restless and irritable, he was staring into the fireplace, in which there was no fire.

He was thinking about the unknown assailant who had killed Carlyle Burke, and about Cassandra, and about his daughters. He wondered whether Cassandra was in the habit of opening her door to strangers. He thought she probably was. She never locked her car, and he had noticed when he drove her home last night that she'd just opened her front door and walked right in. He couldn't believe it. Surely what happened to Burke should have taught her that even in Sechelt caution ought to be a way of life.

He got up to refill his glass. He'd been reading lately about attacks on young women at the University of British Columbia. There were special campus buses to take female students from the library to brightly lit city bus stops. But even that wasn't enough. Some "jerk shitrat," to quote Sokolowski, was attacking women in the library now, right in the stacks.

Alberg sat down heavily, worrying about his daughters. The campus at the University of Calgary was smaller; did that make it safer? He had drilled it into them for years: Keep your doors locked, always secure your car, carry your key ring with the keys sticking out from between your fingers, walk in light, lock all doors as soon as you're in your vehicle, run, scream. . . .

Maybe they'd like to get jobs in Vancouver for the summer. He would suggest this. If they liked the idea, maybe he could help them find work. Maybe they could spend weekends with him, and he could teach them how to sail.

He wondered if they had boyfriends, serious ones, who might screw up his plans. Should he write the girls directly? Or should he contact their mother first, sound her out about their situations?

He pulled from his pocket a letter he'd received that day from his younger daughter, Diana, the one with long straight hair and a grin like a meteor. His daughters were taking intersessional courses; it worried him that they were trying to do too much, right after completing a full winter session.

Dear Pop, he read.

Life is frantic these days, frantic, but I've only got one more exam and then it'll be all over until September. Geology. The worst of them all. I was really glad when I got my schedule that it came last. I'd have more time to study for it, right? But now here I am, I've got to write the damn thing tomorrow and of course I've put it off and tonight's the only time I've got left. It's not as important to me as the other two so I studied like mad for them and now I'm not ready for geology. It's not important to me but I've got to have it, and I'll just DIE *if I fail it, I'll be so* FURIOUS *if I have to take the damn stuff again next year. And now here I am writing to you instead of using the last hours remaining to me. Sigh.*

I wish I could talk to you face to face, Pop. This letter-writing stuff is the shits. When are you coming out here??? Don't you have some perpetrator to chase across the Rockies? Seriously, I hope you're happy and not bored in that place. I'm sure it's very pretty, though, it looks like it from the pictures you sent, and you must have friends by now, right?

I love you and miss you. Wish me luck in geology. I know you would, if you were here, and you'd give me a pep talk, too. I probably never told you, but I used to like your pep talks.

Love,
Diana

P.S. Janey's only taking two courses in intersession, and she sailed through her damn exams without a ripple of fear. She keeps trying to give me advice. She calls it sisterly love; I call it condescension.

P.P.S. Mom is fine. We saw her last month, on the long weekend.

He wished he could hug her, and smooth the hair away from her face, and study her face for signs of worry or weariness, and find none, and send her back to her books with a kiss on the cheek and words of faith and confidence—a "pep talk." It was good to know she liked his pep talks, though he wouldn't have described them that way. The phrase implied a stalwart self-confidence he had never felt when trying to help his daughters.

Her letter had been mailed the day of her exam; it was over, now. He would call her tonight, to see how she'd done.

He tried to remember what he'd been doing while she was writing it, hunched over her paper in the University of Calgary gym. She had probably marched in there wearing an old pair of sweats, he thought, smiling, no makeup, her hair tied back in a careless ponytail, nails bitten to the quick, head swimming, filled with irrelevancies. She would sit down, drop her huge denim bag on the floor, and clutch her forehead. It would take several seconds for her eyes to actually focus on the first question.

If she'd written it Friday morning—he got up and went to

the kitchen to freshen his drink—that would have been, let's see... He thought about it idly as he dropped ice cubes into his glass. He was at the office on Friday, going through the paperwork on the Burke homicide. There hadn't been much there, just the autopsy report. Then he'd had lunch with Cassandra.

If Diana had written the exam in the afternoon, he thought, adding a small amount of scotch to the ice in his glass, then he had been at the funeral, or maybe in the library....

He went back into the living room and stood looking out the window. It was dark, now, except for the splash of light near his front gate, from the streetlamp.

Cassandra. She made him feel good. And she tasted wonderful. He smiled, thinking about her....

And after the library, he'd gone to George Wilcox's house. That was late afternoon, but Diana could have been writing her exam then, too, while he was in Wilcox's house....

Alberg stood very still.

He thought about going through the door and looking around the living room, automatically filing things away. He did it all the time, everywhere he went; it was instinct, by now; he imagined his brain filled with little slots, each crammed with observations, some useful, some not.

He fixed his concentration, his drink forgotten.

And he remembered.

He had stood in the doorway again just last night and had looked around, puzzled. And now he knew why. Now he knew what had been different about George Wilcox's living room.

He put his glass down carefully on the table next to the wingback chair. He struggled hard against leaping to conclusions.

But he got his jacket from the hall closet, pulled the living room curtains closed, turned on the porch light, and left the house.

CHAPTER 18

George was spooked by the place.

He felt when he arrived at Carlyle's beach as though he'd skulked his way there, although he hadn't. He had walked upright—as upright as the weight over his shoulder would permit—and hadn't tried to crunch quietly across the rocks, and hadn't hastened crablike and stealthy when he'd had to walk past a lighted-up house. But now, arriving on Carlyle's quiet silver beach, he felt furtive, all right. His heart thumped in his chest, irregular beats of alarm. He had to stop to rest.

He sat on Carlyle's silver lawn with his back against a tree, the burlap bag beside him. He felt rough bark against his shoulders and the back of his head. In a circle beneath the tree a permanent layer of needles had killed the grass. It was a thin cushion for him to sit upon. From the branches above came the scent of pine.

He stayed there for several minutes, looking across the lawn at the high laurel hedge that grew all the way down to the beach, taking occasional uneasy peeks at the house. It was out of range of the moonlight but it had a slight glow anyway, it seemed to George, but he knew that was just the whiteness of its paint against the blackness which surrounded it.

He waited until he felt somewhat restored, then got up and carried the burlap bag over to the rowboat.

He dragged it off its four-inch wooden blocks without great difficulty. The oars which were stored beneath the seats clanked, and clanked again when he tipped the boat over.

The tide was high, but there were some sharp-looking rocks on the strip of sand between the lawn and the water's edge. George cleared these away, put the burlap bag in the bottom of the boat, and set to work dragging it, bow first, down the gentle slope of lawn and into the water. He took it slowly, sometimes no more than a few inches at a time. He was making some noise, all right, but he didn't think it was enough to be heard by anyone living in the houses above the beach. Of course, somebody could be standing at an upstairs window this very minute, gazing out at the moonlit sea before closing his bedroom curtains and climbing into bed. If it happens, it happens, thought George; but he couldn't prevent himself from glancing up. And of course it was Carlyle's house which looked back at him, still and curious; he tried not to imagine malevolence.

It was about ten feet long, Carlyle's aluminum rowboat, and looked to be in good shape even though it must have been a couple of years since George had seen him use it. Carlyle used to go out fishing in it. Sometimes while George was in his garden he'd see him rowing away out there. Sometimes he'd plant himself in the sea right off George's garden and sit there, puffing on his goddamn pipe, wearing a big straw hat, holding that stupid fishing line over the edge of his boat.

George stopped and leaned against the rowboat, mopping his forehead with his big handkerchief. He took off his pea jacket and tossed it into the boat and rested for a minute. Then he began again, pushing at the stern, then trudging around to pull for a while at the rope attached to the bow. Eventually he felt hard wet sand beneath his feet and looked over his shoulder to see the ocean reaching for his shoes. He went back around to the stern and pushed hard three times, stopping to rest between pushes, and felt the bow become suddenly weightless.

He got hold of the rope, threw it inside, and cautiously gave two more pushes. Then he clambered in from the stern and sat on one of the rowboat's two seats. He fumbled for an oar, stood up and pushed himself off, then sat down quickly and got the other oar, fixed them both in the locks, and began to row.

Alberg sat at his desk with the Burke file in front of him, absorbed in the autopsy report. He wanted to be absolutely sure—and he couldn't be, of course, until he got the shell casing and turned it over to the pathologist. "Well, what do you think, doc?" he'd say. "Is this it? Is this the thing came crashing down on old Carlyle's skull and put out all his lights?"

He couldn't understand why the old man hadn't gotten rid of them earlier. Maybe, not so deep down, he wanted to be caught.

Alberg's sense of exuberance was very strong. He was trying to dampen it—let's have the Nordic caution, here, he told himself—but it was the other part of him that wanted to handle this. His Irish mother's genes were screaming, "Get moving, you cold-headed bastard; prudence never got you anything but another night in the same room." He marveled at it. He could actually hear her.

He put everything neatly back in the folder and put the folder neatly in the filing cabinet in exactly the right alphabetical slot. He read a cryptic note from Isabella: *Vet says don't worry, a parrot's not a bat.* He turned out his desk lamp, put on his jacket, and left his office. He even stopped to have a few words with the constable on night duty. He was absolutely under control.

But as he unlocked his car he was hot in the cool of the evening, and felt light on his feet, as if he'd lost twenty pounds, and he did not for some reason dare to take a deep breath.

Nowhere in his mind was there room for George's roses, or George's unsteady old hands pouring three glasses of lemonade from a crystal pitcher.

CHAPTER 19

George rowed in a southwesterly direction out into the bay, at an angle from Carlyle's house, which had not been his intention. He had originally decided to paddle straight out from the beach almost due west, drop the bag when he'd gone about three hundred yards, then row straight back. But on second thought he hadn't liked the idea of Carlyle's house watching him as he carried out his task, as if some part of it—the drainpipes, for instance—might raise themselves from the ground and commence to point, accusingly. A man can't always control his imagination, he thought, especially when he's physically weary and somewhat distraught. He thought it not a good idea in this case to try. So he rowed southwest, and Carlyle's house was soon out of sight behind the black mass of the laurel hedge.

It was extremely quiet out on the water. George could see no other boats. Every once in a while he raised the oars and drifted for a few seconds, listening. He was almost out of earshot of the sea's insistent caressing of the shore, and the only other noises were those of an occasional bird and, from far away, a large vehicle gearing down for one of the highway hills. Soon even these sounds were so smudged as to be indecipherable, and all he heard was his oars dipping, pulling, rising through the black water, and, when he paused now and then to rest, the dreamy sensuous lapping of the sea at his little boat.

He was rowing straight out from shore, now. The land

receded, slowly, and the light from the stars and the moon intensified. He looked left and saw that he'd gone only about half the distance he needed to go; he wanted to row out until he was even with the end of the spit which formed the northern edge of the bay. He figured that was about three hundred yards, and at that point the water ought to be deep enough to gulp down the shell casings and swallow them whole. He had to get out there as quickly as possible, before the tide turned; he wasn't sure there was enough strength in his arms to try to row against it.

It was a relief not to be able to see Carlyle's house. It had looked so vacant, even though it was still full of Carlyle's possessions. He remembered that they were his possessions, now, and this came again as a terrible shock. He tried to imagine himself sitting on the white piano stool, his hands poised above the ivory keys of the white piano; it had candle-holders, he suddenly remembered, sticking out from the front of it. . . . He recalled one night when Carlyle had put candles in them and turned out all the lights and sat down and played. George couldn't remember whether this had happened in Sechelt, before Myra died, when they sometimes went to see Carlyle, or in Vancouver, a long time ago. Carlyle's hair had been pale in the candlelight, he remembered; but before it was white or gray it had been blond, so that didn't help. He couldn't remember Carlyle's hands on the keyboard—his fingers had moved too quickly. But he remembered the music: Chopin, it was. And when he finished, Carlyle had quick put his hands in his lap and spun around on the stool, a big smile on his face. The candles made funny shadows. Carlyle had looked like he had no eyes.

George checked the shore far away on his left and tried to row harder. Clouds had begun to gather in the west.

It must have been in Vancouver, he thought, because Audrey was there. When Carlyle spun around, smiling, she went up to him and put her hand on his shoulder, tentatively; Carlyle had lifted her hand to his lips and kissed it, and patted it, and then looked at George and winked.

What the hell did that mean? thought George furiously,

rowing. What the hell was the meaning of that wink? He tried to sort this particular memory from the others that were crowding into his head, clamoring to be heard and seen, but it faded on that wink. ...

Next he remembered Carlyle sitting on a bar stool. George was sitting next to him. Carlyle was holding a glass of beer in both hands. He was slumped over. George was filled with distaste and alarm; he was afraid Carlyle was going to burst into tears and wondered if they'd be low, racking sobs or silent, just salt water pouring noiselessly down his face into his drink. It'll ruin that beer, George remembered thinking. He had put his hand in his pocket, ready to haul out his handkerchief. But Carlyle hadn't cried after all. He shook his head and gave a kind of a laugh and then he looked up sideways at George. "You don't know what the shit I'm talking about, do you, fella, do you, George, old sock, old buddy, old pal." George couldn't remember what the hell either of them had been talking about.

Again he glanced to his left. He seemed to be making progress. He was sure the end of the spit wasn't as far behind him as it had been the last time he looked. ...

One morning in autumn, during a spare period, he had left the staff room to go to the office. He'd walked down the middle of the wide hallway lined with lockers. Drones and murmurings issued from the classrooms as he passed them. The floor gleamed in the light from the big glass front doors at the end of the hall, and George had a secret inside him; he'd applied again to teach in Germany. (He was almost unbearably excited at the possibility of living in another country. He couldn't talk about it much to Myra, couldn't hope out loud that this time they'd get to go, because it meant too much to him. For Christmas she gave him a set of luggage. He was furious with her at first, because he thought she had tempted the gods. But she told him he didn't have enough faith, and in January his application was accepted. He had felt a new and different kind of respect for Myra, from then on.) He was walking along the shiny waxed floors holding onto his secret and looking down the long hall at the sunshine coming through the glass at the end of it when a door burst open ten or fifteen feet in front of him and a student hurtled out, stumbled, and grabbed at the opposite wall. Before George could get himself together to go to the boy's aid Carlyle strode out, banging the door behind him. He yanked the boy around; Carlyle was a tall man, and the boy only came up to his chin. "You little punk," said Carlyle, in a raspy whisper that echoed down the hall. He seized the boy by the shoulders and banged his head against the wall. "You son-of-a-bitching little punk," he said.

And then, gripping the student's shirtfront with one hand, with the other Carlyle took the boy's left wrist and twisted his arm back into an awkward, unnatural position. He kept pressing and pressing, his eyes on the boy's face. George watched, stupefied, for several seconds before he managed to uproot himself and walk quickly toward them.

"What's the trouble?" he called out in what he hoped was an authoritative tone.

It was as though they hadn't heard him. They were looking directly into each other's eyes. The boy's face was creased with pain and fear and was very white; his freckles stood out like blood blisters. Carlyle's stare was intent and curious as he pressed the arm back, and back—

"Hey!" said George loudly. He put a firm hand on Carlyle's shoulder. He saw Carlyle's pressure on the boy's wrist relax, allowing the arm to fall forward. Still Carlyle held his wrist, and the front of his shirt. The boy's eyes rolled toward the ceiling. His lips were quivering.

"What's going on?" said George.

Tears appeared at the corners of the boy's eyes. Carlyle let go of his wrist. He did up a button on the boy's white shirt, which had come undone during the one-sided fracas. He tugged indifferently at the shirt, smoothing it. Then he reached out and with no expression at all patted the boy's cheek, his hand lingering there, smudging the tears.

He turned to George, his eyes bright. "No trouble," he said. He pulled down his shirt cuffs and adjusted his tie. "A small difference of opinion. That's all." He turned and went back into the classroom without giving the boy another glance.

George turned to the student, who began shoving his shirt

back inside the waistband of his cords. "Are you sure you're all right?"

The boy wiped his mouth with the back of his hand.

"What the hell happened?" said George.

But the student refused to answer. After a moment he went quietly back inside the classroom. . . .

George stopped rowing. He hung onto the oars and rested his face on the backs of his hands. The muscles in his shoulders were fluttering. He checked his coordinates: the end of the spit of land was almost directly opposite him, on his left.

He hoisted the burlap bag up onto the edge of the boat and pushed it over. It made hardly any noise as it hit the water. He leaned over and watched the ripples from its passage into darkness disappear. He waited, watched, but it didn't return to the surface.

Wearily, he turned the boat around. The moon was to his left, now, halfway between the horizon and the top of the sky, and sometimes it disappeared briefly behind a veil of cloud stretching across the sky from the west. Ahead of him lay the ocean, a black carpet to nowhere; he could see it rippling.

He thought about turning around again and continuing to row out to sea, watching the shore as it retreated farther and farther and then disappeared. He would row on and on through the soft warm night until his arms collapsed and the weight of them pulled him into the bottom of the boat, where he would sleep until awakened by the day. Then he would sit up and look around and find himself approaching a small uninhabited island. He would let himself drift onto its beach and he would climb out and lie down on the sand, and on the softness of the sand with the sea kissing the soles of his feet he would sleep while the hot sun soothed him and he'd never wake up, just sleep there forever on the soft sand, in the hotness of the sunshine.

Except that there wouldn't be any sunshine tomorrow. The clouds were coming.

The muscles in his shoulders burned. He glanced behind him, to see how far he had to go, and kept on rowing. . . .

She ran up to him, her arms filled with lilac. He remembered

thinking that she ought to be queen of that festival they had
somewhere down in Washington, a lilac festival, the color of
the flowers suited her so well. She thrust them into his hands
and threw her arms around him. The lilacs were smothered
against his chest. He felt her cheek against his, and smelled
the lilacs, and ever since that day Audrey never came into his
mind without bringing with her the softness of her cheek and
the scent of lilac.

"Please be happy for me, George, like Myra is," she said.
"We're going to be married, Carlyle and I."

If he'd had that kind of shock now, at age eighty, he would
have died of it.

"You can't do this," he had said, incredulous and appalled,
clutching the lilacs. But she laughed, and put an arm around
his waist, and led him into the kitchen where Myra waited,
smiling, ready to open a bottle of wine in celebration.

If only he could have found, somewhere, the right thing
to say!

He knew he wouldn't convince Myra. Whatever he said to
Myra sounded weak and desperate because she couldn't know
what lay behind his fear, he had never told her; she could not
possibly have understood the bleakness, the sickness that struck
at his soul, when Audrey said it: "We're going to be married,
Carlyle and I." The more he railed against it, the more impatient and exasperated Myra became. "What have you got
against him, for God's sake? Isn't she entitled to a life of her
own? Are you going to keep her chained to you—to us—
forever?"

But Audrey understood. She knew exactly what he feared,
and why. But she refused to discuss it. So he had said, "He's
too *old* for you!" and God knew that was true enough, there
were twenty years between them. And he had said, "I don't
like him!" and that ought to have been enough; oh, Christ, if
only that had been enough. . . . She would have been sixty-
four, now, he thought: a woman in her prime.

He hadn't given up. Not until the last minute. On the day
of her wedding, in desperation he told her about the episode
in the school hallway. He told her other things, he gave her

other examples of Carlyle's meanness, his cruelty. He rattled them off with an urgency that caused his face to flush and his heart to beat fast: Carlyle's snide remarks about his colleagues; his contempt for his students; his hatred of women, hidden behind a facade of gallantry; his loathing for animals; his appalling rages—George held his sister by her shoulders on the day she was to be married and forced her to listen to him, and when she averted her head, refusing to hear, he shook her violently and flung her aside and saw in that gesture all the things he feared for her.

From the chair into which she had fallen, Audrey said nothing.

"Do you *want* this?" George shouted, almost weeping. "Don't you see what you're *doing*?"

"What I see is that you can't forget things that should be forgotten," said Audrey. "But I can, and I will. You've made sacrifices for me, I know that. You made them for her, too, I remember that. You couldn't help how it ended. You've got to stop torturing yourself." She got up to embrace him, but he wouldn't let her. "You're a good man, George," said Audrey, who was crying, now. "I know you mean well. But you've got to stop this. I'm going to marry him. You're wrong about him, I know it."

He hadn't been able to find the right words. He had failed her, and for that he never forgave her, and in the end it had killed her.

He looked behind him. The shore was still a long way off. He saw the moon strike from between two clouds and lay a cool white path across the water, pointing obliquely at the land.

He didn't remember the wedding. He had no recollection of it at all, although he knew he'd been there. He'd given his sister away.

George hurt all over, now. The oars weighed a hundred pounds each, and the ocean had transformed itself into molasses, or tar. He had to stop after every two or three strokes, breathing heavily, to flex his shoulder muscles and let his head drop while he tried to relax and strengthen himself.

He knew his failure had killed her. He was certain of it. And all three of them were therefore culpable: Audrey, Carlyle, and George himself.

He had put his own guilt in abeyance in California, working furiously all day and gardening himself into exhaustion in the evenings. Back in Vancouver he thought he had come to terms with it, even put it finally to rest, by growing and nurturing with increasing skill the living things that Audrey had loved.

Years later they had moved here, he and Myra. "It's the twilight of our years, my love," she had said, smiling, teasing him. They bought the little house by the sea and he started his small garden and they went to Vancouver to see Carol every month or so and everything was hunky-dory.

And then Carlyle had popped out of those goddamn laurel bushes and George's guilt made a swift return, supplanting almost everything in his life, creating dreadful, terrible flashes of things in his head.

But he got it under control.

Until Myra died. He felt so vulnerable, then. He thought about moving to Vancouver, living with Carol, who was all alone now, too—but his garden, his garden—and then last Tuesday...only six days ago, he thought: less than a week ago....

He stopped rowing, lowered his head, and rubbed at his eyes.

...he sees him shout at her, roar at her, his eyes bright and his face shiny with sweat. She stands before him full of sweet reason, and it means sweet bugger-all. His hand snaps back and he hits her in the face; George sees her mouth bleed...

But *is* it Carlyle? *Is* it Audrey?

He jerked up his head and started rowing again, hard, pain grabbing at his shoulders.

...she hits the floor, her limbs flying like those of a doll...he crouches; his fist buries itself fast and hard in her stomach...

But *whose* limbs? *Whose* fist?

He shook his head violently; he would not do this must not do this will not think of this...

George was weeping now, hot tears gushing as he rowed.

There was nothing to look at in front of him but blackness, and to his right, the soft slow-moving land, lightless, edged by a ribbon of silver sand. He rested again on his oars and knew he was too tired to take the boat back where he'd gotten it. He changed course, heading straight for his own beach.

Could he have been wrong about Carlyle? Had the past laid such a black shadow upon him that he couldn't see to make rational judgments? Had he struck Carlyle because of the past, only the past, a time of which Carlyle was innocent, of which he should have remained ignorant? Had he killed him only because he was afraid to hear things he knew were true, and thought he had learned to live with?

Was it possible that Carlyle wasn't guilty, after all? Was it possible that he hadn't deserved to die?

Aching with exhaustion, sick with uncertainty, George rowed still harder, battling the tide.

CHAPTER 20

Alberg drove slowly from the detachment office down the hill and turned onto the highway leading south through Sechelt. He made himself keep his eyes open as he drove, looking for the vandals who had twice broken into Pete Venner's corner store, on the watch for the kid who liked to roar through town at sixty miles an hour flashing his father's Trans-Am under the streetlights, and dutifully watching, too, for an old VW van with rainbows on its sides.

He saw only quiet streets. Almost everything was closed, now; it was after ten o'clock. There were no bars or beer parlors in the village itself, only restaurants where you could order wine or beer with your meal. There was the government liquor store in the shopping center, which closed at six, and there was a lounge in the new hotel down by the water; never any trouble there, the clientele was middle-aged and subdued.

It was a short drive to George Wilcox's house. Alberg pulled up in front and switched off the engine.

The house was dark. The neighbors' houses were dark, too. The stillness made him uneasy, and for a minute he wished he were on Denman Street, in Vancouver's West End. Everything was open there, bars and restaurants and movie theaters, and there was lots of noise. Kids with punk haircuts swished along the sidewalks on skateboards, and the traffic was bumper to bumper, and bicycles weaved among the cars, and English Bay at the end of the street was still crowded even at this hour, and up and down the streets and alleys prostitutes male and female young and old sold themselves while trying to avoid being "pressing and persistent." And children were selling themselves, too. Whenever he thought of the West End Alberg thought of Stanley Park, vinegary fish and chips, and perversion.

He got out of the car and went through the gate up to George Wilcox's front door. He knocked softly, waited, knocked again, waited, knocked harder. Nobody came to the door. He couldn't hear a sound.

He made his way around the side of the house and looked in the windows of George's bedroom. It was empty, the bed made. He went to the other side of the house, squeezing between the house and the cedar hedge. The living room windows were too high; he couldn't see what was on the sills.

The cedar hedge made a ninety-degree turn at the end of the house and it was too thick to push through. Alberg went around the other way, to the back yard, and got the ladder from the toolshed. He carried it around the house to the living room side. He leaned it against the house and climbed up until his eyes were level with the windows.

On the sill to his left he saw the three china flowers set in a base, the two Hummel figurines, the empty pipe holder. On the other sill, two Toby mugs, a pair of brass candlesticks and a candle snuffer, a wooden salt shaker and pepper mill. The objects had been distributed so as to fill evenly all the available space on the windowsill. When he had first seen them they were closer together, and first in line had stood two forty-millimeter shell casings; he remembered thinking they were probably from a Bofors gun, and noticing the decorative work that had been done on them.

He climbed down and returned the ladder to the toolshed. He knocked on the back door, but nobody answered. He tried the door; it was locked.

Alberg stood in the middle of the lawn, his hands in his pockets, looking at George's garden and wondering where he had buried them. Then he turned and walked over to the canvas chair and sat down. He put his hands on its wooden arms and crossed his ankles.

He knew he'd hear George when he came home. He'd hear the front door open and close, and then light would flood into the garden from the kitchen; he was pretty sure George would fix himself some tea or some lemonade or something before he went to bed.

The moon shone fitfully from behind the passing clouds. The tide was going out; there was a narrow strip of hard wet sand between the water and the rocky beach. The sound of the sea lapping at the land was hypnotic, soothing. He heard a bird, maybe crying out from a dream; a dog barking, from far away; and sometimes a little whisper from George's garden, as a breeze passed through it.

Eventually Alberg became aware of a new sound. He realized that it was the sound of oars.

He stood up and went down the lawn toward the beach. The slap of the oars against the water was uneven; there wasn't a great deal of strength behind it; the oars penetrated shallowly and often seemed only to shudder against the surface of the water. Alberg stared out at the sea and finally almost dead ahead saw a black shape hunched over in a small rowboat, its back to the shore. The shape stopped to rest, leaning on the oars. Then it bent again to its rowing, weak and strained; the oars lifted, struck the water, were dragged ineffectually back.

The moon suddenly poured white light from a hole in the clouds and, like an actor stepping into a spotlight, George Wilcox rowed his small boat out of the darkness and into its radiant trail. Alberg watched without moving as slowly the old man traversed the wide streak of silver washed upon the water. He rowed laboriously, awkwardly, with an immense and terrifying dignity, moonlight clothing him and his boat in a cool silver glow.

"You crafty old bugger," Alberg whispered.

By the time George reached the rocky beach, the moon was once more veiled. Alberg waited until the bow of the rowboat ground upon sand, and George climbed wearily over the side. As he reached for the rope, trying to beach the rowboat, Alberg waded through the water toward him.

George stared at him, hanging on to the edge of the boat.

Alberg reached past him and grabbed the rope. George let go, and Alberg pulled the boat across the beach and up onto the lawn, next to the toolshed. He got George's damp pea jacket from the bottom of the boat and waited for George to slosh through the water and over the rocks and into his back yard.

"What were you doing out there at this time of night, George?" said Alberg, conversationally. He held out the jacket, and George took it. The old man was bent over and hobbling. "Where'd you get the boat? It's your friend Carlyle's boat, isn't it?"

"It's mine, now," said George. "Or so you people tell me. Everything's mine, now. Isn't that what you said?"

"Not quite yet, George. We have to sort out the business of the homicide, first. Keep the crime scene sealed, and all that. There's a corporal on duty at the house, you know. You didn't know that? Yeah, he's there. Must spend all his time around front. I'll have to have a word with him."

"You do that," said George.

"No, I'm afraid you're going to have to wait awhile before you stake your claim to Carlyle's loot, George. Taking his boat—that could get you into trouble."

"The corporal and I, we're in trouble together, that's the way I figure it," said George. He began shuffling toward his back door. Alberg followed.

"Do you own a blue sweater, George, by any chance?"

"I used to, policeman. I don't any more," said George.

"You must be worn out, George, after all that rowing. You rowed quite a distance, too, I guess. Had to make sure the water was deep enough."

George unlocked the door and opened it and reached inside to turn on the kitchen light. "I don't know what the hell you're talking about." He turned around and grasped the doorway, a hand on either side, holding himself up. His face was gray with exhaustion. His pants and shoes were soaked and dripped seawater onto his kitchen floor.

"You couldn't just dump them anywhere," said Alberg. "If you didn't take them far enough out they'd probably get washed up on somebody's beach, right?"

"Good night," said George, and made to close the door.

Alberg held it open. "I'm real sorry about this, George," he said softly. "I really am."

"Good night," said George, and tried again to close the door.

"You should have gotten rid of them right away," said Alberg. "I have to look for them, now. Now that I know they're out there, I have to look for them. And I'm going to find them."

"I don't know what the hell you're talking about. Look for what? Look for them, go ahead, look for anything you damn feel like looking for, just let me get to bed."

"In a minute," said Alberg, still holding the door open. "I think you should know what I'm going to do. First I'll send out the divers. You know we've got a couple of divers, don't you?"

George looked at him grimly, shoulders hunched, white hair disheveled, pants still dripping. He was trembling from cold and tiredness.

"They might find them, they might not," said Alberg. "Depends on how far out you managed to get. If they don't, then I call in the sea search people from Vancouver. Now this is a very special outfit, George. They do lots of work for us. They've got a big boat with all kinds of special gizmos on board."

"I don't give a good goddamn for your gizmos. I don't know what the hell you're babbling about. I go out for a little row, I go too far for my own good, I come back wrecked, all I want to do is get to bed, you babble on to me about gizmos. Go away." He pulled again, weakly, at the door which Alberg continued to hold open.

"They've got underwater cameras, and side-scan sonar, and believe me, George—" He leaned closer to the old man, who pulled away, and whispered, "There is *nothing* those guys can't find. *Nothing*." He shook his head in admiration. "They've found something as small as an engagement ring, George, in two hundred feet of water. Do you think they won't be able to locate a couple of World War Two shell casings?"

George looked steadily at Alberg. He stood as straight as his screaming shoulders would allow. "Are you trying to scare me?"

Alberg let go of the door and stepped back. "I thought there might be something you'd like to tell me, Mr. Wilcox."

"You thought wrong, sonny. I've got nothing to say to you. Nothing." He closed the door, slowly and quietly.

Alberg went around to the front of the house and got into his car. He wasn't sure how he felt. He could identify several things—frustration, exhilaration, excitement, resolution—but there were other things shuffling uneasily around inside his brain that he was less anxious to put a name to.

He drove directly to the detachment office, where he called the divers and told them to meet him at the police boat as soon as the sun was up.

CHAPTER 21

When George awoke the next morning, one week after the murder, he felt like something washed up by the tide, scoured and bloated. His aches were so deep, so significant, that for several minutes he didn't even try to move. But he had to go to the bathroom. He attempted to push himself up with his elbows, but it was too painful. He seriously considered, then, relieving himself right there in his bed. Incontinence, though— that was the end, that was death.

He eventually got himself into a sitting position on the edge of the bed. The aches were concentrated in his shoulders, the back of his neck, his hands, and his thighs. It was obviously important to be active today. Maybe by nightfall the pain would have subsided into stiffness. He groaned as he shoved himself off the bed with arms that trembled. He staggered, shoulders hunched and knees bent, into the bathroom.

He had dreamed not of shell casings or Mounties, bloodied rugs or jail. He had dreamed of rowing, and of the fraudulent sea, which in his dream had transformed itself from the calm blue splendor of the last weeks into titanic fury. He flailed at it with useless oars, clung tight to his small rowboat, and the sea flung him from wavetop to wavetop, into chasm after chasm, until finally it hurled him onto a small island which at first seemed to be deserted, and then he saw Carlyle sitting on a big rock outside a log cabin. Carlyle was puffing on a pipe and singing "When the Saints Go Marching In," and on a clothes- line behind him hung a row of salmon, attached to the line with wooden clothespins, and they were flashing and flipping in the sun, still alive.

George hobbled into the kitchen to make coffee. He had spooned decaffeinated granules into a cup and was sitting in his chair, hands on his knees, waiting for the kettle to boil, when he became aware of faint shouts.

From his window he saw the R.C.M.P. boat out on the water, about a hundred feet offshore. There were two men on board who appeared to be staring down at the sea. Then a black shiny figure popped out of the water slick as a seal, and George knew the divers were at work.

The clothes he had worn last night were still in a heap on his bedroom floor.

It was cloudy today, as he had expected.

He took the kettle off the stove, put on an old hat, and went painfully out into his garden. He watered the flowers and the vegetables. He did some weeding.

The R.C.M.P. boat moved slightly farther out, stopping somewhat north of George's beach.

He mixed up a batch of insecticidal soap and washed the aphids from his rosebushes. He thought he ought to mow his small lawn, and the one in front, too, but his shoulders hurt too much.

After an hour or so the boat moved slowly southward, past his beach, and anchored there; meanwhile George got a small pair of clippers from his toolshed and deadheaded the roses and the marigolds. Then he picked some peas and took them into the kitchen. While he was inside, he took three aspirin.

When he went out again he saw the divers climb aboard the R.C.M.P. boat and watched it move quickly across the water and disappear around the spit.

George sat down heavily in his canvas chair. It was still hot, despite the cloud cover.

He heard it long before he saw it. He didn't recognize the sound of it, but knew before it hove into view what it must be. And then it appeared, cutting a frothy swath through the steel-gray sea, a twenty-five-foot aluminum boat with a peculiar radarlike structure mounted on its deck. George watched it come to a stop about two hundred feet from shore, almost directly out from his beach. There were two men on board. He watched them fiddling with something; then he thought he saw them lower something overboard.

George stood up quickly. He had to bend over, pressing his hands against his thighs, until the pain there diminished.

He went almost blindly through his house and out the front door and, once on the road, turned himself toward Sechelt. He began to walk along the dusty shoulder. He was shuddering, despite the warmth of the day, and in his chest was a great lump which he banged at with an ineffectual fist.

"You have been seen," said Phyllis Dempter, "on the beach, with a Mountie. Practically holding hands, I'm told." She was lounging against the counter, behind which Cassandra sat labeling books for the reserve shelf. "When did all this begin? Did you get yourself arrested? Is that how it started?"

"Nothing has started, Phyllis," said Cassandra. She taped a label marked VANDERBERG on a copy of James Michener's *Space*. "We've had lunch, and we went for a walk on the beach. No big deal, believe me."

"Then why is your face pink?" said Phyllis. She began to laugh.

"My face is pink because you're embarrassing me. This is no place for a discussion of my personal life." Stephen King's *Pet Sematary* was put aside for Mrs. Callihoo, a widow who operated a day-care center in the basement of the United Church. "Besides," said Cassandra, "I blush easily."

"No, really," said Phyllis, leaning farther across the counter. "Tell me. How did you meet him? It couldn't have been your ad. Could it?" She looked intently at Cassandra. "You mean to say it was? It *was* the ad?"

"Shut up, Phyllis. We're not alone in here." Behind the partition separating the counter from a large work area, a volunteer was sorting returned books.

"I told you," said Phyllis complacently. She stood up and tucked her bright red shirt smoothly into her jeans. "My dad's having a hell of a good time through the ads. I told you something would come of it eventually. When do I get to meet him?"

Cassandra wrote FRATINO on a label and affixed it to *Cold Heaven*, by Brian Moore. "I don't even know whether I'm going to see him again," she said. "I'm thinking about putting in another ad."

"Liar," said Phyllis. She picked up her purse and the two books she'd checked out. "But that's okay. Be closemouthed. It's typical. You jabber away a mile a minute, but never about anything important. You give yourself away, you know, Cassie." She reached over to pat Cassandra's hand. "But I love you anyway."

As she left the library, George Wilcox came in. Cassandra's smile faded. She got up quickly and went to him. "Mr. Wilcox. What's wrong? What's the matter?"

He looked at her vacantly. He was wearing earth-stained pants held up by suspenders, a white shirt, soiled and rumpled, and a shapeless felt hat, gray, with a drooping brim. On his feet were tattered old running shoes. His face was crumpled and weary. "I forgot my books," he said, and she saw panic in his eyes.

She asked the volunteer to take over, grabbed her purse from under the counter, and ushered George gently out the door, down the sidewalk, and into a small coffee shop.

It was lunchtime. Most of the stools at the counter were filled, and many of the tables. Cassandra stood just inside the door, her arm around George protectively, and willed the couple at the table in the corner to leave. George stood quietly, his head bowed; every once in a while he pounded his chest, almost tentatively.

"Do you hurt somewhere?" she said, bending to speak directly into his ear. "Does your chest hurt?"

He shook his head, slowly.

The people at the corner table stood up. The man left a tip while the woman started for the door. Cassandra led George over and sat him down; she exchanged a nod with the departing customers, whom she saw sometimes in the library. She and George sat without speaking as the waitress, who to Cassandra's relief was a stranger to her, cleared the table and gave them menus.

"What have you eaten today?" said Cassandra.

George lifted his head and pondered this. "Nothing, I think."

She ordered for them both: coffee for her, beef barley soup and a glass of milk for George.

"I've been working in my garden," said George. "Forgot to change my clothes. Forgot my books, forgot to change—I'm getting senile, that's what it is."

"That's *not* what it is," said Cassandra.

"Oh, yeah? What then?" He seemed genuinely curious.

"I don't know. You don't look well. You keep putting your hand on your chest. Doesn't it feel right, in there? Should I take you to your doctor?"

"Doesn't feel right at all, no," George agreed. "No doctor, though. I don't think so. No."

He looked with interest at his soup, which had just been placed in front of him. He took a sip of milk. "Don't care much for milk," he said. "But it's good for you, I admit it." His shaky fingers struggled with the small package of crackers that had come with the soup. Cassandra took it from him and opened it. He ate one of the crackers, slowly, and drank some more milk.

"Eat some soup," said Cassandra.

George picked up his spoon. "You and that Mountie, coming up from my beach like that; it gave me quite a turn."

"I should have called and asked if it would be all right. It was thoughtless of me. I'm sorry."

"I like showing off my garden, though. It's just that..." He put his hand over his eyes.

Cassandra gripped his other hand, which lay on the table. "Mr. Wilcox," she said. "What is it? Please, what is it? What can I do for you?" She heard laughter from the counter, and the waitress taking orders from the table nearest theirs, a few feet away.

George lowered his hand and put down the soupspoon. "I remembered on my way here," he said thickly. "I was trying and trying to remember when I'd seen it before, his fear. And on my way here, I remembered." He looked at Cassandra intently. "Did I ever tell you about my sister?"

The waitress approached with a coffeepot. Cassandra waved her away. "No, you didn't," she said to George.

He was straighter in his chair, now, and he'd stopped touching his chest. His hands were in his lap. Cassandra wondered if he had any grandchildren, and if he'd ever told them stories.

"Her name was Audrey," he said. "I won't tell you about her. It would take too long. Maybe another day. But she got married to Carlyle, do you see, that's the thing, and I was there, at the wedding. But I couldn't remember it, couldn't remember anything about it, whether she got married in a church or a registry office or somebody's house or what." He leaned toward Cassandra. "I gave her *away*, for Christ's sake, and I couldn't remember anything about it." He slumped back in his chair and looked away from her, over her shoulder, unfocused. "It's because we were angry with each other about it, I think. And we stayed angry." He looked again at Cassandra. "I still don't remember where it happened or what her dress looked like, or Myra's, or whether there were flowers all around, or what. But just today, on my way here... I remember this, now. When the time came I got up from where I was sitting and went to stand beside her, to give her away, and... Carlyle was on the other side of her. I turned my head, very slowly—it was as if the whole thing was happening in slow motion—and out of the corner of my eye I saw Carlyle's head turning, too. I wanted to look straight ahead, then, at the minister or whatever the hell he was, but I couldn't; my head went right on turning and then we were staring at each other, Carlyle and I, over the top of Audrey's head; I looked right at his eyes, couldn't help myself, and I don't know what I expected to see; I probably expected he'd grin at me or maybe even wink, the son-of-a-bitch—but he didn't. His face was white as marble and his eyes were full of fear. Terror. The man was terrified." He looked out toward the window. "I should have stopped it, do you see," he said dully. "Right then and there. I should have stopped it. regardless."

"Is the soup all right?" said the waitress, standing over them.

"It's fine," said Cassandra. "He's just letting it cool." The waitress left, and Cassandra turned back to George. "I think everybody gets nervous when they get married. That's what I've heard, anyway." She was prattling, and told herself to stop it. "I know my mother was. And my father."

"I couldn't remember when I'd seen it before," he said, nodding at his soup. "It bothered me a lot, because it was the only thing that really shook me up, when the other thing happened. I shouldn't say it, but it's true, that fear in his eyes, it was the only thing that shook me up about that whole business the other day. And I knew I'd seen it before, but I couldn't remember. But I've got it now. That's when it was, all right. At first when I was thinking about it I thought maybe it was at the funeral. That would make sense, I thought. But it wasn't the funeral, Christ, no, it wasn't the funeral." He grasped the table, as if he were about to overturn it. "Christ, no, nothing but tears at the funeral, all the tears you'd care to see, all that Christly weeping and grieving, the great big soppy lying tears of a crocodile." He held on to the table, breathing heavily.

Cassandra sat tense, ready to restrain him, or comfort him. After a while she saw his hands relax. He fumbled a paper napkin from the container on the table and wiped his face. Then he looked up at her, and she was greatly relieved to see that he was calm.

"I don't deserve your attention, Cassandra. But I appreciate it more than I can say."

He'd gotten his dignity back, she didn't know how.

She smiled unsteadily. "You're my friend, Mr. Wilcox."

She insisted on driving him home.

Back at the library, she sat by the rest of the books awaiting reserve labels but did no more work.

She was trying to determine where her duty lay.

She heard it clearly: "that fear in his eyes, it was the only thing that shook me up about that whole business the other day."

What whole business?

She was sure, *convinced*, that she had misunderstood him.

Yet her hands, clutched in the lap of her full-skirted yellow dress, were cold.

Through the window, she saw the cloud-covered sky and wondered when the rain would begin to fall.

CHAPTER 22

He had had no food today, except for a cracker and half a glass of milk, and he knew food was important to a body his age. But he didn't want to eat. Even the peas on his kitchen counter, fresh picked that morning, didn't appeal to him.

He shuffled into his bedroom and got a large manila envelope from the bottom of a drawer. In the kitchen he closed the curtains so as not to see the search vessel doggedly combing the bottom of the bay, putting all its gizmos to work in its relentless search for Carlyle's shell casings. He figured the staff sergeant was probably out there on that boat. Maybe he'd fall overboard and drown.

George sat in his old leather chair and unwound the red string that secured the flap of the big brown envelope. He turned it upside down and shook it and the letters tumbled onto his lap, letters written in a small neat hand on onionskin which the years had tinged with ocher and caused to become slightly brittle. He arranged them chronologically, and as he handled them was faintly surprised that they produced in him no immediate turbulence.

From the day of her marriage in May until August, when George and his family left for Germany, he spoke not a word to Carlyle and saw his sister only three times. This upset Myra and Carol greatly, and he knew they were extremely disapproving of him, but he couldn't help himself. He couldn't bear to see Audrey and Carlyle together. It wasn't a great deal easier to see her alone, either, knowing when they said goodbye she would return to that man. Besides, on the few occasions they did get together, usually arranged by Myra, they invariably quarreled.

So it wasn't surprising that in the thirteen months she lived after George's departure, she wrote them only eight letters.

He looked at them now, such a pitifully small pile, sitting in his lap, and wondered why he was doing this to himself, torturing himself in a useless search for affirmation of something he had believed with all his heart until the moment he had hit Carlyle on the head, cutting off his vicious ramblings forever.

Her letters were at first filled with bright chatter about her piano students, her garden, learning to run Carlyle's house the way he liked it run. She didn't speak about her private thoughts; for all they knew, she didn't have any. It was frustrating to read these letters, which to George described a cardboard-cutout world, a stage set occupied by marionettes. Yet he couldn't blame her for not stretching her hand across the rift that separated them; it was up to him to try to repair the damage he had inflicted upon their relationship.

Eventually, he did so. He wrote to her at Christmas, when he and Myra and Carol had been away four months, and tried in his clumsy way to make things right. "Just tell her you love her," Myra had said. "That's the most important thing." And so he had done that.

She wrote back to him immediately. His letter of conciliation had obviously made her happy, and he clung to that thought desperately ten months later, when she was dead.

She continued to avoid mentioning Carlyle, but he understood that. She talked a great deal about plants, and about books she had read. Her letters were brief and infrequent, but at least now they were warm and confidently affectionate.

He read them all, now, pored over them with the greatest possible concentration, and he asked himself the same questions he asked every time he read them. Why had she stopped talking about the piano lessons she taught, which had for years given her so much pleasure? Why did she never mention seeing any movies, or going to parties, or having people to dinner?

Was it because then she would have had to refer to "we" and "us"? Did she really believe George would be enraged by even an oblique reference to the fact that she was sharing a house, a life, a bed, with Carlyle?

He sat back and closed his eyes. He should have let Carlyle talk. It wouldn't have done him irreparable damage to hear Carlyle speak of those things which Audrey had apparently told him. And if only he'd let him finish, he might finally have had answers to his questions, answers which, as hard as he looked, he could never find, incontrovertible, in the letters.

He turned to Audrey's shortest letter. It hurt him even to look at it, because it was the last one, and because he had learned later that it must have caused her physical pain to set down even these few paragraphs.

Her handwriting was a clumsy, childish scrawl. The letter made no reference to this.

Dear George, she had written.

I'm addressing this only to you, because I know there are things you still haven't told Myra.

I've been doing a lot of thinking, these past few weeks. Carlyle has been away. He's coming back tomorrow.

I know you love me and have tried to protect me, and I've trusted you all my life. You've been my rock, for as long as I can remember, and before that, too, I know.

I know you think Carlyle is wrong for me. But I can do something about it, George, if I've made a mistake. It hurts me to think you don't believe I can do something about it, on my own. But times have changed, George, and I can, truly I can.

We went through so much together, you and I. I think about it often, these days.

None of it was your fault. NONE *of it. You've never been able to see how much good you did. You've always only blamed yourself for the way it ended. And now you're all set to blame yourself for whatever happens to me, without giving me credit for having sense enough to get out of it myself, if I have to.*

I'm glad Myra takes such good care of you, and Carol is so rational and even-tempered. They don't need (and wouldn't appreciate) the

*kind of anxiety you felt for our parents, and then for me. And I don't
need it any more. So it's time you put it aside, George.*

*I love you.
Audrey*

He distinctly remembered getting this letter. When he had
seen that the envelope was addressed only to him he was
surprised, and filled with concern, too. He had read it pri-
vately, standing by the gate which led to the row of attached
houses occupied by three army officers and their families, and
George and his. He remembered that it was early September
and the trees in the old German town down the hill were
becoming red and gold.

He tore the envelope open and scanned the pages quickly,
bewildered by the awkwardness of her handwriting, looking
for disaster, and then read it more slowly.

He had thought a lot about that letter, during the next couple
of weeks. He saw in it a strong implication that Audrey was
deciding her marriage to Carlyle had been a mistake and that,
if it was, she would get out of it, leave him.

Maybe she was right, he thought. Maybe his sense of responsibility to her had grown unnaturally intense over the
years, blinding him to her very real strength of character.

He had been working on a reply, composing it in his mind,
when the telegram came informing them of her death.

George put the letters back in the big brown envelope and
did up the string that secured the flap.

He rested his head against the cracked leather of his chair.

She had been wrong, after all. She hadn't been able to do
anything about it. Not in time. Carlyle hadn't let her.

It was the autopsy that convinced him. He had insisted on
a complete autopsy. It was the accident which had killed her,
he knew that, and he also knew that Carlyle wasn't with her
in the car. So he wasn't directly responsible for her death. Not
directly. But he was responsible, all right; George had been
certain.

The palm of her right hand bore fresh, barely healed scars.

Her left wrist had been fractured; her right tibia also. The fractures had healed normally. None of these injuries had occurred before George left for Germany. There might have been others—he would never know that; the rest of her body had been too badly broken in the car accident.

He confronted Carlyle at the funeral. Carlyle had wept ceaselessly, telling George that Audrey was accident prone, that she had stumbled and put her hand on a hot burner of the stove, and fallen from the apple tree while trying to prune it, and fallen again while getting out of the bath. Carlyle wept and sobbed, and George didn't believe a word he said and told him he would live to see him burn in hell.

Myra had to drag him away. He was making a spectacle of himself.

George wiped his face with his hands and confronted himself with the same tired questions. Had he misread the letter? Maybe they just argued a lot. Maybe things weren't working out in bed. Had Carlyle beaten her, sent her flying from the house in a frenzy of blind fear? Or had she simply suffered a series of inexplicable accidents, culminating in one which had caused her death?

He closed his eyes and felt fresh tears spill down his cheeks and imagined he heard the search boat's crafty gadgets probing the sea, and he saw Carlyle bleeding into his braided rug and would have given his life and his soul to have heard all of what Carlyle had meant to tell him.

CHAPTER 23

Alberg strode into the detachment office late that Tuesday afternoon in a state of barely controlled rage. His faded jeans were thrust into bright yellow rubber boots, and the sleeves of his shirt were rolled up. His face and arms were reddened by the cloud-shrouded sun.

He stopped at the duty officer's counter. "Is Corporal Sanducci on the premises, by any chance?" he said politely.

"Yes, Staff," said Ken Coomer. He stood up, nervous.

"Send him into my office. On the double."

When the corporal stood before his desk, Alberg looked at him with disgust. "You were on duty at the Burke house last night, right?"

"Right, Staff. Four to midnight." Sanducci stood stiffly. He was insufferably good-looking, thought Alberg, far too popular with women, and much too cocky behind the wheel of a car. He was also intelligent, efficient, and courteous with civilians.

"See anything interesting?"

"No, Staff. Everything was pretty quiet."

"Everything was *not* pretty quiet, Sanducci," said Alberg, softly. He stood up and yanked the venetian blinds to the top of the window. "Tell me, Corporal. Did you spend the whole eight hours planted on the front porch, for some reason?"

"No, Staff," said Sanducci, flushing. "I made regular circuits of the house and grounds."

"And how often did you make these circuits, Corporal?

Once? Twice? How many times did you walk around back?"
His voice was level but cold.

"Hourly, Staff Sergeant. Once an hour. Or so."

Alberg let the venetian blinds fall closed. "While you were
parked on the front porch, Corporal, a whole lot was going
on. You seem to have missed it." He sat down and clasped his
hands on the desk in front of him. "Would you like to hear
about it? Do you want to know what happened there, that
managed to escape your attention?"

"Yes, Staff," said the corporal, uneasily.

"Well, while you were out in front, dreaming your dreams
or whatever it is young corporals do while on a boring assign-
ment like the one you had last night, a tottery old guy came
ambling down the beach. Now we're talking about a really
old person, here, Sanducci, someone you wouldn't think would
have the strength to change a tire. What he did, this declining
specimen of humanity, this eighty-year-old ancient, what he
did was haul the victim's rowboat off its blocks, drag it down
to the water, and row his elderly self out to sea." He looked
at the corporal with an icy calm. "And then, Sanducci—then
he heaved the murder weapon into the drink." The corporal's
face paled. "And where were you when all this was going on?"
said Alberg with interest. "Taking a cigarette break? Peeing
in the bushes?"

Sanducci stood even more stiffly. He looked at a point on
the wall above Alberg's head.

"Get out of here," said Alberg quietly.

A little later, Sokolowski came in.

"I'm going to break that bastard down to constable," said
Alberg, slouched behind his desk. "Third class."

"They didn't find anything out there, I guess."

"They'll never find the goddamn things. We're talking about
four hundred square yards of ocean, rocks all over the goddamn
bottom, some of them as big as a truck." He shook his head.
"The divers never had a chance. The old guy's too smart to
dump them that close in. After four hours the sea search team
gave up on the sonar. Now they're trying the underwater
camera. I told them to keep at it until ten tonight. At three

thousand bucks a day or whatever the hell they're charging us, half a day is all the budget can take."

"Okay if I sit down?"

Alberg waved impatiently, and Sokolowski sat.

"We got that accident report," said the sergeant, "the one from 1956 that killed Burke's wife. It was a single-vehicle accident. She wasn't speeding or anything. Ran off the road into an abutment. Killed instantly."

"Anything on the autopsy?"

"Yeah. They gave her the works. Wilcox—her brother—he insisted on it. Called the Vancouver city police from where he was living in Germany. Death due to injuries sustained in the accident. Nothing suspicious. Vancouver never thought there was, but the guy called, all the way from Europe, and the husband didn't object, so..." He shrugged.

"We're really batting a thousand on this one." Alberg got up to open the blinds again.

Sokolowski tried a grin. "Looks like you got some sun out on that boat. It's always worse, when there's some cloud."

"My face feels like it's been fried."

"Listen, Staff," said the sergeant. "Could be the old fellow was doing just what he said, taking a little row. People do funny things, sometimes."

Alberg opened a drawer in his filing cabinet and immediately clanged it closed. "He was dumping those shell casings. He did it, the crafty old son-of-a-bitch. He smashed that guy's head. I know it. And he knows I know it."

"But why? Where's the motive? Unless he really *did* know he was in the will. But even if he did, there just isn't enough there to make it worth his while to waste the guy." Sokolowski was getting exasperated. "Jesus, Staff, you've got no motive, no physical evidence, not even anything circumstantial to tie him to the thing."

"I've got that Erlandson, who saw him going into the victim's house during the period the coroner says he died."

"Come on, Staff. With his sister there contradicting him every time he opens his mouth?"

"And," Alberg went on stubbornly, "I saw the shell casings

on his windowsill, Sid, and they aren't there now, and meanwhile the stupid old bugger's practically killed himself rowing out into the bay. If that's not circumstantial evidence, I don't know what is."

"Karl," said Sokolowski, "you're the only one who saw them on his windowsill."

"So what?" snapped Alberg.

"And you don't know they were the victim's. You're just speculating."

"I am *not* speculating, Sergeant," said Alberg furiously.

"Maybe they were his own," Sokolowski protested gently. "Like you said before, those things are a dime a dozen."

"Not with *flowers* or some damn thing all over them. If we could *find* them, the cleaning woman would identify them."

The sergeant sighed. "Okay. Say we find them. And one of them turns out to be the murder weapon. You're still not a whole lot further ahead. You can't use Erlandson's testimony, you know that; it just won't stand up. We haven't found anybody who saw the old guy out on the bay last night. And why would he wait almost a week before getting rid of the damn things, if he used one of them to kill somebody with? I'm not saying he didn't do it, Staff. But I'm not convinced. Not without a motive."

Alberg's weariness was catching up with him. His face and arms were burning. "It's got something to do with his sister," he said, and sank back into his chair. "Car accident or no car accident, he blamed Burke for her death."

"That was a long time ago, Staff," said Sokolowski. He hesitated. "He seems like a nice old guy. I kind of like him."

"So do I," said Alberg. "What the hell's that got to do with anything?"

"Hard to believe he'd have the strength for it," said the sergeant. "Knocking the guy on the head, hauling the shell casings home, then rowing far enough out to dump them where they're never going to be found."

"It's the gardening," said Alberg grimly. "Keeps him in shape." He shuffled listlessly through a pile of phone messages Isabella had placed on his desk and pushed them aside. "I want the house searched again." He looked at Sokolowski. "First thing tomorrow. I'll do it, but I need one man to help me."

There was a pause. Then, "How about Sanducci?" said the sergeant.

Alberg gave him a cold stare. "All right. Sanducci. But first I want to know what Corporal Sanducci was up to last night."

Sokolowski got up to leave. "Oh," he said at the door. "I checked the victim out on the computer, like you said. Nothing."

After he'd left, Alberg sat brooding. Then he pulled the phone closer to him and called Cassandra.

CHAPTER 24

Cassandra Mitchell lived in a small house set back from a narrow gravel road above the highway. In her front yard was a prickly, crazily configurated growth called a monkey puzzle tree.

Her living room and kitchen windows looked out across the gravel road and the highway to the brush that bordered the Indian cemetery. In leafless seasons rows of white crosses were visible, and a tall white statue which stood in the middle of the graveyard, and the white fence that surrounded it. Behind the cemetery, the forested land sloped steeply down to the sea. On clear days she could see beyond the tops of the trees and across the Strait of Georgia to a faraway point on Vancouver Island slightly north of the city of Nanaimo.

Her house had two bedrooms. She kept the smaller one as a spare room for friends who often visited from Vancouver, especially in summer. Her own room was so filled with bookshelves, a small desk and chair, and a chaise longue that there was hardly room for her double bed. The chaise sat by a window that looked out over her neighbors' garden. She spent a lot of time in it, reading and watching her neighbors' flowers grow.

The living room had a fireplace and a large glass-and-chrome coffee table and a white leather sofa that was Cassandra's pride and joy. There were prints on the walls—some Emily Carr, and a Paul Klee, and two Matisses. At the end of the living room was a dining area with patio doors leading outside.

The phone was ringing as she came into the house after work on Tuesday. It was Alberg, asking if they might have dinner together.

Cassandra didn't want to see him. He was a policeman. It took enormous effort, as she listened to him, to think of him as anything but a policeman. And she had absolutely no desire to have dinner with a cop: not today. Not after George.

Gradually she became aware that he sounded hoarse and dispirited.

"What's the matter?" she asked, despite herself.

"Just tired. Not a good day. That's all."

She had a quick mind; she could have thought up all sorts of excuses. But in the end she didn't. She invited him to have dinner at her house.

She set the table with candles and a low bowl of flowers. For dinner they would have a stew from her small freezer. It was already in the oven and she was tearing romaine into a bowl when Alberg drove up.

She went to the door to greet him. "What did you do," she said, as he appeared in his jeans and rubber boots, "take the day off and go fishing?"

He came onto her porch carrying a bottle of wine in a brown paper bag. "Sort of," he said. He glanced at the monkey tree. "I hate those things. They look like they've been put together by somebody who's deranged."

"Don't be rude," said Cassandra. "I presume this is for me," she said, taking the bag from his hands. "I might be very fond of that tree, for all you know."

Inside, he pulled off his boots and left them on the mat. "I hope I'm not making myself too much at home, but they'd leave marks all over your floor."

She looked uneasily at his sock feet. "A shoeless policeman in my house." She took the wine into the kitchen. "Does this have to breathe or anything?"

"Yeah. Let me know when it's half an hour before dinner. I'll open it then." He went restlessly into the living room and looked at the prints on the walls.

"I have to finish the salad," said Cassandra from the kitchen. "Why don't you go out back and have a look around?" She heard the patio doors open and relaxed a bit. She hadn't realized she was nervous. Maybe I'm even frightened, she thought, chopping tomatoes and throwing them into the bowl. She would have to be very careful what she said to him, and she wasn't a practiced equivocator.

The door to the patio closed and he joined her in the kitchen. "No garden out there. Only grass. How come?"

"I don't like digging around in the dirt much. I get to look at my neighbors' garden. Sometimes they give me flowers."

He went over to the kitchen door and looked through its window.

The garden next door was terraced up the incline all the way to the woods, which also backed onto Cassandra's property and extended around it to meet the gravel road. Next door there were bushes covered with blossoms, and vegetables growing in neat rows, and banks of flowers near the house.

"Yeah, I see what you mean," said Alberg. "Nice." He wandered over to the counter and ate a slice of cucumber. "Not too good living back-to-back with a forest, though."

"Why on earth not?" said Cassandra, the paring knife poised over an avocado.

"Hard to keep the place secure."

"Good God," said Cassandra. "Secure from what? The deer? They're the only things that come down from those woods. They ate my neighbors' scarlet runners last year. Well, not the beans. They ate every leaf on every stalk, and left all the beans. I guess deer don't like beans." She had peeled the avocado and was now slicing it into the bowl. "Would you like a drink?"

"Oh, God," said Alberg gratefully. "I would."

"Help yourself. There's a cabinet in the living room."

"Can I fix one for you?"

"A small scotch, please, lots of water. There's ice in the top of the fridge."

"I'm serious, you know, Cassandra," he called from the living room.

"About what?" she said, slicing. She wasn't nervous any more. There was no earthly reason why the topic of George Wilcox should even come up. It was herself she had to watch, she thought—not Karl. She was the one who couldn't get George out of her mind, and part of her wanted very badly to talk about him, to someone. But this man was absolutely the wrong person.

He came into the kitchen and rummaged around for ice. "You don't even lock your door when you go out, do you? I noticed that when I brought you home on Sunday."

"All right, all right, I'll lock my door if it's so important to you. But there's nothing you can do about the woods. I'll never be safe from the deer." She washed her hands, dried them, and took her drink from him.

In the living room he sat on the white sofa and she sat in a chair by the window.

"Your face," said Cassandra, "is as red as a lobster."

"It's painful as hell," he said modestly.

She got some ointment from the bathroom and tried to give it to him. He wouldn't take it, protesting feebly. Cassandra took the top off the tube and began applying it gently to his sunburn. He closed his eyes and moaned. She jerked her hand away. "Am I hurting you?"

"No, it feels wonderful. Cool."

"It won't last. But it'll help for a while." She smoothed it over his high wide forehead, his long straight nose, across his cheeks, around his mouth; it was a generous mouth, and there was a slight cleft in his chin. She screwed the top on the tube. He opened his eyes. They were wintry blue, and probably specially trained to spot a lie or an evasion a mile away.

She thrust the tube into his hand. "Here. Take it with you. Put some more on tonight, before you go to bed."

"Maybe you'd do it for me," he said, looking up at her. "Before I go to bed."

Cassandra ignored this and sat down again. She picked up her glass. "How did you get that burn, anyway?"

"I was out in a boat all day."

"Playing? Or working?"

"Working." He drained his glass. "May I get myself another one?"

"Of course. I heard there was some kind of search going on," she said casually as he got more scotch and went into the kitchen for ice. "What were you looking for?"

He put his glass on the coffee table and dropped onto the sofa. "Oh, we took it into our heads there might be a murder weapon out there."

"And was there?"

"Don't know yet. They're still looking. Doesn't look very encouraging, though."

'Has this—uh, got to do with Mr. Burke?"

He looked at her curiously. "Yeah, as a matter of fact."

"Well he's the only person I know of who's been murdered around here lately," said Cassandra defensively. "If you don't want to talk about it, just say so."

"Sorry. I can't talk·about it, really. I shouldn't, anyway."

Cassandra got up to freshen her drink.

"How's your friend George?" said Alberg.

She turned quickly from the fridge; he was out of sight, in the living room. For a moment she couldn't think of a single thing to say.

"Not very well, I think," she said at last, and was surprised at how calm she sounded.

She went back to her chair. She couldn't have denied seeing him. They had been observed by all sorts of people.

"He came to the library today," she said. "He seemed very tired. I drove him home." Stop, Cassandra, she told herself; stop right there.

"Tired," said Alberg.

Cassandra's heart was thudding. This man had her ointment all over his face, his sock feet on her carpet; this man had come to her for food and, presumably, affection; this man worried about her unlocked doors and burglars creeping down on her from the woods: He was not her enemy, after all, she told herself.

But she had to keep her loyalties straight, because that's

what duty was, after all, wasn't it? Loyalty. She had known George Wilcox for years, and an affectionate regard had grown between them; she had met this policeman less than a week ago.

"Yeah," said Alberg, looking at the glass in his hands. "I imagine he's pretty tired, all right."

Cassandra didn't respond. He didn't seem to expect her to.

"It's half an hour until dinner, now," she said.

In the kitchen he opened the wine and Cassandra put rolls in the oven to warm. They were standing back to back, almost touching. She felt the heat from his body, and smelled the sea, and sunburn ointment, and sweat.

"There's no dessert, I'm afraid," she said.

"You warned me I'd be taking pot luck."

He was observing her thoughtfully, standing only a couple of feet away. She slipped past him into the living room.

"Don't you ever wear a uniform?" she said, sitting again in the chair by the window.

"Sure." He was looking beyond her, out toward the highway.

"When?"

He sat on the sofa, holding his glass between his knees, where the denim of his jeans looked thin enough to fray. "I wear it when I go to talk to kids in the schools, or to service club meetings, or when somebody from Vancouver's coming over to inspect. Gotta look shipshape for the brass." He took a drink.

"What about the red one? Do you ever wear that?"

"You mean boots and breeks?"

Cassandra laughed. "Is that what you call it?"

"The red tunic, the boots, the Sam Browne, the breeches—yeah, that's what we call it. Review Order. It's only worn for ceremonial things. I look pretty good in mine," he said comfortably.

She laughed again.

"Well, most people do, I guess," said Alberg with a grin. "Not so much the women. They don't get to wear the Stetson or the breeks—just skirts and a kind of a pillbox hat."

"What a chauvinistic bunch," said Cassandra. "You're undoubtedly a chauvinistic man."

"We're a paramilitary outfit," said Alberg. "What the hell do you expect?" He put his glass down and fell back into the sofa, stretching his arms along the top. "I feel better."

"Three scotches," said Cassandra dryly. "That'll do it."

He sat up. "Two. I don't think it's the booze. I just like it here."

The timer on the stove began to ring, and Cassandra got up to serve dinner.

She lit the candles.

He complimented her cooking, and she complimented his choice of wine.

"What are you doing here, anyway?" said Alberg suddenly. "In Sechelt?"

"Why don't you tell me what you're doing here, first," said Cassandra. "I know you people get moved around. But by the time you're a staff sergeant, surely you have something to say about where you're going to go next."

"I don't know how much to tell you." He looked at the candles and the flowers. "What the hell." He put down his fork and leaned his elbows on the table. "In Kamloops it got to be time for my annual review. Personnel evaluation. I was a sergeant there, in charge of my first detachment. And it was also time for promotion to staff sergeant. There were several places I could have gone. Sechelt was one of them."

He picked up his fork and started pushing salad around on his plate. "Sechelt's what we call a 'jammy' posting. Nothing heavy, a nice place to live, nice people to deal with, for the most part. A quiet place, not much happening. And yet it's close to Vancouver."

He looked up at Cassandra. "My wife and I had decided to separate. I didn't tell the review team. They'd have wanted me to stay in Kamloops, try to work things out. The force gets uneasy about divorce. They feel guilty. And it's true that in a lot of cases it's the job that does it."

"Was it the job in your case?"

He started to rub his forehead, winced from the pain of the sunburn, and drank some more wine instead. "I thought it was, yeah. Maura thought so too, I think. But now—lately— I don't know. Anyway. I was feeling a bit—well, low, and battered." He laughed a little. "A jammy posting sounded like just the thing. And it was on the water, too. So I asked for Sechelt." He spread his hands. "And here I am."

"How long will you be here?"

He looked directly at her. His eyes looked warmer in candle-light, and his hair was the color of wheat. "It's up to me. If I don't screw up, I could probably stay until I retire. I don't think I'm going to screw up. I usually don't."

"Would you want to stay, though?" She made herself take a sip of wine, slowly. "It's pretty dull around here. Especially for a policeman."

"I don't know yet," he said reflectively. "Sometimes I think if I stay in a place like this, a little place, with a lot of ordinary people in it and not a whole lot of—well, hardcore creeps, let's say . . . maybe in a place like this, where most people don't feel uneasy around police officers, some of my cynicism will wear off. Eventually."

"I hadn't really thought of you as a cynic," said Cassandra gently.

"Thank you, ma'am." He smiled. "But you don't know me very well. Yet." There were hollows beneath his eyes—but maybe that was the candlelight, she thought. "Also," he went on, "I think I'm tired of change. I think I want things in my life to stay pretty much the same, for a while."

"You like your job though, don't you."

"Yeah, I do. I sure as hell wouldn't want to do anything else."

"What do you like about it, exactly?"

"Figuring things out," he said promptly. "Talking to people, thinking, finding out what happened, who did it, why they did it—that kind of thing."

"What about . . . justice?" said Cassandra tentatively.

He looked at her quizzically, not quite amused. "Justice isn't up to me. Getting the answers, that's my job. And making sure the Crown prosecutor has enough to go ahead with. And that," he said grimly, "is the toughest part of it all."

Cassandra got up to clear the table. Alberg helped. In the kitchen she reached to switch on the light, but he stopped her.

"No, look," he said, taking plates from her. He put them on the counter and turned her toward the window, his hands on her shoulders. The moon had broken through the clouds to shine bright above the water.

"It's beautiful," she said.

"Is that why you're here? Because it's beautiful?"

"I'm here because my mother's got heart disease," said Cassandra, looking at the moon, which was being obscured once more by cloud. "She's lived in Sechelt for more than twenty years. When my father died, my brother and I decided one of us ought to live near her. Not *with* her, I told him I wouldn't do that, not under any circumstances. But near her was okay. He's married, has kids, lives in Edmonton. I was in Vancouver. It was easier for me."

He turned her around to face him. "What did you give up to move here, Cassandra?"

"Quite a lot, actually. But it'll keep."

"What was it? A man?"

Cassandra laughed. "I said it would keep, didn't I? No, it wasn't a man. I'd been to Europe for the summer and got all excited about traveling. I was going to sell everything I owned and go live someplace strange and foreign for a while."

His lips brushed her cheek. Oh, Jesus, thought Cassandra. She would tell him anything in bed, she knew it: all her hopes, all her dreams, all her worries about George Wilcox.

"What about men?" he said. "Tell me about the men in your life."

"Like hell I will." Cassandra pulled slightly away from him. "Listen, Karl, you're getting too personal too fast."

He wrapped his arms around her and held her tightly against his chest. "I like you. I want to know things about you."

"I'm happy here," she told him, her voice muffled in his shirt. "I like my job and I like this place and I have lots of friends."

"How come you put an ad in the paper?" He was rubbing a big hand slowly up and down her back. "You're wearing a bra."

"I always wear a bra. I put an ad in the paper—it's none of your damn business why I put an ad in the paper."

"Sure it is. I answered it." He bent his head and rested his hot cheek, sticky with ointment, against her temple.

Cassandra pushed herself away. She put her hands on his chest, to keep him at a distance. "All right," she said. "I put an ad in the paper in the hope of finding a pleasant, courteous, not unattractive male person, intelligent and interesting, with whom I might enjoy adequate conversation and spectacular sex."

She dropped her hands. She knew her face must be as red as his.

"Well?" said Alberg. "So?" He held out his arms and capered around in a clumsy circle. "What do you think?"

She made a determined effort not to laugh. "I don't know yet. I haven't decided."

The phone rang.

He dove at her, growling. She fought him off, laughing, and they stood in the darkened kitchen smiling at one another. Then he stepped close and kissed her, and she put her arms around him.

The phone continued to ring.

"Shit," said Alberg after a while. "It's probably for me."

It was Sokolowski.

Alberg told Cassandra he had to leave. He told her he had to interview a suspect in the Burke homicide.

With an odd deliberateness, Cassandra put her hand delicately to her throat. "Anybody I know?" she said casually.

"Could be," said Alberg. "You seem to know everyone in town." He smiled, kissed her again, and pulled on his yellow boots.

She watched him drive away.

She tried to feel relief.

Surely he wouldn't have gone off so cheerfully if it was George Wilcox, his white hair springing from his head in the indomitable waves that so touched her heart, who was sitting patiently in God knew what kind of a rathole of a cell, waiting to be grilled by the Mounties about murder.

But if it wasn't George, she thought suddenly, feeling sick, who *was* sitting there, waiting for Alberg the cop?

CHAPTER 25

"Good dinner?" said Sokolowski innocently from the counter where a constable just beginning night duty was checking the book.

"You're working overtime again, Sid," said Alberg. "Where is this guy?"

Sokolowski pointed. "Right over there."

On the green-cushioned bench in the reception area sat a man about forty, dark-haired, with a beard showing some silver. He was wearing jeans and a denim jacket, and western boots, and smoking a cigarette.

"How did we find him?" said Alberg. From its covered cage next to Isabella's desk, not far from the fish seller, the parrot muttered.

"We didn't find him. He found us. Saw the story in the local rag, he says, and drove right over."

The rainbowed van was in the parking lot. Alberg had stopped to have a close look, on his way in. It was the right van, all right: orange paint underneath, where the gray had flecked away, lots of bluebirds.

"Bring him into my office," said Alberg.

When he got there, Alberg motioned the man to the black chair. Sokolowski leaned in the doorway.

"What's your name?" said Alberg, who was standing by the window.

"Derek Farley. I'm sorry I didn't get here sooner." His voice was deep and melodious. He spoke slowly and deliberately and seemed perfectly relaxed. "I only come into town once a week. Saw in the paper while I was having a meal that you've been looking for me and my van."

"We had a homicide here last Tuesday. I guess you read about that, too."

"Yes. A Mr. Burke, it said. He was one of the people who bought a salmon from me." He pulled out his cigarettes and a folder of matches. "Mind if I smoke?"

"Go ahead," said Alberg. "Where do you live, Mr. Farley?"

The man shook out the match and put it in the ashtray on Alberg's coffee table. "Up near Garden Bay. I've got a little cabin there, out in the bush."

"What do you do for a living?"

Farley grinned at him. "I sell things. Fish, vegetables. It depends on the season. My wife's got a big garden. She's also a weaver. There's a couple of stores—one in Garden Bay, another in Gibsons; we're working on one in Sechelt, here—they take her things on consignment. Ponchos, things like that." He dragged on his cigarette. "I'm a carpenter, too. I do work for people all up and down the coast." He grinned again. "Word of mouth. I'm good at it. Slow, but good."

"Tell us about last Tuesday. That was your day in town, was it?"

"I came down to Sechelt, yes. Let's see." He stubbed out his cigarette. "I've been trying to get it straight. A week ago, that's a long time."

"What time did you leave home?" said Sokolowski. "Let's start with that."

"I left about eight. Had a dozen salmon in the van, packed in ice in washbuckets. Sold about four–five fish in Madeira Park, Secret Cove. Had some coffee and a doughnut at a little place near Halfmoon Bay. It must have been . . . sometime after eleven, I guess, when I got here. I remember I drove right through Sechelt and turned around, figuring to try to get rid of the rest of the fish along the road outside of town, then stop for a bite to eat and head on home."

"And is that what happened?" said Alberg.

"Pretty well. I still had—I had five left when I stopped for lunch. That's right. Forgot I sold one to the guy who runs the cafe at Halfmoon Bay. I remember thinking I should keep on going down toward Gibsons, try to get rid of the rest of them there, but I was pointing in the wrong direction by then." He grinned up at them. "But it turned out okay. When I got back to Garden Bay I went down to the wharf and sold all five to some tourists up from Seattle in two big yachts."

"I'm happy for you, Mr. Farley," said Alberg. "But could we get back to the ones you sold here?"

"Yes, sure, sorry. Well, let's see. I sold two. Now I know you'll want to know what time this was. Let me think...."

Alberg and Sokolowski waited. Alberg picked up a pen that was lying on his desk. Sokolowski shifted in the doorway, turning a page in his notebook. Alberg leaned against the filing cabinet and discovered that Isabella had put a plant on top of it; long leafy tendrils wafted down the side of the cabinet nearest the window.

"It was after eleven when I got here," said Farley, confident. "And it was about twelve thirty when I went into that little place down from the library, to have some lunch. And it must have taken me—oh, say twenty minutes to drive through town and get turned around. So I'd say I was trying to sell my fish from about eleven forty-five until about twelve fifteen." He smiled, contented. "That'd be about right."

"About half an hour, then," said Alberg. "Tell us what you did and what you saw." He moved to the window and peered out at the van from between the slats in the blind. In the light from the building he could see rain spattering the roofs of the van, the patrol cars, and his Oldsmobile.

Farley sighed. "This is tough. Let's see." He looked up at Sokolowski. "You know, I can't possibly remember everything. It was a week ago. Just an ordinary day. I know I didn't see anything particularly unusual. I know for sure I didn't see anything suspicious."

"Try, though, will you?" said Alberg, turning from the window.

"That Burke fellow, I do remember he was the second one to buy. And the last. I pulled over, crossed the street, went through a hedge and down a path. The door was open. I looked around but there wasn't any bell, so I just banged on the door. I remember thinking I ought to holler something, since the door was open, but I couldn't think of anything. So I just waited, and in a minute a voice says, 'Coming.' So I just stood there on the step, holding the salmon, and eventually this tall old man came down the hall toward me."

"What happened then?" said Alberg, after a minute during which Farley frowned at his knees.

"Well, he said, 'Ah, a peddler of fish.' It was obvious; I was standing there holding it. 'I used to catch my own,' he said, 'but not any more,' or something like that. Then he told me he'd buy it because a friend was coming over for lunch and it would be a nice treat." He looked at them and shrugged. "That's it. He gave me a couple of bucks and I gave him the fish, and then I went back to the van. I was getting hungry by this time, so I headed straight for the cafe." He shook his head resignedly. "A lot of people around here catch their own fish. The tourists are your best bet. My wife keeps telling me that, and she's right."

"Can you tell us anything about the inside of Mr. Burke's house?" said Alberg. "Did you notice anything special about it? Anything valuable? Anything worth stealing?"

Farley smiled, slowly. "What are you trying to suggest? That I spotted something interesting and came back and killed the old guy for it?" He looked at Alberg reproachfully. "I never got past his front step. Besides, I am not a thief. Also, I am a pacifist."

"Just one more thing," said Alberg. "This friend he was expecting. Did he say anything more about him? Like, was it a man or a woman, or what time he or she was supposed to arrive?"

"No. Nothing more than I've told you."

"By the way," said Sokolowski. "You left here after lunch last Tuesday, right?"

"Right. Headed back up to Garden Bay."

"How come you're still around today, at this time of night?"

Farley grinned. "I don't keep to a rigid schedule, like most folks. Today I didn't have any fish. Today I was peddling my wife's ponchos. Didn't leave home until noon or so. Had to deal with the place in Garden Bay, then drive all the way down to Gibsons."

"Okay, Mr. Farley," said Alberg. "Thanks very much for your cooperation. Would you leave your address with the sergeant, please? Just in case we have to get in touch with you. And you'd better give him the names of the stores you deal with in Gibsons and Garden Bay, too."

Sokolowski saw him out and returned to Alberg's office, where the staff sergeant sat behind his desk with his chin in his hands. "I guess we've got to check him out, Sid." He touched his nose, gingerly, and tried to remember if he'd brought Cassandra's ointment with him.

Sokolowski slumped in the black chair. "He could have done it," he said wearily. "He could have. But why didn't he take some of that stuff with him? The silver, stuff like that?"

"If he did it," said Alberg, who had found the tube of ointment in his shirt pocket and was unscrewing the top, "it was damn smart of him to wander in here and tell us this tale, before we found him." He dabbed the clear gel on his nose and closed his eyes as his skin immediately cooled; he wished Cassandra was there to do it for him. He sighed and opened his eyes. "Check him out, Sid. I don't think he did it. But it's possible."

"You still want to search the victim's house again?"

"You're damn right I do."

"Sanducci will be at the house at eight."

"Tell him to start without me," said Alberg. "I've got some paperwork to do. I keep trying to forget there's more going on around here than this damn homicide, but Isabella won't let me."

There was a knock on the door, and Freddie Gainer stuck his head in.

"Look at that face," said Alberg to Sokolowski. "He was out on that boat all afternoon too, and is he burned? No. What have you got to report, Constable? It can't be good. You would have radioed ahead."

"Right, Staff," said Gainer. "They've packed it in. No luck. All they found was this." He came into the office.

"What the hell is it?" said Sokolowski.

Gainer held it out. It was still dripping. "It's a burlap bag, Sarge."

"Jesus holy Christ," said Alberg, staring.

"It could have been from anything, Karl," said Sokolowski, also staring at it. "There's probably dozens of them out there. You can't trace those things. You can find them in anybody's garage, or barn, or back porch—"

"Or toolshed," said Alberg, numbly. He looked at Sokolowski. "They're out there, all right, Sid. They're out there. We're just never going to find them, that's all."

Gainer backed out of the office, still holding the burlap bag. "I'll tag it anyway, Staff."

Sokolowski rested his forearms on his knees and stared at the floor. "You know, Karl, I think you may be right. I finally think you may be right about that old guy. I think he was the guy supposed to turn up for lunch. And I think he did it. But you know what else?" he said heavily, looking up at Alberg. "I also think you're not going to get him on it."

"I've got no witnesses," said Alberg, almost cheerfully. "No evidence. And up to now, no motive. It doesn't look good, does it?" He smiled. "Unless I get a confession."

Sokolowski looked doubtful. "He's a pretty tough old bird. And you'd still need corroboration."

"Yeah, I know. But let's worry about one thing at a time. If I can find the motive, let him know I know *why* he did it— then maybe he'll crack. He's not the kind of guy who goes around doing homicide whenever he loses his temper. He's going to want to talk to somebody about it." He stood up, stretched, and turned off the desk lamp.

"Seems a shame," said Sokolowski with a sigh, hauling himself to his feet. "A nice old guy like that."

"A nice old guy," said Alberg, "who snuffed his ex-brother-in-law. You really want him to get away with that, Sergeant? I don't."

CHAPTER 26

George heard the rain fall throughout the restless night, a soft absentminded rain that would bathe his garden and feed it and not pummel it into the ground. He couldn't sleep and found the sound of the rain soothing. At some point he must have slept, though, because he opened his eyes and the night was gone and the rain, too, and through his curtained windows some sunlight was filtering.

He got dressed and went to the back door. He put his gnarled hand around the worn round knob and looked fixedly at the door, not seeing its yellow paint, slightly greasy from six months' accumulation of grime, not able to move, trying hard not to let the moment overwhelm him. Then he turned the knob, pushed the door open, and walked out for the last time into his garden.

He saw that the clouds were fleeing quickly. Those too close to the sun were shriveling into nothing, burning away, and soon the sky would be quite clear again.

George stood on his still-damp grass and watched steam rise from his garden. He touched the marigolds and stroked the petals of the roses and laid his cheek against a hydrangea blossom and cut a big bunch of sweet peas and wished he could pick a zucchini, but there weren't any yet.

He spent considerable time outdoors, inspecting, admiring, approving. He was aware of stirrings and rustlings, fragrances, glorious splashes of color. He heard birds arguing in the arbutus tree, and noticed a new influx of aphids on the roses, and saw that the tide had left new driftwood on his beach.

He didn't know how to say goodbye to his garden, or to tell it that he had loved it.

He went back into his kitchen, put the sweet peas in water, and made himself some coffee. He got a notepad and a pen from his desk in the den—a room he had used scarcely at all since Myra's death—and sat down in his leather chair with his coffee to make a list.

He had a lot to do today. It took him half an hour to make the list. As soon as it was complete, he looked at the first item: *library books*. He would work his way down from the top. That was the sensible way of going about things.

"Wilcox here."

She was ridiculously relieved to hear his voice, even though it was curiously dry and remote.

"Mr. Wilcox? It's Cassandra. I'm calling to check up on you—I hope you don't mind. How's your chest? Did you sleep well? Are you feeling better today?" She got it all out in a rush and waited anxiously for him to reply.

"Cassandra?" He sounded amazed. "Where are you calling me from? The library?"

"Yes. How are you? May I come to see you? I was worried about you yesterday. I'd like to make sure you're all right."

"You were the first thing on my list," he said. "It must be an omen. There are some books I have to return, you see. The only thing is, I don't think I'm up to making the walk into town today, and my car's still in the garage."

"Then I'll come by and get them," said Cassandra. "All right? May I come?"

"Sure. Fine. That would be grand. I want to see you anyway."

Cassandra drove to his house preoccupied and uneasy. When he opened the door she looked at him intently. He appeared calm, and looked back at her steadily. He was tidily dressed and his hair was combed and she smelled fresh coffee. She relaxed somewhat, and smiled, but he didn't smile back.

He led her into the kitchen and insisted she sit in the leather chair. The library books—the two mysteries and the Mozart biography—were in a neat pile on the footstool. He poured coffee, fussed with sugar and milk, and finally settled in a straight-backed chair opposite her.

"I got you here under false pretenses, Cassandra, which until lately hasn't been my nature."

"You mean the books? But I was going to come anyway."

He got up stiffly and picked up from the kitchen counter the crystal pitcher, which was overflowing with sweet peas. "I want you to take these with you when you go," he said. "And the pitcher too."

"I can't take the pitcher, Mr. Wilcox. But I'll take the flowers, with pleasure."

"I want you to have the pitcher." He sat down again. "It's important to me. It was my sister who gave it to Myra and me, for our wedding." He put his hand on her arm, impatiently shaking his head. "Please don't argue with me, Cassandra. I'm trying to get my life in order, here. I need your help for that, and in exchange I want to give you something." He looked at her slyly. "I'm getting rid of everything. I could have offered you my house, or my car."

She spluttered, horrified.

"See?" he said, grinning at her. "You're getting off lightly. Will you take it?"

She hesitated, and watched his smile disappear. "Yes, all right. I'll take it. It's beautiful, and of course I'll take it, if you want me to."

He let go of her arm and sat back. "I'm moving away. Going to live with my daughter, Carol, in Vancouver." He frowned and reached for a notepad which lay on the footstool next to the library books. He took a pen from his shirt pocket and laboriously added something to a lengthy list. "Haven't told her yet," he muttered. "Better give her a call."

"But when?" said Cassandra. "When are you going?"

George put the pen back in his pocket but he held on to the pad, as though it might occur to him to write something else there. "Tomorrow," he said.

"Tomorrow?" said Cassandra, incredulous.

"That's why I had to get these books back to you today, you see."

"Tomorrow? But why? You mean, forever? You're never coming back?"

He shook his head.

"But why? I thought you were happy here. What about your garden? What about the hospital? What about me?" Her voice had risen, and tears were pushing at the backs of her eyes.

"I *was* happy here," said George, taking no notice of her distress. "For a long time. And then Carlyle arrived, and then Myra died, and now I'm not happy any more." He glanced through the window. "What about my garden? That depends on who moves in here, I guess." He turned back to her. "As for the hospital, there are lots of people who can do what I do there. It's just half a day a week. I don't do much. Got good eyesight, so I read to people. Anybody can do that. You could do it yourself, if you wanted to."

"Do you think you'll be happier in Vancouver?" It was a question she knew she shouldn't have asked.

"I doubt it." He leaned toward her, his hands grasping his knees. "The thing I can't stand the thought of, Cassandra, is dying where Carlyle died, and being buried where he's buried. That's the whole thing of it, in a nutshell." He sat back.

"But isn't your wife buried there too?" She needn't have asked that either, she thought; she knew the answer well enough.

He sat unmoving for a moment. His eyes were dry. "Yes. She is."

I could get up and leave now, thought Cassandra. I could get up gracefully and kiss him on the cheek and take the pitcher and the sweet peas and the library books and warmly wish him well and just leave, walk right out to my car and drive away. And he wouldn't think less of me for doing it, either.

They were silent for what seemed to Cassandra a very long time, and in that whole time she never took her eyes from his face.

"Why do you hate him so much," she said finally, quietly, "even though he's dead now?"

"Because I killed him," said George.

Cassandra felt very strange. She heard herself breathing, patiently, and finally realized she was still waiting for him to answer her, although he already had. Maybe she was waiting for him to change his mind, or tell her he'd been joking. But looking at him, at his face the color of cement, at his brown eyes looking steadily back at her, she knew he had told her the truth.

"It's a bad thing I'm doing now, I know it," said George. "I'm using up all our friendship, grown so slow and strong, right now, in this single minute."

"But I'm letting you do it," said Cassandra, numbly.

"I'm not asking you to keep this a secret," he said. "I don't care if you tell anybody or not, or who it is you tell. But I had to say it to somebody, and I knew I'd only be able to say it once, and you're the only person came to my mind."

"Why did you do it?" she said after a minute.

"I don't think I can tell you that part," said George wearily. "It's too long a story. It goes back too far. I thought it was because of Audrey, my sister." He closed his eyes and rubbed at his temples. "But it turns out it's more complicated than that. I didn't have any idea, when I did it, how complicated it was going to turn out to be." He looked at her and tried to smile. "It's all bound up with responsibility, you see. It's a good thing, in the main—responsibility. But I've a feeling, now, that you can carry it too far, or get it all wrong. And that brings me to awful uncertainties about myself."

He squeezed his eyes tight shut, fiercely rejecting the comfort of tears.

"Ah," he said a little later, "you'd think by the time a man gets to my age he'd have accumulated some wisdom around him, wouldn't you?" He looked out again at his garden. "I guess Myra was my wisdom."

Cassandra stood up quickly. He struggled to his feet. She put her arms around him and held him close to her, his thick white hair pressed against the curve of her chin. She looked over his shoulder through the window at his garden, glowing exuberant and abundant against the backdrop of the sea and the summer sky. She had no tears for him, but she held him to her with a fierce protectiveness, patting his back and saying into his ear murmured things meant to be soothing.

CHAPTER 27

It was afternoon by the time Alberg arrived at Carlyle Burke's house. The sun was as bright and hot as it had been before the single day and night of cloud. He thought of the waitress in the diner, as he waited for Sanducci to let him into the house; she had seemed so certain of her predictions, and he had accepted them unquestioningly.

Sanducci had taken off his hat and his jacket, but his shirt looked crisp and the creases in his pants were still sharp. "No luck so far, Staff," he said, as he followed Alberg into the living room. "I've done this room, the kitchen, and the bathroom. There's only the bedroom left, and the room with the piano in it."

Alberg, his hands in his pockets, had wandered over to the window to stand in front of the rocking chair, looking outside. "And that toolshed," he said.

"There's one thing, Staff, before I get back to work."

"Yeah? What?"

"I wanted to speak to you for a minute."

Alberg turned around. "Go ahead."

Sanducci was standing very straight. His black hair gleamed. His eyes were the color of the sea out there. At least his dimple wasn't showing.

"It's about the other night," said the corporal.

"Go on."

"I have to tell you, Staff, that I've been overextending myself a bit lately."

"Overextending yourself? What the hell does that mean?"

"I mean that I've been indulging myself in too many what you might call extracurricular activities."

Alberg walked closer to him. Sanducci stared straight ahead, over Alberg's right shoulder. "Extracurricular activities?"

"Yes, Staff."

"I take it that's a euphemism for . . . women."

"Yes, Staff, I'm afraid it is."

"And what are you trying to tell me, precisely?"

"That I fell asleep, Staff. On the front porch, here. I guess that's why I didn't hear the old guy out in back. I'm truly sorry, Staff."

Alberg stared at the corporal. There was, he realized, considerable envy in his stare. He went back to the window. "I'll do the toolshed," he said.

"Yes, okay, Staff. I'll finish up in here."

"And Sanducci," said Alberg, without turning around. "You don't want to get busted down to constable, do you?"

"No, Staff."

"Then I suggest you start taking a lot of cold showers."

"Yes, Staff." Without looking at him, he handed Alberg the key to the toolshed.

Christ, thought Alberg, trudging out the side door from the kitchen. Where the hell did he find them all? Better he didn't know, he thought; the guy might have a harem of sixteen-year-olds.

The toolshed was much like George Wilcox's, except that it was bigger, dirtier, and less tidy. Carlyle Burke had himself a power mower, instead of a push-it model, and his ladder was an extendable aluminum job instead of a wooden six-footer, and he had a lot of expensive, little-used lawn furniture stacked away in a corner, instead of three threadbare canvas chairs with slivery wooden arms. But his gardening tools were piled in a heap on a counter and looked as rusty as those in Alberg's garage, and bags of fertilizer and grass seed had been thrown in carelessly, to slump against the wall.

The obvious place to start, thought Alberg, sighing, was with the four cardboard cartons on the highest of several shelves lining one wall. They had been marked on the outside with black felt pen: XMAS DECORATIONS. But what the hell, you never know, he thought, and dragged them down.

The place was clotted with spiderwebs. The beam of sunlight which struggled through the single dirty window was choked with dust. Alberg carried the boxes out onto the lawn and sat on the bench there while he went through them.

There were boxes of tinsel, some unopened, some half emptied, with silver strings seeping from them. There were gaudy garlands of orange and blue—odd colors, he thought, with which to bedeck a Christmas tree. There were boxes and boxes of ornaments, and string after string of lights, ranging from tiny blinking ones to the large kind used to decorate the outdoors. Three cartons he opened, emptied, sifted through, refilled, and replaced on the shelf in the filthy toolshed.

But the fourth carton didn't contain anything having to do with Christmas. It was filled with women's underclothes—panties and bras and slips and garter belts—and with nylon hose, and negligees, and lace-trimmed pajamas. And it was at the bottom of this carton that he found an ebony box about six inches by eight, bearing on its lid, in gold, the initials AMW.

This, thought Alberg, is why Carlyle Burke willed George all his possessions; he wanted him to find whatever's in this small black box. He thought it inexpressibly tasteless, or perhaps simply malevolent, that it should have been buried under a pile of what must have been Audrey's underthings.

Alberg let the clothing slip languorously through his hands. She hadn't been a slim woman—not fat, but not thin, either. She had been feminine, but not lusty; her nightgowns were long-sleeved and scoop necked, threaded with now-faded ribbon, and her underwear was pretty but not particularly seductive. He sniffed at it cautiously and smelled only mustiness.

He put the box next to him on the bench while he slowly packed the clothing, neatly, almost tenderly, back into the carton. He took both box and carton into the toolshed and put the carton back on the shelf.

He pulled out a lawn chair, wiped from it spiders and their

webs, and set it up in the tremulous shaft of sunlight from the
window. Then he sat down with the ebony box.

It contained several pieces of jewelry: a cameo pin, a gold
filigree necklace, a topaz ring, and a wide gold bracelet with
no engraving inside. And beneath the jewelry, a small pile of
letters.

Alberg put the jewelry back in the box, closed the lid, and
arranged the letters according to date.

He sat for a moment with them in his lap. Subdued sunlight
washed upon them, made uncertain by dust and a grime-
streaked window. He was profoundly reluctant to start reading.

But after a while, he did.

He soon realized they were letters exchanged between Carlyle
Burke and his wife over a period of about six weeks in the
summer of 1956; Burke was in Victoria, apparently taking
courses at the university there, and Audrey had remained at
home in Vancouver.

Alberg read through them once quickly, then started over
again, paying particular attention to certain sections, certain
phrases.

You bring it on yourself, Audrey, you know you do, Carlyle wrote
on July 3. *You can't help yourself. Having a kid wouldn't make any
difference—you sure as hell ought to know that....*

Why can't we admit it? said Audrey a week later. *There's no
shame in it. We can just say we've made a mistake, and get a divorce,
and go on with our lives.*

We have NOT *made a mistake,* wrote Carlyle on July 13. *I've
always had trouble with my temper, I've told you that, time and time
again. It's part of being a man, for God's sake. Women have to
understand that, if they want to live with a man.*

July 23: *Some men do that kind of thing, of course I know that,*
Audrey replied. *Who could know it better than I do?... I cannot
live in fear. It's a terrible, terrible thing, living in fear, and I am
not going to do it again.*

Don't talk to me about your goddamn George, said Carlyle, near the end of July. *Look at him, off in Europe. They never give single men that kind of opportunity. Talk about prejudice—just try being a single man past thirty-five or so! And now they tell me fifty's the cutoff—I can't even apply again! So don't talk to me about George. And you know he's no better than the rest of us. You've told me yourself, for God's sake, what he's capable of. Are you MAD? Are you out of your MIND? To imply that the little bursts of temper that happen to me are as bad as what HE did?... We can keep ourselves under control, Audrey, if we try. It just takes work, that's all. ... I'll never hit you again. I can promise you that. I DO promise you that. We can't humiliate ourselves, for God's sake....*

August 9: *I just don't know if I can believe you,* wrote Audrey. *You don't understand about George. It wasn't the same kind of thing at all. I should never have told you, but I thought it would HELP you, Carlyle. Oh, God ... I don't want to fail, either. But if I can't believe you then I'm going to leave you, Carlyle, I swear it. I just can't go on like this. I WON'T go on like this.*

Alberg refolded the letters and put them back in the box, under the jewelry. He sat for a long time, holding the black box in his big, long-fingered hands, running the tips of his fingers over the initials on the top, aware of the smoothness of the ebony, warmed by his hands.

It had been like watching bits and pieces of an old movie, starring actors he had heard of but never seen before. He felt dazed, disoriented.

Maybe that's what did it, he thought, sitting in Carlyle Burke's dusty toolshed. Maybe Carlyle invited him over and spilled his guts, told him everything, confirmed all of George's worst suspicions.

And confronted him, probably for the first time, with whatever it was that George had once done that had let Carlyle Burke feel less corrupt by comparison.

He got up slowly, folded the chair and put it away, and, still holding the ebony box, went out of the toolshed and locked it behind him.

He told Sanducci to stop the search.

When he got back to the office, for some reason not clear to him he didn't tag the ebony box but put it in the bottom drawer of his desk.

Then he went off to see George Wilcox.

CHAPTER 28

George was trying to pack. The clothes hadn't been difficult.
He'd just shoved them all into the suitcases he and Myra used
to use when they went traveling. There was still room left in
them, enough for whatever personal things he decided to take
with him, but the problem was that in wandering through his
house he couldn't find anything except clothes that he wanted
to bring.

He had called a real estate agent and told him to put the
house up for sale. Maybe he should sell all the furniture with
it. What use would he have for furniture, anyway? Carol had
a big two-bedroom apartment filled with her own stuff; she
certainly wouldn't need any of his. He didn't have anything
really good, anyway; he and Myra had spent all their extra
money on trips, and never regretted a penny of it, either.

Maybe he should take his slides and photo albums. And
he'd have to take his books. And surely there must be lots
more things, he thought with growing desperation, that he
couldn't bear to leave behind. He stood in his kitchen looking
around but couldn't see a single thing he didn't mind abandoning.

Then through his window he saw his garden, and lifted his
hands and made a strange sound in his throat. He wouldn't
want to take it with him even if he could: he didn't deserve it
any longer; his life-guilt was much too heavy. It hurt his soul
to see it spread so joyously out there, unaware that he was

deserting it, but he refused to step outside. Never again would he go out there.

He went into his den and sat in the chair behind his desk, wondering what to do next. He'd called the garage where his car was being repaired and told them to sell it. He'd phoned the matron at the hospital and let her know he wouldn't be going there any more. Anybody else who ought to know he would write to from Vancouver.

He folded his arms on the desk and rested his head there, and he heard Carlyle's nasal voice again, but this time he was too tired, too tired to get up and get himself some coffee or sweep the floor or do anything, anything at all, to push that voice out of his head. . . .

How had he persuaded him to come? How had he done it, anyway?

"George, it's Carlyle," he'd said briskly. "I'm not feeling too well these days, George, don't think I've got much longer to go, and I want to get some things said while there's still time. Don't do it for *me*, George"—he'd chuckled, here—"I know you'd never do anything for me, but do it for Myra. You know how she was always trying to make things right between us. And do it for Audrey, George. Come to see me. Just once more."

Carlyle had stopped driving, stopped going out to Old Age Pensioners' things. There was some talk around the village about his sudden inactivity, and George had believed when he called that there might be some truth to the rumor that he was failing.

So he'd gone. For Myra? For Audrey? He doubted it. He'd gone out of a dark curiosity, a rancorous desire to see his own good health substantiated by a pale and wraithlike Carlyle, dying.

It was hard to tell about these things, but he certainly hadn t looked like he was failing.

He'd just wanted to vent his spleen, that's all, thought George bitterly, lifting his head from his arms. He was always a venomous bastard and maybe he finally got bored, having to be always on his best behavior in a town the size of Sechelt. And when Myra died, the buffer between him and George was suddenly gone.

Anyway, he'd called, and for whatever reason, George had answered the summons.

He'd knocked on the half-open door and heard Carlyle call to him from the living room. "Come!" he'd sung out, like he was a king or some damn thing.

"What is it, Carlyle? What do you want from me?"

"Oh, George, just look out there," said Carlyle from his rocking chair. "Did you ever think we'd be living in a place like this, you and I, only half a mile apart, looking out at such a beautiful sight?"

"We wouldn't have been," said George, "if I'd had anything to say about it. Not both of us."

Carlyle glanced over his shoulder. He gave him a grin and one of his ludicrous winks. "Funny, isn't it," he said, "the tricks that fate plays."

"Just say what you have to say, Carlyle, and then I'll be getting on my way."

"I'd hoped you'd stay for lunch," said Carlyle. "I just bought a salmon."

"I don't care for fish."

Carlyle sighed. He seemed tired; perhaps that was why he wasn't getting out of the rocking chair. "Well, at least have the courtesy to sit down, George," he said.

"I have no intention of sitting down. Just say what you've got to say, and if you don't say it fast, I'm going."

Carlyle, looking out at the sea, rocked, and nodded, and rocked.

"Okay. That's it. I'm on my way."

"Not so fast, George." Carlyle turned around and hooked an arm around the back of the rocking chair. His voice had lost its warmth. "I've gotten pretty sick of you over the last five years. Everywhere I go, there you are with your long face and that perpetual scowl. It wasn't so bad when Myra was around—she kept you under control, Myra did. But ever since you buried her, George, it's gotten to be a bit much. Oh, I know you talk about me," he said, turning back to the window.

"I've never said a goddamn word about you to anyone," said George, furious. "I don't like the taste of your name in my mouth."

Carlyle was silent for a moment, rocking gently. "It's too bad we couldn't ever get to be friends, George. I wanted that, you know, especially in the beginning." He was speaking quietly, almost to himself. "I thought you were a man I could get to know, confide in—I thought I might have found a real friend. Never had many of those. Never had any, when you come right down to it. I haven't the faintest idea why I thought you might turn out to be my friend. It was your eyes, I think. So stubborn and unwavering. And something about the way you walked, aggressive and hesitant, all at the same time." He turned around again, slowly. "But that never happened, did it," he said bleakly. "I ended up with your sister, instead." He threw back his head and laughed. "Oh, God, that was the biggest mistake I ever made."

"It was a bigger one," said George huskily, "for her."

When Carlyle looked at him this time there was grief on his face, and in his watery blue eyes. George didn't believe it for an instant.

"I didn't want her to die," said Carlyle, heavily. "I loved her. As much as I could. You jumped to a lot of conclusions about me, George. Some of them were accurate. But some of them weren't."

"You killed her," said George. He stared at Carlyle, open-mouthed, hardly able to believe he'd said it. "You killed her," he said, more belligerently.

"You do insist," said Carlyle coldly, staring back at him. "on missing the point." He deliberately turned his back on George. "She was a foul driver, and she finally managed to kill herself. I'd never let her drive, never, not while I was in the car. I tried to stop her that day, as a matter of fact, but she was in a state, as usual, wouldn't listen to me."

"You made her go," said George. "You frightened her into going."

Carlyle turned around again, slowly, smiling. "Ah, George. Did you hear what you just said?"

George felt the earth shift beneath his feet.

"I didn't make *her* do things, George," said Carlyle, petulant. "She made *me* do things." He shifted himself around in the rocking chair, clumsily, it seemed to George, and looked again out at his garden and the sea. "You should have told me," he said. "You had a responsibility to tell me what I was getting into. How was I supposed to know, for God's sake? And then *she* told me, finally, when it was too late. Oh, she told me, all right, she told me everything," said Carlyle, rapidly, nodding, rocking.

George began looking desperately around the room. He thought he was looking for something close enough to grab, hang on to, something he could lean on while he made his painful passage out of the house, away from the sound of Carlyle's voice.

Carlyle glanced over his shoulder at him. "I'm talking about your sister, George. Your family. Pay some respect, George. Pay some attention." He watched until George became still, then smiled and once more arranged himself to face the sea. "There was nothing much you could do about it, was there? Although you certainly tried, like a good son, a good brother. But that sort of thing is contagious, in a way—did you ever think of that? It's ironic, but they get to like things that way. That's what I think, anyway. Do you see what I mean? So the damage was already done, George, long before she met me; probably before you decided to take matters into your own clumsy hands. . . ."

George saw the shell casings sitting on the bookshelf, and suddenly his feet were no longer nailed to the floor.

Carlyle shook his head regretfully at the ocean. "It must have been a terrible scene," he said, "just dreadful, such an awful thing you did, and all the time—you'll never know— maybe they *liked* it! After all," he said, beginning to turn, "she didn't let you save her in the end, did she, and Audrey—"

George struck him.

He sat upright, now, at his desk, his heart beating fast, looking out the window, not seeing his garden.

A long time later he noticed that the sun was getting low, and he was hungry.

He forced other things from his mind and thought about tomato soup.

Then he made himself think about his daughter. She had sounded happy that he was coming. She'd been suggesting it for months, ever since her mother died.

George tried to remember if she had a balcony. Maybe he could grow things in pots.

But he knew he never would.

CHAPTER 29

For several minutes after he knocked on the door, Alberg heard only silence within the house. He was just about to go around to the garden and have a look there when the door opened and George Wilcox was looking up at him.

"You know," said George, "I kind of thought it might be you. The perfect end to a perfect day, as they say."

He looked disarranged. The deep waves in his hair were askew, as though he'd been abstractedly running his hands through it. The ubiquitous gray cardigan was absent. He was wearing an open-necked white shirt which revealed the sagging flesh of his neck, wide maroon suspenders, shapeless gray pants and scuffed leather slippers.

"Cassandra been talking to you?" said George.

"Cassandra?" said Alberg. "No. Why?"

"Oh, I don't know. The two of you seem to be pretty thick these days." He opened the door wider and gestured to Alberg to come in. "I thought she might have told you about my plans," he said, as Alberg squeezed past him into the long, narrow living room.

"What plans?" His eyes went automatically to the place on the windowsill where the shell casings had stood, and he felt a welcome rush of anger. Nice old guy or not, the man had killed someone.

It was hard to believe, all right, he thought, watching George shuffle slowly toward the kitchen.

"What plans?" he said again, following the old man into the

den, where a large suitcase, half filled with clothing, lay open on the desk.

"I'm moving," said George. "To Vancouver. I'm going to live with my daughter."

Alberg leaned against the doorway. He told himself to remain calm. He told himself to be patient. He reminded himself that George Wilcox was no fool.

"What brought this on?" he said, watching the old man stuff a couple of books into the suitcase. There was a pile of them on the desk, next to a framed photograph, face down.

"People dying brought it on," said George. He got two more books from the pile and fitted them in. "I figure I'll be better off living with somebody who's still a long way from crapping out."

"What about your garden?"

"What about it? There's gardens in Stanley Park. Stanley Park's practically across the street from Carol's place." He glanced up at Alberg. "Sit yourself down in the chair, here." He pushed it toward him. "I don't like you looming in the door like that. You're blocking some of my light."

Alberg sat. For a while they didn't speak. George continued to pack, stuffing books in among pajamas and pants and socks and underwear. Finally he picked up the photograph. He studied it for several seconds, then abruptly held it out to Alberg. "This is my sister," he said. "Audrey."

Alberg, accepting the photograph, saw something in George's eyes: whether irony or amusement, he couldn't tell.

He looked at George's sister.

His shock was almost physical. The hair was shorter, and done in a pageboy style now out of fashion, the nose was slightly longer, the mouth was slightly smaller, but the resemblance to Cassandra was striking.

Alberg looked from the photo to George; he knew his astonishment was obvious. But George was busily packing more books, looking, Alberg thought, like a squirrel creating his winter's cache.

"I thought you might like to have a look at her," said George, "seeing you've expressed such a curiosity." He took the phot graph back and packed it carefully between two flannel shirts. "I'd show you the one of Myra and Carol, too," he said, "but it's already packed away." He straightened up and rubbed the small of his back. "Time to take a break. Bring that chair into the kitchen. We'll sit in there for a while."

He looked at Alberg, waiting for him to stand and pick up the chair, and Alberg realized that there was to be no discussion of the resemblance between his sister and Cassandra Mitchell.

He got up and moved the chair and sat in it quickly, before George had a chance to make him take the leather one.

"Now," said George, arranging his hands in his lap, "since you didn't know I'm leaving, you haven't come to say goodbye. And since you didn't find anything out there in the ocean that's got to do with me, you haven't come to arrest me for anything. So tell me, policeman. Why are you here?"

He would miss coming to this house, Alberg realized. He would miss the flowers in the garden, and the sound of the sea on the beach, and sitting like a benevolent hunter in George Wilcox's kitchen, reluctantly enjoying his company.

"I've come to tell you a story," he said, and smiled, and stretched out his long legs.

"I'm a busy man," said George shortly. "Got no time for stories. Not today."

"It won't take long," said Alberg. "I might get some of it wrong, but if I do, you can correct me."

"It's your story," said George. "Why should I correct you?"

"It's *your* story," said Alberg. "I'm only telling it." He pulled cigarettes and a lighter from his pocket and reached for the ashtray on the tobacco stand next to George's chair. "Do you mind if I smoke?" he said politely.

George didn't answer, just stared at him, stubbornly.

"Last Tuesday morning, Carlyle Burke phoned you," said Alberg. He lit a cigarette and put the package and the lighter back in his jacket pocket. "He asked you to have lunch with him. Now we both know how you felt about old Carlyle, so I won't even speculate about how he persuaded you to go, but he did, and you went." He leaned toward George. "You didn't intend to kill him. I'm sure of that. You're not a killer, George."

He sat back. "At least you weren't, until last Tuesday."

"I don't have to listen to this." George was pulling at the tufts of stuffing that protruded from a break in the seam of the leather chair. Alberg remembered sitting in that chair and doing the same thing.

"No, you don't," he said quietly.

George said nothing.

"You went into the house and Carlyle, for whatever reason, maybe just because he was a spiteful old bastard, talked to you about things you'd just as soon never have heard. And finally you couldn't stand it any more, and you hit him on the head." He looked at the old man closely. "Is it too hot for you, George, sitting in the sun?"

George said nothing. His face was crumpled and still.

"You probably didn't mean to kill him, even when you hit him," said Alberg. "Sometimes it's harder than you'd believe, to kill a man. Sometimes you have to stab and bash away at him until you're both soaked in his blood and the other guy's still yelling, still crying out, maybe praying, or calling for his mother and yet he won't die, he just won't die."

"You speaking from personal experience?" said George. "Is that your police brutality kind of thing you're talking about?"

"And other times," said Alberg, unruffled, "one little smack seems to do it, and the guy stands there bewildered, looking down at this dead person and wondering how the hell he got that way."

He took a final drag on his cigarette and stubbed it out. "That's the way I figure it happened with you. One little smack, probably didn't feel like much to you, just enough to shut him up, that's probably what you thought. And then there's the man lying there dead."

"With his eyes open," said George, involuntarily. He pulled himself upright, flinched from a twinge somewhere, and let himself sink back into the chair. "I know that," he said carefully, "because I found the body. His eyes were open. I remember that."

"Then," said Alberg, "you realized what you'd done. Not much you could do about it. You could have called us, of course. Maybe that didn't occur to you. Maybe you thought you'd do it later, after you'd watered your roses. Or maybe you decided you could get away with it. Anyway, you found something that would hold the shell casings—probably in the kitchen, since that's the only place you left any prints—and you dumped them into it and lugged them home." He shook his head admiringly. "It was clever to take them both. We wouldn't ever have known they were missing, if it hadn't been for his cleaning woman."

The color had seeped from George's face. He wasn't moving at all.

"Now what I do not understand," said Alberg, leaning forward, elbows on his knees, studying George intently, "what I simply cannot comprehend, George, is why, when you got those things home, you didn't get rid of them right away. You could have buried them in your garden or put them out with the trash. But what do you do? You put them up on your windowsill, bold as brass, if you'll forgive the pun."

George looked back at him, silent and gray.

"Of course you were lucky, too," said Alberg. "Damn lucky. You were seen going into Carlyle's gate by three people. Two of them saw you at two thirty, when you found the body. One of them—unfortunately, he's what we call an unreliable witness—one man says he saw you a lot earlier. That fits with the time of death. It also fits the story of the man who sold Carlyle the salmon. Oh, yes, we found him, George; or, rather, he found us. He says Carlyle was expecting a guest for lunch. And I figure that guest must have been you."

He lit another cigarette and crossed an ankle over his knee. He wondered why he wasn't enjoying himself.

"So here's the other thing I don't understand, George," he said. "Why the hell did you go back there? Did you start wondering if he was really dead, and decide you'd better hie yourself back on up to the house and finish the job?"

"Watch yourself, policeman," said George, struggling with exhaustion.

"Or did you just want to sneak another peek at him lying there, dead as a doornail, eyes staring at nothing, his head resting in a pool of his own brains and blood? Was that it, George?" said Alberg, with contempt. "Did you really hate him that much?"

"You stupid miserable cop," said George. He looked completely drained. He had barely enough strength to push himself out of his chair. On his feet he glared down at Alberg, almost swaying. Slowly he bent close to him. "Okay, policeman," he said. He jabbed him in his chest. "Now you just sit there and keep your goddamn mouth shut and let *me* tell *you* a story."

Painfully, awkwardly, he paced the small room. "He went into the war," he said. "I was ten years old. Up to then it wasn't so bad. He had a barbershop. Drank some, got into a temper now and then, threw things around sometimes. Scared the piss out of me, but he never hurt anyone. Then he went into the war. Gone four years, he was. When he came back. . . .

"God help us, I don't know what happened to him over there. Maybe nothing. Maybe he'd have worked himself into it anyway. He was no saint before, that's for sure. It turned me into a pacifist, him coming back from the war like that, but maybe it wasn't the war's fault, who knows?"

He went to the window and stood, still and stooped, looking out. He seemed calmer, now.

"I was fourteen when he came home. He went back to the barbershop. Drank more. A lot more. Threw things around more. Then he started to hit her." He looked over his shoulder at Alberg. He looked extremely old. "They've got a name for it now," he said. "Battered wives, they call them. There are places they can run to. But not then."

He turned back to the window. "Not then. No relatives, either. We lived up in Yale, right where the Fraser Canyon begins. You think Yale's a small town now, you should have seen it back then. Dirt roads, wooden sidewalks."

He stopped talking. Alberg heard no birds, no wind, no sea.

"And no help," said George, despairingly. "There was no help." He stopped again, then went on. "I couldn't believe it, at first. The first couple of times I saw it happen, it was like my eyes were bugging out of my head and my tongue was frozen in my mouth and my feet were permanently attached to the floor. She'd scream at me to get out, go, run, and the first couple of times I did."

He turned slowly to Alberg. "And then one day I stopped running. He came at her and I yelled at him. 'Don't touch her,' I said. 'Hit *me*,' I said." He shrugged. "So he did. Knocked me flying. And *then* he went at her. It was pretty bad," he said, nodding at the floor. "Pretty bad. Then I got to be sixteen, and Audrey was born."

He sat down again, slowly, stiffly, his knees together, his hands clenched in his lap. "I'd been thinking before about my dilemma. I just wanted to get the hell out of there, just get the hell right out, as soon as I finished high school. Make my way down to Vancouver, live a life of my own, and forget all about him." He looked up at Alberg. "Trouble was, of course, how could I leave my mother? He was going to kill her one day, I knew it. And then Audrey was born...."

"I hated them both," he said, striking the arm of the chair with his fist. "How could they do it, sleep together, have another child, for Christ's sake!" He wiped his eyes with his hands.

"And this one was a girl," he said dully. "Right from the start, he couldn't stand her. He wasn't so fond of knocking me around, any more. I was as big as he was, by then, and he knew I wasn't afraid of him any more. He used to wait until I was out before he'd beat up my mother. But when that little girl arrived..." He leaned back and closed his eyes. "Ah, I just knew that was it. I couldn't leave. I could never leave the two of them. He'd kill them both."

Alberg waited.

Finally George sat up and rubbed his eyes. "I'm not going to go on and on about it. I stayed there for ten more years. He drank more and more. I loathed him and lost all respect for my mother. But I loved my sister, and I was goddamned if I was going to leave her with him.

"I thought about sneaking away with her. I should have done it. If we'd been able to get to Vancouver, nobody would have found us.

"But I didn't do it. I just got crummy wretched jobs around town and lived at home and kept her with me all the time she wasn't at school. I even dragged her bed into my room, eventually, because—he'd go in there at night, and I'd hear her scream and my mother and I would get to him at the same time and she'd be screaming too and I'd pound at him with whatever was handy and he'd try to fight me back but he was too old by then, too old and too drunk."

He stopped. "It's a lovely tale, isn't it, Mr. Alberg? I'm sure you've heard it before, a man of your experience, a man who knows how long it takes some people to die."

He looked away, out at his garden.

"One day," he said, "I don't know why, but I was out, for some reason, and Audrey wasn't with me. She was ten. I came home and I could hear it from outside the house: her screaming, my father roaring, my mother screaming." He gave Alberg a distorted smile. "Lucky we didn't have neighbors living close by, huh? Do you think that's why he got the place? Because nobody could hear what was going on inside?"

He got up again and went to the window. "I practically broke the door down, getting in," he said bleakly. "He was beating her with a stick. Her face was bleeding, her hair was matted with blood. Her hands and arms were bleeding, too, because she'd stretched them out, see, to ward him off. My mother was clawing at his back. She was a small woman. I don't even think he felt her.

"I ran right through the house to the mudroom in the back and got the shotgun and loaded it and ran back into the room where they were and shot out all the windows. That stopped him, all right."

He looked around the kitchen, but Alberg didn't think he saw it.

"I pointed the shotgun right at him," said George, detached. "I told him to get the hell out and never come back or I'd blow his goddamn head off. He stood there, lurching around the room, waving his hands and swearing at me. He wouldn't come close—I think he knew how badly I wanted to do it blow his head to kingdom come."

He turned to look at Alberg. "But he wouldn't go, either. I think he was so drunk he couldn't quite figure out what I was yelling at him. Meanwhile there's Audrey on the floor, bleeding and crying, and my mother looking wildly around, not knowing what to do."

George shuffled around behind the leather chair and hung onto its high back. "I dropped the shotgun and shoved him out of the house. The car was sitting out there. An old Model T. I pushed him into it—he stank of booze and he could hardly stand up, but I shoved him into the driver's seat and got the car going. 'Drive,' I said to him. 'Drive, you son-of-a-bitch. Get the hell out of here.' Then I ran back into the house, to see to Audrey."

He pushed a hand through his hair and looked almost bewildered, for a moment. Then he let himself lean heavily upon the back of the chair. "My mother was with her, by then. I'll give her that. She was crooning at her, looking over the— injuries. I came charging in and I said, 'The bastard's in the car, it's pointed up the canyon road, if there's a Christ in heaven he'll drive himself over the cliff.' I was shouting and shaking all over."

He looked directly at Alberg. "But then my mother heard the car rev up and start to move away, all jerky-sounding. Her head came up and she scrambled to her feet and she ran out after him. She was screaming at him, telling him she was sorry."

He leaned forward a little, looking at the staff sergeant intently. "Did you get that, Mr. Alberg? She was telling him she was sorry."

"I got it, Mr. Wilcox," said Alberg quietly.

George gave a shuddery sigh. He had aged, shockingly, since Alberg had come into the house. "I went outside," he said. "I saw her running after the car. It wasn't going very fast. I watched her, didn't even yell at her, and I saw her get herself onto the running board, and open the door, and climb into the car."

Alberg watched him carefully.

"I fixed up Audrey as best I could. Had to take her to the doctor, though, for stitches."

Alberg waited.

"It was such a long time ago," said George. He was ancient, now, his skin the color of parchment. "Sometime that night, or maybe it was early in the morning, I can't remember, they came to tell us the car had gone over the cliff."

He looked up. "It was a minister and a Mountie, as a matter of fact," he said, "who came to tell us that."

He came around the chair, holding on to it, and sat down. "That's it, Mr. Alberg," he said. "I killed my parents. I killed them both. That's what it comes down to. And I've got absolutely nothing more to say to you."

After a while, Alberg got up and left.

CHAPTER 30

"You might want to look in on your friend George," said Alberg when she opened the door. He looked haggard and depressed.

"Where is he?" said Cassandra, who was in her nightclothes.

"At home."

"What's the matter with him?"

Alberg looked beyond her, into her house. "He's very tired." He leaned against the doorframe. "Why didn't you tell me he was moving?"

"Why *should* I have told you?"

Alberg sighed. "May I come in? Just for a minute? I won't stay long. I've got to get home. . . ."

They went into the living room, where a crystal pitcher filled with sweet peas sat on the glass coffee table. Cassandra noticed that he looked at this for a long time. He would recognize the pitcher, she knew.

"He's very fond of you," he said.

"Yes," said Cassandra. "And I'm very fond of him." Her eyes were filling with tears. She clenched her fists.

"He did it, you know," said Alberg, still looking at the flowers in the crystal pitcher.

"Did what?" said Cassandra.

He turned slowly to look at her. She watched his face as the thought first skittered across his mind, then skittered back, grew still, and took root there.

"You knew," he said.

"Knew what?" said Cassandra, desperately.

"Oh, for Christ's sake, Cassandra, stop playing games with me. He did it. He killed him. How long have you known?" They were still standing, and he seemed to tower above her, his eyes icy and his face pale. "When did he tell you? Did he run to you that same afternoon, weeping on your shoulder, because you remind him so much of his sister? How long have you known?"

"Stop shouting at me," said Cassandra, suddenly strong. "If you want to speak to me in my own house you will sit down and speak to me like a civilized human being, not a frustrated damn cop."

He opened his mouth, closed it. "Tell me," he said grimly, and he didn't sit down.

"Tell you what? I have nothing to tell you."

"For Christ's sake, Cassandra—" With an effort, he lowered his voice. "We're talking about a homicide."

"I know what we're talking about," said Cassandra. "You don't have any evidence, do you? And he hasn't told you anything, has he?"

"He told *you*," said Alberg bitterly. "I know he did."

Her anger drained away. She was regretful and heavy-hearted, looking at him. She wanted to embrace him, as she had embraced George, and try to comfort him, as she had tried to comfort George.

"Karl. Listen to me." He turned hostile eyes on her. "I can't help you. Even if he *had* told me he did it, and I reported this to you, it wouldn't help you much. If," she said carefully, "if he had told me he committed a crime, I would have rummaged around in my library. And I would have found out that a confession like that isn't admissible evidence, it's hearsay." She looked away from him. "You'd have to get corroboration even if he confessed to you directly. Which he hasn't." She looked up at him. "And which he won't."

He moved toward the door.

"No, please."

He waited, not looking at her.

"He's a miserably unhappy old man," said Cassandra. "He's

giving up everything he loves—his garden, his life here. He is not in any way a danger to anyone. And he's my friend."

Alberg looked at her with contempt. He went to the door.

"Is your job so simple, Karl? Is your job really so damned cut and dried?"

She had to raise her voice and speak very quickly to get the last words out before the door slammed behind him.

CHAPTER 31

The next day Sid Sokolowski was standing by the counter making conversation with the duty constable when he heard the front door open. He turned, casually, and saw George Wilcox.

"Who's in charge around here?" said George. He was dressed in a brown suit Sokolowski figured must be almost as old as he was, and a brown tie, and was wearing a brown hat with a narrow brim from which sprang a small green and red feather.

"Staff Sergeant Alberg is in charge, sir," said Isabella, looking him over. "What's the nature of your business?"

"That parrot is the nature of my business, madam," said George, waving toward the bird. "It's my property, and I've come to claim it."

Sokolowski had disappeared down the hall. He now hurried back into the reception area, followed by Alberg.

"Good morning, Mr. Alberg," said George.

"Good morning, Mr. Wilcox," said Alberg.

"May I have a word with you in private?"

"Sure. Come to my office."

George didn't sit down, when offered a chair. He wandered curiously about, looking out the window, sticking a finger in the soil of the ivy that still sat on top of the filing cabinet, finally coming to rest behind Alberg's desk, facing the wall on which hung the photograph of the staff sergeant's daughters.

He studied the photograph absorbedly for several seconds while Alberg, moored awkwardly in the center of his office, watched him and grew increasingly irritable.

"Well?" he said finally. "What is it that you want, Mr. Wilcox? Have you changed you mind? Want to sign a statement?"

The bitterness in his voice startled him, and it seemed to startle George Wilcox, too. He turned from the photograph and looked at Alberg.

"They're beautiful young women, Mr. Alberg," he said. "I envy you. I understand you're divorced. Divorce won't hurt them. At least, not for long."

He walked around to sit in the black chair, allowing Alberg access to his own swivel chair and the comforting paraphernalia that cluttered the surface of his desk.

"I came to tell you something," said George. He took off his hat and held it in his lap, stroking its feather. "There's life," he said, "and there's conscience, and there's fate, and then there's law, Mr. Alberg. I've struggled with three of them, and I've decided to avoid a struggle with the fourth."

Alberg felt unutterably depressed.

"And it's not as though the struggling's over with," said George, so softly that Alberg had to strain to hear him. "I don't even know if I had reasons for some of the wrong things I've done. I don't even know if things are really as complicated as they seem to be or if—if it's just that I was plain wrong." He put on his hat, adjusting it with fumbling fingers. "I thought it might give you some satisfaction, if I told you that."

The white waves of his hair swept out beneath the brim of his hat, echoing its curve. As he got unsteadily to his feet, it struck Alberg for the first time that an eighty-year-old man probably didn't have much longer to live.

"I meant it about the parrot," said George, as they went slowly down the hall. "I have to take it with me." He stopped out of hearing range of Isabella. "The other stuff. If it turns out that it has to come to me, like the will says, I've made arrangements to have it all sold."

"Planning another trip on the proceeds?" said Alberg.

George looked up at him. Defeated, he shrugged. "I've got to take the damn bird, though," he said obstinately.

Back in the reception area, Alberg grasped the handle of the cage, through the cloth, picked it up, and handed it to him. "Be my guest," he said.

The parrot shrieked.

"We'll miss him," said Isabella.

"I'm sure he'll miss you, too," said George.

"Give him some cheese now and then," said Isabella. "It seems to keep him calm."

"Does it, now," said George.

"How are you going to get him home? Have you got a car? Where do you live?" said Isabella.

"I have my own personal taxi, madam," said George, "which is right now waiting to deliver me to the bus station." He went out the door without another glance around him.

Alberg, through the window above the green-cushioned bench, saw Cassandra's yellow Hornet waiting at the curb. Before he turned away he saw her reach across the front seat to open the passenger door for George.

Twenty minutes later, George and Cassandra were sitting side by side in the waiting room of the small bus station. They were surrounded by three large suitcases, a cardboard carton tied with heavy string, and the parrot's cage, cloaked in its red-and-white checked cloth.

Alberg came through the door and walked directly over to George. He didn't acknowledge Cassandra's presence.

"I have something for you," he said, handing George a brown paper bag. "Don't open it until you're on the bus."

He turned and walked away before George could say a word.

Cassandra reminded herself that he was just a cop, a stubborn, coldhearted cop whom she'd known for precisely six days.

When the bus came, the driver loaded George's three suitcases and the cardboard carton into the bottom of the bus. He expressed dismay about the parrot but was finally persuaded to let George carry it on his lap.

Cassandra tried to embrace him but it was difficult because he wouldn't let go of the cage, from which issued a series of ever more piercing cries, or the brown paper bag. She contented herself with kissing his cheek and patting his shoulder and making him promise to write to her.

George, as the bus left, waved until Cassandra was out of sight.

He had managed to get a seat by a window and the bus wasn't full so he stashed the parrot on the seat next to him, where it gradually quieted.

He wiped his eyes and pushed his handkerchief back in the pocket of his suit jacket and undid the jacket buttons and sat for some time, looking out the window, with the brown paper bag in his lap. He had felt the outlines of its contents through the paper and thought he knew what it was.

Eventually he took it out, and as soon as he saw it he was stabbed with love, and grief, and a terrible sense of things having gone wrong. AMW—Audrey Marion Wilcox. He and Myra had given it to her, on her twenty-first birthday, which had fallen two days before the birth of Carol.

He held it tightly for a while, before he lifted the lid and saw the jewelry, all of it familiar, all of it gifts from him: the bracelet, for her eighteenth birthday; the necklace, for Christmas the year after he and Myra were married; the ring, for her thirtieth birthday, shortly after they had moved from Saskatchewan to Vancouver; and the cameo, sent to her from Germany after he and Myra and Carol had taken a trip to Italy in the spring of 1956, just a few months before her death.

He had seen the letters beneath the pile of jewelry, of course, as soon as he'd opened the box.

But he closed the lid and contented himself with caressing the initials, embossed in gold, until the bus had reached Langdale and been loaded onto the ferry and disgorged the driver and most of the passengers to seek refreshment in the cafeteria or the sea wind on the sun deck or the spectacular views from the glass-enclosed lounges.

Then he opened the box again, and took out the letters, and unfolded the top one.

You bring it on yourself, Audrey, you know you do. .

CHAPTER 32

July 29, 1984

Dear Mr. Alberg:

I think I'm dying. I say this with some astonishment but with little dismay. I've been very lucky. No awful disease has claimed the last months of my life, as it did Myra's. I don't even feel any real symptoms, just a gradual seeping away of something important.

If you get this letter—WHEN you get this letter—you'll know I'm right. I'll be dead. It's a peculiar feeling, I'll tell you, writing this, imagining you in my head and not knowing when you'll get to read it. It could be you'll be all gray-haired and stooped over by then, though I doubt it. Could be you'll be dead yourself before it ever gets sent, though I doubt that even more.

I wonder if Cassandra has told you by now about my talk to her. My "confession." She asked me to write to her from Vancouver but I couldn't. She's written to me (those librarians, they're worse than policemen or reporters, the things they know about getting information), but I haven't answered her. I couldn't. It didn't seem right, somehow.

Anyway, if she hasn't told you I'm telling you now. I don't think I would have bothered, except that you gave me those letters. I think you did it because you wanted to help me a little. It was a compassionate gesture, and for that I thank you.

I've done a lot of not good things in my life. I've done some terrible things in my life. But you know, Mr. Alberg, what the worst one of them all might have been? I've been giving it a lot of thought.

I stopped writing, there, for a minute, just to think it over again, it's such a peculiar idea. Yet I think I'm right. I think the worst thing I ever did was not to let Carlyle be my friend.

Isn't that odd? Isn't that peculiar?

But I think that's what it was, all right.

I liked you, Mr. Alberg, despite it all. I know it was a hard time for you. Mounties like to get their man, and all that crap.

*But just think how much harder it would have been—*MIGHT *have been—if I'd planned the whole thing. I'm a pretty good planner. You might never have figured it out at all. And wouldn't that have been a whole lot worse for you?*

George Wilcox

CHAPTER 33

Alberg folded the letter and put it back in the envelope.

It had been sent to him at home. He had read it sitting at the dining table in his living room, on a day in mid-August. The old man hadn't outlived Carlyle Burke by much, he thought. A little over two months.

He got up, now, and went to the big window that looked out onto the road and his hydrangea bushes, smothered in huge blue blossoms. It was five o'clock on a hot, sunny afternoon.

He went to the telephone in his kitchen and put through a call to his daughters in Calgary.

"Hi," he said, when Janey answered.

"Daddy!" she said. He tried to listen dispassionately, objectively, but he couldn't help it; he heard joy in her voice whether it was there or not, and put his head in his hand and let the tears come.

"Where are you?" she said excitedly.

"Gibsons," he said, and cleared his throat.

"Oh. I thought you might be here. In Calgary." Surely he couldn't have mistaken her tone; surely there was real disappointment there.

"No, I'm here. At home. I just wanted to hear your voice."

There was a short pause. "Daddy?" she said "Are you all right?"

He started to say sure, fine, put on his hearty reassuring-father act but it wouldn't come, it just wouldn't come.

"Not really, sweetie," he said. "A friend of mine died. I'm a bit sad." He lifted his head from his hand in amazement. A *friend*?

"Oh, Daddy," she said. "I'm so sorry." Another pause. "I wish I were there. I'd give you a hug and try to make you feel better. Like you used to do with us."

"Did I?" he said, astonished.

"Of course you did." He waited, holding his breath, but she didn't even add, in that dry, detached tone that struck him to the bone, "Whenever you were available, that is."

"I love you, Janey," he said.

"And I love you, Daddy."

"When are you coming out here?" He tried a fatherly chuckle, meant to reassure her.

She put her hand over the receiver and mumbled something to someone in the room with her. Oh, Christ, he thought, she's got her boyfriend in for the night. He tried to blank it from his mind.

"Just a minute, Dad," she said, and then Diana was on the phone.

"Labor Day weekend," said Diana.

"Labor Day weekend what?"

"We're coming out there," she said.

"Out here? We? You mean you and Janey?"

"Of course I mean me and Janey. Who else? You want to see Mom, you've got to make your own arrangements. I take that back," she said quickly. "Yeah, we'd like to come out for the long weekend. Okay with you?"

"Okay with me," he said, smiling.

When he'd hung up the phone he leaned heavily against the kitchen counter. What was he: father, friend, cop, what? He slumped there for a long time, trying to figure it out.

Eventually he became aware of an unfamiliar sound. He cocked his head, trying to identify it, then sprang away from the counter and hurried through the door into the sun porch. He peered through the screen, and there she was. Gently, slowly, he opened the door, and the cat undulated through the opening. She stood looking up at him, meowing.

"It's over there," he said, pointing.

She followed his gaze and ambled over to the blue bowl, and he watched her, and became horrified. He went to her and crouched down, examining her without touching her. She was bloated around the middle.

As she lapped contentedly from the blue bowl, lifting her head every now and then to glance at him, unafraid, even friendly, he looked her over more carefully.

When she finished eating she looked around, spotted the cardboard box full of clean rags and stepped delicately inside, turned around several times and arranged herself contentedly.

He thought he heard her purr.

It occurred to him that she was there for the duration.

He went into the kitchen and, without letting himself think about it, called the library.

"Cassandra?"

"Yes."

"It's Karl. Karl Alberg."

"You're the only Karl I know."

He tried to think, looking into his porcelain sink, rust-marked.

"I got a letter from George Wilcox," he said. "He's dead."

"I know," said Cassandra after a minute. "I got one too. And a package."

"A package? Not the bloody parrot."

"No. Some jewelry."

He remembered a wide gold bracelet, and a large ring, and thought of the crystal pitcher.

"My daughters are coming out here," he said. "For the Labor Day weekend."

"That's nice," she said politely.

"One more thing."

"What is it?"

"I've got a cat here. Did I ever tell you about this cat?"

"No, you didn't. We didn't know each other very long," she said.

"Yeah, well, it's a stray. It goes away for a while, comes back for a while, goes away for a while."

"Are you at work?"

"Work? No. I'm on a day off."

"Okay. Go on."

"Well, it's come back. The cat."

"It that bad or good?"

"It's good. I've been waiting for the damn cat since April. Been leaving milk out every night and everything. Damn cat never showed up."

"But it's back now."

"Yeah. I think it's pregnant."

Silence.

"It's very big around the middle."

Silence.

"I don't think it's going to go away again. Until after it's had its kittens."

Silence.

"Cassandra?"

"Yes?"

"I don't know what to do."

"Well what do you expect me to say, for God's sake? Cats have kittens, that's part of being a cat."

"Yes, but it's my goddamn responsibility!" he shouted. "And I don't know what to do!"

Silence.

"Karl?"

"Yeah."

"There are lots of books in the library. I'm sure there's one here that will tell you how to help a cat have kittens."

"That's a very good idea," said Alberg thoughtfully. "I don't know why I didn't think of it myself." He grinned. "I'll be right down."

ABOUT THE AUTHOR

L. R. WRIGHT, who worked as a journalist for twelve years, has published three previous novels: *Neighbors*, *The Favorite*, and *Among Friends*. Her latest novels are *The Suspect* and *Sleep While I Sing*. She lives in Vancouver, British Columbia.